Also By Cathryn Grant

THE WOMAN IN THE CHURCH

AN ALEXANDRA MALLORY NOVEL

CATHRYN GRANT

The Woman In the Church

CHAPTER 1

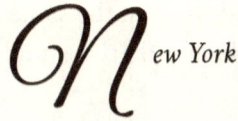 ew York

* * *

I'D KNOWN Stephanie was up to something with her new, slick look. She'd spent a lot of money to change how she presented herself, and it was clear it wasn't about a man. It had to be about her career, and that made me wonder how it played into Trystan's demand that I become her mentor.

So far, her personality hadn't changed to match her appearance. I wasn't sure it ever would. Although she looked quite nice—successful and approachable—her religious zeal was part of her DNA. I couldn't imagine her doing a makeover on that. She was still a woman bleeding desperation, and I had a feeling her desperate blood was going to get all over me.

Now that Trystan had made it clear I was going to mentor Stephanie whether I liked it or not, I was trying to figure out precisely what that meant. First of all, he wanted a written plan for my mentoring project. I suppose most people would search the internet for information on what positive mentoring relationships entailed, what the desired outcomes were, and how to be successful as a mentor. But what I really needed to know was how I was going to tolerate the over-sensitivity and short temper and neediness and self-doubt that were Stephanie. Tips on navigating those obstacles were not to be found on the internet.

Stephanie was not going to like, or willingly accept, a single piece of advice I gave her on how to become a good photographer, which was Trystan's goal. I had no idea what Stephanie's goal was, and maybe my first step should have been to ask her that question. But I didn't do that. I was looking for the easiest path possible—the strategy for wrapping this up in the shortest amount of time I could manage.

I was pretty sure Stephanie would appreciate that. She didn't want to be around me any more than I wanted to be in the same room with her. However, she did want my job, and that was not going to happen.

I was an excellent photographer. The skills I possessed could not be taught. I could not teach Stephanie to look at people with detachment. I could not teach her to talk to them in a way that made them forget about the photographer and their tendency to perform for the camera. I could not teach Stephanie how to interact with people in a way that enticed them to let down their guard and say what was really on their minds. These skills led to photographs that exposed what was below the surface.

None of those things had been covered in the photography class I'd taken. They weren't covered in any photography class and probably not in a classroom at all. I just knew these things because I'd spent my life watching how people behave. Stephanie, it seemed to me, had spent her life watching for people to make mistakes.

She was so enthralled with her religious views, she was blind to the true nature of other people.

I couldn't understand how she'd managed to raise a dynamic, savvy daughter like Eileen. It was a mystery, and I wondered if even Eileen or Stephanie knew the answer to that question. Eileen had none of her mother's religious rules and none of her mother's anxious, awkward neediness. It was that neediness I disliked most of all. It was exhausting and off-putting. Being around her made most people feel as if they had to take care of her, watching out for her feelings. That was not the way to become a competent, confident professional photographer.

Stephanie was dangerous. Fanatics always are. They don't think things through, and they aren't careful. They have an agenda that drives everything they think, say, and do.

I was dangerous too, of course, but in a different way. My danger was calculated and planned. Stephanie was the type who could easily get lost in her own fantastical view of the world and end up doing something that destroyed the lives of people around her—our small consulting firm, her daughter, maybe even herself. But mostly, me.

This mentoring thing seemed like a test of some kind. If I didn't do it in a way that was acceptable to Trystan, I might lose a job that kept me entertained and paid me quite well. It wasn't as if I had a solid work history with excellent references that would easily get me a new position, especially one with the freedom and creative energy this one offered.

Sure, Tess would give me a good reference. So might Trystan if I didn't drive my mentee over the edge, but that wasn't enough.

I didn't want to go back to social media management or data analysis or any of the things I'd done in the past. I liked taking pictures, and I didn't want to stop. I liked watching people through a camera lens. So for now, there was no choice but to help Stephanie become a photographer, starting with a plan for how I would hold her hand and make her feel she could trust my advice and trust me. Because that's what a mentor does. I did Google that part.

CHAPTER 2

On Monday morning, I went into the office at quarter to six. I printed out the mentoring plan I'd developed the night before. It was three pages. The cover was a photograph of a camera. It was placed on a table covered with a red cloth tossed in disarray, so the folds enveloped the camera and made it look like something exotic and almost seductive.

I left the office and took myself to a diner for breakfast. I figured Trystan could see the mysterious appearance of the plan on his desk, leaving him to wonder when I'd placed it there. He would be forced to read it first instead of showing up in my office doorway to talk about it before he'd absorbed the details.

The document had one pillar of the plan on each page.

The first page explained that Stephanie would take several photography courses. She needed to learn the mechanical features of the camera Trystan would be purchasing for her. She also needed to take a class dedicated to photographing people. I didn't point out that such a class hadn't been required for me because I knew how to make people feel loved by the camera. I had no doubt Stephanie would make them feel judged, and I wasn't going to try to explain that to her or Trystan. She would argue with me, and the intensified power struggle would add weeks to the process. She needed a teacher who would lay out the principles of taking good portraits. Even though that wasn't really what we did, it was the closest she would get. She could choose whether she would follow the suggestions or not.

The second page listed four upcoming client appointments where I thought it would be appropriate for Stephanie to join me. I'd written steps for what she would do at each one—first, simply sit in the background and observe me, followed by increasing involvement over the course of the four appointments.

The third page outlined her homework assignments. After each client session, she would provide a written report of what she'd observed. Since Trystan was insisting on a written document from me, I would require the same from her. Besides, how would he know how much effort I was putting into mentoring her if it wasn't written down? It was unlikely he would get that information from Stephanie.

I imagined that her verbal reports back to him would involve complaining about me and mischaracterizing me, if not downright lying about me. That's what she'd done so far, and there was no reason to think she'd changed. Her written report required answering specific questions about the actual photography session, unrelated to me.

I took a small bite of bacon and sipped some coffee. The coffee was adequate, strong enough, but lacking in flavor. I put up with it because the food at this diner was amazing—perfectly cooked bacon, firm eggs with creamy yolks, none of the white jiggling and running around like a yolk wannabe. The toast was delicious, made from bread that tasted homemade. And they served real butter in a dish, not tiny packets with barely enough butter to fit on the end of a knife.

While I ate, I listened to the people around me, talking about politics and the stock market, shopping, and kids. It was a pleasant background hum. There was a lot of talk about children, lots of anxiety in the voices. Listening to passionate complaints about toddlers who would eat nothing but fruit and cheerios, or climbed out of their beds seven or eight times during a two-hour period in the evening, teenagers who didn't want to get out of bed at all and refused to eat fruit at all, was maddening from the outside. I couldn't imagine being responsible for trying to shape a human being to fit into society.

Maybe that had been part of what had drawn my parents to such a dictatorial, restrictive church. Maybe they liked having the certainty that came from following our church's directives on how to raise children. There must have been some comfort in not having to make a hundred decisions every week about striking the right balance.

I wasn't sure why my thoughts were traveling in that direction and why those conversations stood out from the others taking place around me. Possibly, I was feeling like a parent with my new responsibility for Stephanie.

I finished eating, left my mug mostly full with the second pour of coffee, and walked to a specialty coffee shop to order a latte before returning to the office.

When I stepped into our small lobby, I was juggling my coffee and the outdoor clothes that I'd peeled off in the elevator. I went to my office and dropped the coat, scarf, hat, and gloves on the guest chair. I took the coffee to the window. The sky was white but without the promise of rain or snow. The overcast had settled down four days earlier and appeared to be planning to stay through the end of February. It threw a bleak mood over the city.

I took a sip of coffee.

"There you are."

I turned to see Trystan in the doorway.

"Thanks for the plan." He held up the packet of paper I'd left on his desk. "Right on time."

I smiled and took another sip of coffee.

"Let's discuss it." He turned and stepped out of sight.

I sighed. I followed him to his office, where he closed the door. I settled in a chair across from him. I thought of all the conversations we'd had in which I was seated in that functional chair. It struck me that it was a somewhat subservient position. In an office, the person in the visitor's chair is not the one in charge. The occupant of the office has a larger, more comfortable chair, information at his or her disposal through a desktop computer, and the power to dismiss you when they're done talking. I suppose the visitor can get up and leave when she or he chooses, but when it's a boss and employee, that's not a likely scenario.

"Is something bothering you?" he said.

I laughed. "Studying my microexpressions?"

"Maybe." He gave me a smile that seemed genuine.

"What did you want to discuss?"

"I asked you a question."

"Nothing is bothering me."

"You looked uncomfortable."

"I'm not."

He nodded. It was clear he didn't believe me. "So...why did you suggest the extra photography class for Stephanie? It seems like overkill. What we're doing isn't formal portraiture. I think—"

"I think she needs more confidence."

We stared at each other. I had the sense he was waiting for me to say more, but what else was there? She did need more confidence, and he knew it. And by confidence I meant, some actual skills to give her confidence, not her delusional opinion of herself.

"And what is the purpose of these written reports each time she goes to meet a client with you? Since you'll be observing everything she does, a report seems unnecessary."

"To cement in her mind what she learns."

"You're treating her a bit like a child, don't you think?"

"You asked me to mentor her. Doesn't mentoring mean holding someone's hand? Metaphorically?"

"Not exactly. It's more of a peer relationship."

"I don't think that's true."

"I'm just concerned that your obvious antagonism toward her is going to show. This needs to be a respectful relationship. You need to help her be successful."

"I get that."

"I don't think written reports are necessary."

"I do."

"Please don't be antagonistic, Alex."

"I'm not. And if you recall, the antagonism goes both ways. So don't put this all on me."

He sighed. "Are you committed to helping her succeed?"

I couldn't answer. Of course, I wasn't. I preferred being the only photographer. I didn't want a backup, and I didn't want to interact with Stephanie any more than I absolutely had to.

"I'll take that as a *no*," he said.

"I didn't say that."

"But you didn't answer."

"I'm thinking about how I want to say this."

"It's a yes or no question."

"I don't think I need a backup. And to be honest, it seems like you don't trust me to do the job."

He put his hands behind his head and leaned back slightly. "If we want this company to grow and take on more clients, which I hope you want as much as I do, we need two photographers. I already explained that. It has nothing to do with trust."

Funny that we were talking about trust, the very thing Stephanie was never going to give me. This was a ridiculous plan and a waste of everyone's time.

He lowered his hands to his desk. "I'd like you to go with her when she picks up her camera. You can introduce her to Leon."

I rolled my eyes. I couldn't help it. I knew I looked like a put-upon teenager, but it felt as if my eyes rolled of their own accord, my body knowing as well as my mind did that mentoring Stephanie was a doomed proposition. Trystan wanted us to be tightly-knit colleagues, friends even. He was not going to give up.

I wondered whether he knew the same about me. And the same about Stephanie, for that matter.

CHAPTER 3

*W*hen Alex and Diana had gone to lunch without inviting her, Stephanie had pushed aside the feelings of rejection and took the opportunity to drop by Trystan's office. It gave her a chance to talk to him without being overheard, to make sure he was serious about her new role.

His door was open, but he was staring so intently at his computer screen he didn't notice her.

She cleared her throat.

He looked up. "Oh, hi."

"Do you have a minute?"

"Sure."

She entered and sat across from him.

Still looking at the computer, he asked, "What's up?"

"I wanted to thank you properly for giving me a chance as a photographer." Although she smiled, her stomach knotted as she spoke. Her heart raged at her—why had she *said* that? She didn't want to *thank* him for something she'd had to beg for. Something that belonged to her, that was originally *her* idea. Why did she say things she didn't mean, things that made her look weak? She'd come in here feeling grateful, driven by the thrill of knowing she was finally getting what she wanted. But it wasn't until the words came out that she realized she didn't owe him gratitude.

"Of course. Anything else?" he said.

She folded her hands. She needed to turn his thoughts back to realizing how much she deserved this. It seemed as if he viewed it as a treat he'd handed out because she'd eaten all the food on her plate like Stephanie had done for Eileen when she was a toddler. "I knew at the start that taking photographs of our clients was better done by someone who understood the vision of the company, someone who had intimate knowledge of how you interact with clients and of the clients themselves. When we were hiring contractors as photographers, it wasn't nearly as effective."

He nodded.

Why couldn't he acknowledge that it was her idea? He knew it, but he refused to say the words. He was incapable of giving her the credit for contributing something valuable.

"Do you remember that conversation we had?" she asked.

"Why are you bringing this up?"

She wanted to smack him. His smile was condescending, telling her that her presence there was pointless. He seemed confused about why she'd even asked for a minute of his time. "I deserve to be the photographer, and I'm just glad you've recognized that."

He sighed. The sound of it was deep, and exaggerated, and designed to let her know she was causing him grief. She decided to ignore it.

"Let's just move forward," he said. "You'll be taking some classes. Alex has worked up a mentoring plan."

"I'm not talking about her," Stephanie said. "I wanted to remind you that I have a lot of untapped potential."

He nodded.

Why was he being such a jerk? He couldn't acknowledge anything positive about her. Although, maybe she was being too argumentative. There was a balance between thanking him for something she deserved, which was demeaning, and reminding him of what she had to offer, making sure he was fully aware of her abilities. She leaned back in her chair. "I know I'll do a good job at this, and I'm really looking forward to showing you how much insight I have into our clients. I think it will help them get more value out of your—"

"Good." He glanced at his computer screen. "Has Alexandra gone over the mentoring plan with you?"

"No. But—"

"That's strange. You should touch base with her before you go to lunch."

"Isn't that her job?"

"What do you mean?"

"She's the mentor. Shouldn't *she* be reaching out to *me?*"

His lips tightened. He glanced at his computer again. What was so fascinating on his screen? He looked at it so frequently she had the impression he was watching a movie.

"Don't be childish, Stephanie. Just touch base with her."

"She went to lunch."

"Fine. Then talk to her when she returns." He forced a smile onto his face.

"I was thinking. I can start the photography class right away. I don't need her help with that, obviously." She laughed. "To be honest, I'm not sure the mentoring is really that useful."

"You need to observe her process."

"She didn't observe anyone's process. She just went with you to meet clients. I think it would be better if I did the same."

"We've already set this up, and we all agreed to it. I want you and Alex to be on the same page in how you approach and handle clients. That won't happen if you just tag along with me. The—"

"I wouldn't be *tagging along!*"

He sighed more deeply this time. She knew she was getting on his nerves, but she couldn't stop herself. The way he was treating her was wrong. Alex was not a professionally trained photogra-

12

pher any more than Stephanie was. She had no special skills, no degree in anything that Stephanie was aware of. Trystan was treating Stephanie like a second-class citizen instead of a key part of his client interaction. She belonged in meetings with him, not getting mentored by someone who had no idea what she was doing.

"Maybe that was a poor choice of words," he said.

"It was."

"Calm down," he said.

"I'm calm."

"You're not. Your voice is getting louder, and I can see your agitation all over your face. This is one of the things you need to learn from Alexandra. It's important to maintain your composure no matter what happens with a client. No matter *what*."

She stared at him.

"Do you understand?"

"No matter what? That's pretty broad."

"I don't mean something inappropriate. But what I do mean is that you can't be emotional like this. The men and women we work with are used to having power, used to being deferred to. If you perceive their behavior as rude or insulting, you have to keep your feelings from intruding. You're there to perform a service for them."

"I know what our clients are like, Trystan. I've been here a lot longer than Alex. I know—"

He raised his hand, telling her to stop. "I'm not arguing with you. I'm telling you why mentoring is useful. We should all be eager to learn and grow."

"Are you eager to grow?" She knew she sounded rude...rude and uncooperative. This was going all wrong, an, as always, she couldn't figure out where she'd gotten off track.

"What is it you want?" He glared at her. "You pushed hard to be given an assignment as a photographer. You have that. I've asked you to spend some time with Alex, getting familiar with a process she's already established so we can provide a uniform experience to all of our clients. They come first. Always. You seem very dissatisfied, and I'm not sure why." He folded his hands and rested them on the desk. He glanced at the computer, letting his attention linger.

"I want your respect." She was as surprised by her answer as he appeared to be.

"What makes you think you don't have it?"

She closed her eyes for a moment. The longer she stayed, the more she said, the worse it got. She needed to leave. Immediately. Even though she was quite sure she did not have his respect. Less so now. She stood. "It's good to hear you say that." She turned and walked out, glad that even if she'd lost the entire battle, she'd had the final word. A tiny, meaningless victory.

Tonight, she would spend time reading her Bible and praying specifically and in great detail about this situation. She needed to feel strong and powerful, and competent. She needed to prevail over Alexandra and Trystan. So far, that hadn't happened.

CHAPTER 4

*S*tephanie and I met outside the camera shop. I gave her a fake smile, and she did the same to me. I pulled open the door and stepped out of the way so she could walk inside. She gave me a dirty look, no doubt seeing clearly that I was setting myself up as the alpha dog by taking control of the door. I followed her inside.

Instead of waiting for me to walk toward the shop owner to introduce her, she charged ahead, slipping her arms out of her coat sleeves as she walked. Under a very nice camel-colored wool coat, she wore a skirt that most women her age wouldn't dare to. I had to admit it looked good on her. The skirt was paired with brown tights and boots. Her top was longish, which made the skirt seem even smaller. From the back, she looked not much older than me.

Leon Sharp, the shop owner and the instructor for all the photography classes, stood at the counter. He smiled at our approach. A box containing Stephanie's camera, the same model as mine, sat on the counter beside him. As he had for me, Trystan had called ahead to order the camera. He had not ordered a video camera for Stephanie as he had for me, and I wondered if he'd forgotten because our video shoots were rare or if that missing camera said something about who was going to get the plum jobs. I hoped it was the latter.

"Hi Alex," Leon said. "Good to see you again." We shook hands, and I asked how business was going.

He shrugged, rolled his eyes, and smiled, all at the same time. I took this to mean he was doing well, despite challenges. I sensed Stephanie growing impatient while Leon talked about how he was offering more classes and private lessons to compensate for a slight downturn in sales as phone cameras became more and more sophisticated and fewer people bought small pocket cameras. Now, SLRs were the primary sellers—with much higher price tags—but lower volume.

I nodded, giving him a sympathetic look. "Your classes are awesome, so I'm glad those are going well."

"Thanks for saying so. We've added more to the mix."

"Every single time I point my camera, I think about some of the things you taught me about lighting," I said.

Stephanie leaned on the counter. "I can't wait to get started."

I introduced Leon to her, and they shook hands, an exchange that went surprisingly smoothly, considering Stephanie's eagerness to make sure she got herself into the center of the conversation and the aggressive way she shoved her hand at his. Her desire to be noticed didn't bode well for her success with clients.

Most people who know me would consider me one of the more self-absorbed people they've encountered in their lives. I know this about myself, and I've been told this, repeatedly. But I don't *need* to be the center of attention. I enjoy it when I am, and I put myself there when it serves me. But it's obvious to me that taking interesting photographs requires becoming a part of the camera. For the hundredth time, I had an almost visionary foresight into how Stephanie would behave around our clients, and it was not going to produce useful photographs that allowed Diana to get inside their heads and assess weaknesses that blocked their potential.

I reminded myself, also for the hundredth time, that was out of my hands. Leon could try to help her. I wondered if Trystan would consider her failure a mentoring failure. I hoped not, and I needed to figure out a way to make clear to him, without him writing me off as catty and childish and territorial, that some skills cannot be taught. I needed to make sure he understood that any failure was on her.

I left Stephanie and Leon chatting about her new camera and drifted off to look at the displays.

There were some new models since I'd acquired the one I used. I spent a few minutes reading the brief descriptions printed on thick cards displayed beside each camera. Some of the terminology told me nothing, and as I looked at them and imagined their weight, I wondered if it really mattered. All the high-tech features in the world wouldn't compensate for weak instincts.

I put a lot of weight on instinct. In everything. A lot of people can't do the same because their instincts aren't as finely tuned as mine. After a life spent trying to stay out of trouble, trying to keep myself from being found out, I'd polished mine into something that resembled a beautiful, elegant sword—sharp and efficient.

As I moved to the next display, the quiet of the shop, disturbed only by the low voices of Leon and Stephanie, allowed me to hear the urgent vibrating of my phone inside my bag. Knowing I wouldn't be getting a new camera, uninterested in what Stephanie and Leon were talking about, I pulled out my phone.

In the center of the locked screen was a message from Kent. I swiped and opened it.

Kent: *Dinner at my apartment? I'm making barley and vegetable soup. I have fresh sourdough. And wine.*

Alex: *Yum. When?*

Kent: *Tonight.*

Alex: *OK.*

Kent: *Had a shock today. I'll tell you all about it.*

Alex: *What happened?*

Kent: *Pretty sure I saw Victoria. She looked completely different.*

Alex: *Probably wasn't her.*

Kent: *I think it was.*

Suddenly, Stephanie was standing beside me, holding the bag with her new camera. "Who are you texting with?"

I angled my phone so she couldn't see it.

"Sooorrrrryyy." She drew out the word and made a face. "I didn't realize it was a *secret.*"

"No secret. I just don't like showing my messages to the whole world."

She laughed. "I'm not the whole world."

I moved away from her. I looked at the screen. Kent had sent another message—a single question mark.

Alex: *She left New York.*

Kent: *She explicitly told you that?*

Alex: *Talk tonight. I need to get going.*

He didn't respond to my last message. That made me wonder about the dinner invitation. Was it really a dinner invite, or was it about his sighting of Victoria? The thought seemed paranoid, but there's instinct and paranoia, and sometimes the line gets blurred. A thought that seems paranoid is often my gut, whispering that there's more to a situation than is obvious on the surface. Some call it paranoia, some call it being careful. As the founder of Intel was famed for saying—*only the paranoid survive.*

I put my phone in my bag.

"Should we get coffee?" Stephanie said.

"I think I've had enough caffeine today."

I felt my phone vibrate again. I couldn't resist, even though I knew Stephanie would be trying to read upside down. I pulled it out to see the final message from Kent.

I'm 99% sure it was her. I wonder what happened.

It irritated me that he was suddenly interested in Victoria's behavior. When I wanted to know more about her and Rafe, he'd stonewalled me until I was forced to dance too close to the open arms of the FBI.

This wasn't good. I couldn't have Kent's interest turn to speculation about the identity of the woman seen going up to a hotel room with Rafe the day before he was found dead. *Any* speculation is not a good thing.

CHAPTER 5

*T*he camera orientation class was scheduled to start at one o'clock on Saturday. Stephanie was walking in the door of the camera shop at ten minutes to one. She wanted to be sure she got the best seat. She wanted to be sure she could watch the others arrive instead of feeling them staring at her, assessing her the moment she opened the door.

The shop itself was empty, so she walked through and down the short hallway to the door with a placard reading, *classroom*.

She knocked, then realized it was silly. She opened the door and went inside. The room was empty. She'd hoped Leon would be there. If she could talk to him before class, she could cement her position with him. He would be inclined to pay her more attention, to make sure the others saw that she was intelligent and not such a newbie as they were, even though using a fancy, complex camera like the one she now possessed was outside of her experience.

In the days since she'd taken the camera home, she'd watched several YouTube videos about its features, so she felt like she wasn't starting completely in the dark.

She took a chair facing the door at the front end of the long table. On the wall to her right was a large whiteboard. The name and model of the camera were written in red marker. Otherwise, the board was wiped clean, gleaming and reflecting the fluorescent lights, making her eyes ache as she stared at it.

She opened her case and lifted out the camera. She placed it on the table and put the case on the floor beside her purse. It was tempting to pull out her phone, to find something to occupy herself while she waited, but perhaps whispering some silent prayers would be a better use of her time. Prayer would ensure she was spiritually focused, making sure her ego didn't get out of control, which it was already clamoring to do, was important to making sure this went well. It was critical that she walked out of this class knowing more than Alex. A lot more. And there it was, ready to trip her up—her ego, screaming for recognition before the class had even started. She took a deep breath. Before she could let it out, the door opened.

Two women and a man walked in. Although they'd arrived together, it was clear from the way they quickly moved away from each other that they were strangers.

The first woman with dark, shoulder-length wavy hair, sat across from Stephanie. She smiled but said nothing. The man, with longish blonde hair, sat beside the woman, moving his chair closer to hers. She looked at him with a sharp expression, and he moved the chair back to its original position.

The other woman was young—barely over twenty if Stephanie was guessing correctly. She looked younger than Eileen. She had long brown hair that she wore in a fishtail braid. Her face was thick with makeup, although it looked nice. She walked around the table and pulled out the chair beside Stephanie's. "Okay if I sit here?"

Stephanie nodded.

The girl placed her enormous designer handbag on the table in front of her, then nudged it to the left to make room for her camera bag. The handbag was soft red leather with an engraved gold-plated bar dangling from it, but Stephanie couldn't read it from where she sat.

"I'm Tamara," the girl said. She smiled at each person in turn. "I'm super excited about this class. It's so great to be here. I wonder if we'll get to go on field trips to take pictures."

The others smiled at her, including Stephanie. Prompted by her cheery attitude, they gave their names—Jason and Eileen.

"That's my daughter's name," Stephanie said, immediately regretting giving away a piece of her personal life so easily.

Eileen smiled and nodded but said nothing.

"Oh, how old is your daughter?" Tamara asked.

"She's grown. About your age."

"You don't look old enough to have a daughter my age," Tamara said.

"Thank you." Stephanie wasn't sure it was a compliment, but *thank you* was the only appropriate response.

Leon stepped into the room and greeted them. After that, there was no more chatter as he asked them to introduce themselves and then dove into an explanation of the camera's key features, telling them he would start with basics to ensure they were all using the correct terminology. He spoke for nearly the entire hour, pausing only to answer questions. At the end, he asked them to take pictures of objects in the room, just to get the feel of working with the camera. "It's too cold to go outside. Next week, if this weather continues, I'll choose an indoor location where you can get more practice."

While Leon began offering individual help, starting with Eileen, Tamara turned toward Stephanie. "Can I take your picture?"

"I think we're supposed to photograph a chair or something like that," Stephanie said. "Maybe your purse."

"People are more fun, don't you think? And you're so pretty." She smiled.

Stephanie felt her skin grow warm. "Okay."

Tamara took several photographs, the second batch assisted by Leon, who had made his way to their side of the table by then. Stephanie took several photographs of Tamara and was thrilled with the results. Wowing Trystan wouldn't be difficult at all. The camera did half the work for her. She wanted to laugh, thinking what a big deal Alex had made out of this. She was glad Tamara had given her a chance to jump right in to photographing a human being.

When the class was over, she and Tamara followed the others to the door and out into the cold, overcast afternoon. Eileen and Jason began walking in opposite directions.

"Want to get a cup of coffee or tea or something?" Tamara asked.

Stephanie considered this. The girl was so young. Watching her in class, Stephanie had decided Tamara was definitely several years younger than Eileen. It was strange to have a classmate younger than your daughter. It gave her the irrational feeling that she was somehow responsible for the girl.

"Don't say no. Please. We can talk about the class and review what we learned."

Her words made Stephanie feel even more awkward. It sounded as if Tamara were in high school and wanted to study for a test with a friend. Stephanie didn't need to review anything. Using the camera was actually quite straightforward.

Tamara tugged on the strap of Stephanie's camera bag. "My treat. Just half an hour. I know you have time."

"Okay. Sure."

Tamara raised her hand and hailed a cab. As it pulled to the curb, Stephanie took a step back. "Can't we walk? There's a—"

"I'm not walking in this weather." Tamara shivered and smiled. "Get in. I'll pay."

Stephanie slid into the cab, and Tamara asked to be taken to the Lotte.

"I live in the opposite direction," Stephanie said. "I—"

"It's only five minutes."

"Not on the subway."

Tamara settled her huge purse on her lap. Both camera bags were on the seat between them. "I'll treat you to a cab home."

"I can't accept that."

"My mom is a VP at Bloomies. And my dad…" She laughed. "Don't worry, it's not a problem."

Stephanie felt oddly ashamed. She nodded and looked out the window, feeling trapped into something that was sucking her deeper into a place where she wasn't sure she wanted to go.

At the hotel, they sat in the coffee shop and ordered cappuccinos. Again, Tamara's red purse was front and center, sitting on the table between them.

"Should we put that on the floor?" Stephanie said. "It's going to be crowded when the coffees arrive."

Tamara shook her head. Her braid flopped over her shoulder, and she shoved it out of the way. "I like to keep my eye on it."

"Sure," Stephanie said, "But can't you put it between your feet or something?"

Tamara leaned forward. She lowered her voice. "My gun's in there, so it's pretty important to be sure there's no way someone can grab it."

"Oh."

"I probably shouldn't take it everywhere, but a woman alone in Manhattan…" She shrugged and smiled. "You can't be too careful."

"I usually feel safe enough," Stephanie said. "Of course, I don't go out late at night, so maybe—"

"You just never know. Especially riding the subway. I'm surprised you don't have one."

"You can't just carry it around in your purse unless you have a permit."

Tamara shrugged. "Who's going to know?"

"Some buildings want to look in your bag if they have a security check."

"They aren't that careful unless you're going to a show or a concert, I guess. They never take stuff out. My gun is small, so it's not that heavy, and I always make sure to have other heavy stuff in there, so they think the weight is from something else."

"I can tell you've thought it through."

Tamara nodded. She settled back in her chair as the cappuccinos were placed on the table. She picked up three sugar packets, tore off the tops in a single move, and poured the contents into her drink. She stirred quickly and took a sip.

Stephanie glanced around the room. She supposed if your mother was a VP at *Bloomies*, and your father was something that couldn't be mentioned, you had enough money in your family that if you were cited for carrying a concealed weapon, you were confident you could easily sidestep any legal issues.

"I'm honestly surprised you don't have one," Tamara said. "Most of my friends do. And my mother and her friends also."

Stephanie picked up her cup and took a sip to test the temperature. The drink was delicious.

"Especially someone as pretty as you. And with such nice clothes. You would be a target for mugging for sure."

Stephanie rarely, if ever, thought about being mugged or assaulted. As she'd told Tamara, she didn't go out late at night. She went to church functions, but they never lasted much past nine. There were almost always other pedestrians in the area, making her feel safe when she was walking home from her subway stop.

"Have you ever shot anyone?" Stephanie asked.

"Once." Tamara looked down at her coffee cup. She ran her finger around the rim, licked the chocolate powder off her finger, then shivered. It was hard to tell if the shiver was from the unsweetened cocoa or the recollection of shooting someone.

"That must have been awful," Stephanie said.

Tamara kept her gaze on the coffee cup. "It was necessary."

Stephanie wasn't sure what to say. How did Tamara define

necessary? What had happened? It sounded horrible like it had been something outside of her control.

Silence filled the space between them, enhancing the nearby voices of two men discussing the challenges of dog ownership in New York City.

"Anyway," Tamara said, "you should think about it. Seriously."

After that, they talked about the class, about Leon, about why they wanted to learn about photography. Stephanie explained her job, and Tamara informed her that she simply liked to take classes. She was planning to take a few more from Leon. "I like to learn things—I take art appreciation classes, poetry, stuff like that. I like learning."

"That's good," Stephanie said.

Later, as Stephanie settled into the cab that Tamara had paid for, Stephanie leaned back against the seat and thought about the gun. Tamara had let her look inside her purse, and she'd seen a glimpse of the tiny thing. It looked so exotic, a weapon that a glamorous woman in a 1940s film might carry.

She couldn't imagine owning one. It seemed so wrong—not trusting God to protect her. And the thought of shooting, possibly killing a human being, was horrible. She put her hand on her belly to still the waves roiling through her.

Then, out of nowhere, an image of Alexandra's face formed in her mind. She gasped as she realized why.

"You okay, Miss?" the cab driver asked, looking at her in the rearview mirror.

She nodded. "Yes. Fine."

Tamara insisted it had been *necessary* to shoot the person she'd killed. What did that mean? She supposed if your life were threatened, it would be necessary to defend yourself. Or if someone you loved was being harmed. What would she do if someone attacked Eileen? She thought about that disaster of a man—Jim Kohn. And now Eileen had a new boyfriend. What if he turned out to be equally harmful to Eileen's mental health? What if he assaulted her? Stephanie couldn't imagine a scenario where she might witness something like that, but what *if?*

Would she have the courage to shoot? Would she consider it *necessary?* Absolutely. Jim Kohn had almost killed her daughter—not physically, but emotionally. Spiritually. And in some ways, yes, physically, because Eileen had teetered on the edge of anorexia when she was seeing him...and long after.

What if it was *necessary* to kill Alexandra? She closed her eyes and imagined holding that small gun in her hand, raising the barrel toward Alex's smug face, pressing carefully on the trigger. She imagined the shock on Alex's face, the sudden quelling of her attitude.

Stephanie's eyes flew open. What was *wrong* with her? Those thoughts were awful. So ungodly! It horrified her to think there was something like that blooming inside her.

"You sure you're okay?" the driver asked.

She nodded vigorously. She turned and looked out the window, forcing herself to forget the relieved, victorious feeling that had flooded her when she imagined pulling the trigger of a gun and watching Alex die. A clean, bloodless death. She didn't like violence, so she hadn't allowed that to intrude on her fantasy, but the freedom would be exhilarating.

She wondered if she was going to hell.

CHAPTER 6

*I*t turned out that I didn't eat Kent's barley soup on Tuesday evening after all. I told him I had a headache. Usually, I like facing things head-on. It wasn't like me to put off something difficult, to try to avoid a confrontation. But this was too serious. I needed time to think. I was also confident he might see my rejection of his invitation as a suggestion that I didn't care about his supposed sighting of Victoria. As if the whole message exchange was completely unimportant to me.

Had he seen her?

I'd assumed that she'd left New York when she moved out of her apartment, fleeing the consequences of her fraud after Rafe's death. But maybe not. Maybe the FBI had caught up with her. Maybe she was required to stay until they finished their investigation. Maybe the defense attorney she'd said she knew had told her it was better to stay until things were resolved. Maybe he'd said running away would make her look guilty. If she stayed, they had a better chance of making sure that the fraud committed by her and Rafe was placed solely on his plate.

It wasn't as if Kent seeing Victoria, talking to her even, meant I was exposed. Victoria didn't know I'd killed Rafe either. She had no information to give Kent. But a curious guy like Kent, freshly curious, might ask a question that would get Victoria thinking along a different line than she usually did. Who knew what might come out of a conversation between two people who were acquainted with me, discussing the murder of a guy whom both of them were aware had been hitting on me, a guy whose background I'd been probing?

It wasn't a huge problem, but the risk of a lot of pointed questions wasn't outside the realm of possibility. It concerned me. I needed to be calm and in absolute control when I saw Kent. I needed to make sure I had answers to all the potential questions I could think of. I also needed Kent to cool down and forget whatever had popped into his head to worry about.

We rescheduled for Saturday night. Again, he was cooking. Tri-tip, this time.

This time, there was plenty of time to allow time for dressing nicely, carefully making up my face, and figuring out how I was going to get his mind off Victoria permanently. I wore dark pink leggings and a matching top that was open in the back, with a few straps crisscrossing over my shoulder blades. I put on makeup and dark lipstick. I brushed my hair until it was silky smooth.

I took a bottle of expensive vodka with me, even though I knew he had plenty. I also brought a brand new jar of olives. Alcohol would help settle him, and olives would help settle me.

At seven, I knocked on his door, loud and firm—in control.

Kent swept me into his apartment with one arm around my waist and a long, deep kiss. I leaned into him, enjoying several minutes without whirling thoughts, feeling only his body and mine. For those minutes, I wasn't plotting my next move and calculating how I was going to make Kent forget my previous obsessive interest in Rafe—an interest that had finally turned to murder. An interest that would *not* be my undoing.

After several minutes we moved away from each other. Kent

took the vodka out of my hand. I closed the door and turned the deadbolt.

I sat on the couch as he suggested, waiting while he opened a bottle of wine. He brought me a glass, told me to change the playlist if I preferred something different, and assured me I could enjoy doing nothing for the next ten minutes until the meal was ready.

I sipped the luscious Cabernet and let the music swallow me. As I relaxed, I decided there was no way Kent would manage to put together Rafe's murder and all my earlier questions about him, along with my dogged pursuit of the former occupant of my apartment. In my mind, those things had loomed large, but to Kent, they were a few isolated conversations. I was being overly cautious. My gut had veered off toward paranoia for a short while. Now, I saw that it would all be fine.

After several more sips of wine, he invited me to the table.

He didn't mention his Victoria sighting all through dinner—tri-tip cooked perfectly, roasted Brussels sprouts, brown rice with nuts and currants, and a salad. Despite the churning of my thoughts, I relaxed enough to polish off the entire meal, including a second serving of tri-tip and Brussels sprouts. It was the perfect meal for a cold, gloomy evening.

We still had a bit of wine left when we moved away from the table and settled on the couch. We talked about work, and I told him how much I disliked being a mentor.

He informed me that the practice of mentoring was a joke. Mentorship, according to Kent, was a concept devised by HR departments to make sure they could point to a list of accomplished tasks that proved they were helping employees develop their skills, preparing them for advancement in the company. In reality, advancement came from being in the right place at the right time or kissing up to your boss's boss, or, in too many cases, screwing over your peers to make yourself look good.

It was a cold and cynical view, but we had a good time

laughing over the absurdity of what Trystan had asked me to do. Then we moved on to trying to figure out how I was going to get the upper hand with Stephanie. Kent had no useful ideas.

Before we knew it, the wine was gone, and he'd mixed martinis. We were sipping them and not talking.

A moment later, he put down his glass. He knelt on the floor and pulled off my boots. I closed my eyes and enjoyed the pampering gesture, the firm touch of his hands on my feet and ankles. His hands moved away from my feet, and just as I was thinking about opening my eyes and taking another sip of my drink, he spoke. "Hey, I know what I meant to talk to you about. Victoria."

My eyes opened and gazed into his. I put the glass on the table and tucked my feet up beside me on the couch. I was going to remind him he couldn't possibly have seen her, but decided to wait. Maybe this was nothing, and I didn't need to make it into something by saying too much, too soon.

"She looked really different," he said.

"How did you know it was her?"

"She walked past me. I was sitting at the counter in a coffee place, looking out the window. She was only four or five feet away. And she looked right at me. She didn't recognize me, maybe she couldn't see me through the window, but she turned her face toward me. It was kind of surreal. Almost like she felt me there, even if she didn't recognize who it was."

"Interesting."

"She was dressed in business clothes—high heels. Her hair was longer, and it wasn't in those little spikes."

"She said she was leaving New York."

"Well, she didn't. I wonder if she decided she needed to be here to pressure the detectives about putting more effort into finding out who murdered Rafe."

I shrugged.

"You don't care?"

I tried to think what most people would say in this sort of situation. Kent knew I wasn't a fan of Rafe's, so I didn't need to pretend too much sadness. But still, they'd been my neighbors. No one likes to see anyone murdered. "It's so awful what happened, but from what the police said to me, they thought he was with a hooker. And they found drugs, so…"

"Just roofies. Hardly any alcohol in his blood," Kent said.

I picked up my drink and plucked an olive off the stick. I popped it into my mouth and chewed slowly. "How did we get off onto this subject?"

"Because I saw Victoria, and I wondered if you have any idea why she would lie about leaving New York."

"Maybe she didn't lie, maybe she changed her mind."

He picked up his drink but didn't swallow any. He sat staring at the olives.

"You don't like your martini?" I asked.

He put the drink down. "It's not that. I'm just wondering about the two of them. It seems odd that she moved out right away after he died."

"She wanted to escape the memories, I suppose."

"She didn't even say goodbye."

"Were you close?" I took a sip of my drink and ate another olive.

"It just feels off."

"Why?" It was a risky question, but it had to be asked. I stared at my drink and longed for an endless supply of olives to give me something to focus upon.

"Knowing how they tried to involve themselves in everyone's lives, then having him wind up in a hotel on the other side of the city—dead? A hooker? *Maybe?* They don't even really know. And then Victoria disappearing like that. Doesn't it seem…questionable?"

"They were strange. Who knows what they were involved with."

"True." He pulled me closer and kissed the side of my neck.

I placed my drink on the table and turned toward him. He did the same. We kissed for a while, and I slid my hands up his shirt.

He pulled away. "I can't stop thinking about it. After all the questions you had about them just a few weeks ago, I can't believe you're not more curious." He laughed and kissed my nose.

"I was curious because I felt like they wanted something from me. Now..."

"Now, what?"

"I guess I've lost interest."

"Well, isn't that convenient?" Even though there was no discernible movement, I felt like his body wasn't as close to mine as it had been. I felt his mind moving even further away. He didn't sound like he was accusing me of anything or that my response set off alarms, but he wasn't far from that line of thinking.

I kissed him and pulled him toward me. I wasn't sure it was the right thing to do. I couldn't assume he wouldn't bring it up again. But at least I knew where his thoughts were leading. It might be time to put some distance between us...after the evening was over.

While we were in bed, I was extremely distracted. I couldn't get a good sense of how curious he was and how shocking my sudden loss of interest appeared to him. Was it just a passing comment, or did he have other, more intrusive thoughts beyond what he was telling me?

CHAPTER 7

The photography class, the cappuccinos with Tamara in an upscale hotel, and the revelation of the girl's gun made Stephanie feel like she'd lived a life other than her own that day. Nothing felt normal. She hadn't done her laundry and the errands that occupied most Saturdays. She hadn't given a thought to her daughter, aside from those brief moments in class, which left her feeling disconnected and outside of her own skin.

Now, she sat on her bed, pillows behind her, nibbling a tuna sandwich.

The most shocking thing was, she wasn't all that curious about what her daughter was up to. She was mostly thinking about how Tamara had repeatedly said that Stephanie was *pretty*. Had anyone ever called her pretty? Not that she could recall, unless it had happened when she was a small child, and of course, those memories were lost forever.

She was also thinking about that gun.

When she'd stepped out of the cab in front of her apartment building, she'd looked around with fresh eyes. Was that man who stood on the corner smoking scoping out the women coming and going from her building? Was he looking for someone who appeared vulnerable? A woman who walked without a sense of purpose or was distracted by her phone. A woman who wasn't paying attention because her thoughts were consumed by her job or her children. Easy prey. She shivered.

She'd never been attacked, and she'd never known anyone who had been. It was something you read about, something you knew happened regularly, but that seemed far outside your experience. Something you occasionally feared and tried not to dwell upon. It was one of a hundred tragedies that happened to *other* people. Like the September eleventh terrorist attack or cancer or getting fired or date rape or any dreadful event that was so enormous, it damaged your life forever. She felt she'd had her share of misfortune and pain. But for the most part, it seemed as if God had His eye upon her, keeping her safe. He'd promised He would, and even though she knew it didn't always work out that way for others, it had for her. So far.

However, God had not watched over her when it came to her career...although, maybe that was an ungrateful thought. She was taking photography classes. Trystan had bought her an expensive camera and promised that her responsibilities would be expanding. So wasn't that from God's intervention? She'd been too impatient.

Still. Eileen had been hurt dreadfully. Where had God been during that whole ugly episode? A gun would not have helped Eileen because she'd invited that creep into her life, welcomed him, exposed her heart to him, and allowed him to chew it up and spit it out. Just as Stephanie had allowed it with Eileen's father.

Stephanie dropped the corner of the bread crust onto her plate and moved the plate to the nightstand. She pulled her knees up toward her chin, hugging her legs close. There was a jumpy, anxious feeling inside her chest.

She straightened her legs again and climbed out of bed. She carried her plate to the kitchen and removed a half-empty bottle of wine from the fridge, filling a glass almost to the top. The bottle had been in the fridge for weeks. She rarely drank wine, and neither did Eileen. At least not at home. Stephanie was pretty sure Eileen drank when she went out with friends, especially with Alex. She suspected Eileen drank a lot with Alex.

She raised the glass to her lips and took a long swallow.

After a second sip, she returned to the bedroom, closing the door behind her. She settled into bed and placed the glass on the nightstand. Why did she feel so edgy? She knew the answer but didn't want to think about what it meant.

It was the gun.

Something about it had thrilled her. The sense of power that would come from carrying a weapon in her purse. The secret knowledge that she would always have the upper hand. No matter what happened, she would possess something that others didn't know about, something that had the potential to make her feel safe; and not just feel safe, but give her the knowledge that her safety was guaranteed.

But why? There hadn't been a single time in her life when she even came close to feeling like her life was in danger. Had such a thing really happened to Tamara? Had it truly been *necessary* for her to kill someone? She should have asked for details. Was the shooting recent? Had Tamara been assaulted? It wasn't as if you heard stories every day of someone defending herself with a gun. Stephanie was sure a story like that would be headline news. Maybe it hadn't happened in New York, although Tamara's accent suggested she'd lived in New York most, if not all, of her life.

She took a sip of wine.

If she had a gun, she could be rid of Alex. It would have to be the right set of circumstances, of course. There was no way Alex would ever be inside Stephanie's apartment again, so shooting her for being a threat inside her home wasn't an option.

What might happen that would make it *necessary* for Stephanie to pull the trigger? And get away with it? She couldn't have a situation where she wound up in prison. It would have to be at the office. Possibly at a client's, but the presence of other people would make the situation more complicated. It would have to be a time when she and Alex were alone in the office. At night, most likely.

If Stephanie suggested they review photographs and Alex began giving her a hard time…She could imagine Alex telling her the photographs were terrible. Stephanie might get angry and grab Alex's arm. Alex would be furious if someone grabbed her with any force. Especially if that someone was Stephanie. Without a doubt, Alex would fight back, she'd fight back hard.

Stephanie put her hand on her arm and rubbed it gently, imagined grabbing Alex's upper arm, squeezing tight, pulling Alex roughly toward her. What would Alex do then? She would say something caustic, for sure. What else? She would try to pry Stephanie's fingers away. Then what? She wouldn't stand for it, that was definite.

Stephanie took another sip of wine. She was getting carried away, veering into a dangerous fantasy. After all, she didn't own a gun. And if she did, she would never dare to shoot someone. It was wrong. The most terrible thing a person could do, or *one* of the most terrible things. Her fantasy meant nothing. It was the thrill of imagining a situation that would make her life so much better. It wasn't an actual *plan* for which she had to work out specific, reasonable details.

After two more sips of wine, she returned the glass to the nightstand, where it settled with a loud click.

The details of the situation didn't matter. She could imagine what she pleased—they would be looking at photographs, and Alex would make one of her awful comments. Stephanie would demand she apologize, and Alex would laugh at her.

She would take out the gun, and Alex would laugh again, telling her that she was too weak to carry out her threat. Alex would laugh harder and give Stephanie that condescending look, the way she moved her eyes slightly to the side, lowering her lashes and letting her lips slide into a smirk. She would say Stephanie had no clue how to use a gun. She would tell her she was being silly and to put it away. She might even try to grab it out of Stephanie's hand.

The moment she did that, Stephanie would raise the gun and fire once. The bullet would penetrate Alex's skull as if there was nothing there but butter.

Diana and Trystan would rush into the room, telling her they'd overheard everything, that her life had been in danger and she was so brave to shoot.

No, that wouldn't work. It had to be more dramatic. Her life would need to truly be in danger in order for a shooting to be considered *necessary*.

She swallowed more wine. It was terrible to be thinking like this. She would have to confess her sin later. But for now, she wanted to ease her tension with wine and a fantasy that would relax her body and allow her to drift to sleep.

CHAPTER 8

*T*hirteen days. It's not very long, but it can also seem like a lifetime, depending on what's been occupying your attention. When you murder a man and hurry a woman out of your life, when you meet new clients and take soul-revealing photographs and start mentoring someone you'd like to have disappear from your workplace and have sex four or five times and go running every other day, it can feel like a very long time.

Time is strange and easily distorted. Looking back a few months can stir up the sense that the months, the years, are flying past. Sitting in an office staring at a computer can make an hour feel like two days.

In this case, thirteen days felt like months.

That's how long it had been since I'd lit a cigarette, inhaled the calming smoke, and blown it out like a mesmerizing, ephemeral work of art.

I thought about it every day. I tried not to, but my brain wouldn't let go. There was no doubt my entire being was addicted to nicotine, as well as to the habit itself.

I loved smoking. But I loved my body more, even the parts I couldn't see—my lungs, first of all, those spongy pink things that filled themselves with oxygen and kept me alive. I doubted mine were spongy and pink, but I hoped for the best. I hoped I hadn't overdone it, and I was confident they would slowly shed the black, thick tar that had collected there. I loved my heart and the way it beat triumphantly when I ran or lifted heavy weights. I wanted those parts of me and the connecting miles of blood vessels to be strong.

I'd pushed my habit to the limit, letting it creep further into my thirties than I'd planned. Of course, when you take your first hit of a cigarette, you aren't making plans. You're trying it out, trying it on for size, trying to imagine yourself as an adult. You're picturing yourself as a woman with a certain level of sophistication and a lack of caring about anything but that present moment and the pleasure of smoke moving in and out of your body.

I missed smoking. I didn't doubt for a second that I'd made the right decision, but I missed it. Terribly. I missed it so badly I ached. It was a little unsettling how strong that ache became at times. I was shocked to find myself waking in the morning with thoughts of a cigarette. I was even more shocked to find myself gazing wistfully at the most down-and-out people on the street and feeling a common bond because they held a cigarette between their fingers, and I knew what they were feeling in that moment.

I missed standing on the roof of my apartment building, looking out over the city, and letting my mind drift with the smoke. I missed taking a mid-day break and escaping from the office with something clear and definite to do—a structured way to spend my time. A purpose. I missed the nicotine, and I missed the sense of relaxation.

It's difficult to put immediate pleasure to the side for the sake of healing something you can't see and never will.

On Sunday, recalling my evening with Kent, I very much wanted a cigarette.

I pictured myself climbing the stairs to the roof, sliding a cigarette out of a box that existed only in my imagination because there wasn't a single pack, not even a stray cigarette, in my apartment. I would lean on the concrete edge that ran along the rooftop, looking down at the people walking by, unaware of my presence. I would slowly inhale, hold the smoke, and think about Kent. I would review his questions in my mind.

I would blow out smoke and consider his mood. Was he truly disturbed about my relationship with our former neighbors, or was he just mindlessly talking about something for which he had no answers and was thus curious? I wanted to know what he'd hoped I would say. I wanted to know what he believed about Rafe's murder, if he believed the police hadn't dug deeply enough.

The question about how I should have handled our conversation about our neighbors tickled and irritated my brain like gnats buzzing inside my head. The belief that smoking would settle and clarify my thoughts screamed at me. It was a lie, really. I knew there was nothing about the smoke or the ritual or the nicotine that did anything of the sort. Possibly the habit, but that was all. I simply needed to adjust my habits.

I changed into running clothes and shoved my feet into athletic shoes, yanking the laces tight. I did some stretching on my living room floor, grabbed my keys, phone, and earbuds, and went out. I walked quickly to Central Park. The sidewalks were too crowded to allow a comfortable run to the park entrance.

When I reached the edge of the park, I started a slow jog. I increased my pace, running along familiar paths and past iconic landmarks. After a little over a mile, my head began to clear. The desire to fill my lungs with smoke had evaporated as easily as the smoke itself might have.

As my thoughts settled and stopped chasing each other in circles, I began to see more clearly that I'd only made one simple mistake. I'd hounded Kent for information about my neighbors for weeks. To suddenly show no interest in who had murdered Rafe was jarring to him. I must have given the impression I was keeping something from him. It was possible he thought I knew more, that the police had provided information to me that they hadn't given him. He might also think I'd spoken quite a lot to Victoria and knew more than I was saying about Rafe's life and how he'd ended up dead in that hotel room.

The next time I saw Kent, I would have to be more forthcoming. It was tricky, it was walking close to the edge, but it had to be done. Otherwise, my disinterest would continue to stir his interest. Maybe I could think of another plan to divert his attention.

CHAPTER 9

Stephanie didn't often think about her marriage. It had ended so long ago, it almost seemed as if it had happened to another person. It seemed as if Eileen belonged only to her, and no one else had been involved in her conception or witnessed her birth and the early years of her life. No one else had fed and clothed and housed her. No one else had worked to shape her soft, pliable mind. And for the most part, as far as feeding and raising her, Stephanie truly had been on her own.

She wasn't sure why she was thinking of her marriage now. Possibly the comment about her prettiness had done it. She didn't recall Tom ever calling her pretty. He must have. When they first met? When they were engaged or just after their marriage or on their wedding day itself? Why couldn't she *remember*? A couple didn't fall in love, get married, and have a child without some exchange of compliments about the other's appearance.

Had he said anything about how she looked on their wedding day? All she remembered was the face of the preacher. Other than that, the images in her mind had evaporated into thin air. How awful was it to remember nothing but the preacher?

Maybe she couldn't remember because she'd worked so long

and so hard to put Tom out of her mind entirely. The quiet click of the door, which had previously marked the start of her evenings, and now signaled his abrupt exit, was the last she'd ever heard from him.

Tom had brutalized her without ever raising his hand. She knew that now, but it had taken many years with her Bible study group for abandoned women to open her eyes to that fact. According to one of the women in her group—she couldn't even recall that woman's name now—verbal abuse was more destructive than physical abuse. It battered you on the inside. Bruises and scratches, and even broken bones could be healed. Damage to your mind, to your opinion of yourself, to the way you interacted with the world took serious effort to heal. Sometimes, it never did.

She still wasn't sure why she was thinking of all this now.

Well, maybe she did know—it was Tamara and her gun.

What would have happened if she'd shot Tom? Early on, before he told her hundreds, thousands, countless times that she was stupid, that she was a terrible mother, that she couldn't cook to save her soul. Of course, there was no real justification for shooting someone in those circumstances. Your life had to be under physical threat to justify killing someone. Everyone knew that.

It was so confusing, thinking that internal damage was worse than bodily harm, when you could justifiably shoot someone for one and not the other. It was totally unfair. Who made those laws? Who had decided that if someone had a knife to your throat and if you somehow extracted a gun from your purse and pulled the trigger, you would be given a free pass? But if someone looked you directly in the eye and said you didn't deserve to have a child, the one good thing in your life, you were not allowed to kill him?

The problem was when Tom walked out of her life, others had stepped up to take his place. Not other men who loved her, but people who wanted to make sure she knew she was a semi-worth-less human being. A manager in her previous job was one of the first. That man nit-picked at every single thing she did, right down to the way she signed her emails. Then there was that bitch who was the mother of Eileen's best friend at her elementary school. That woman never said anything overt, but she undermined Stephanie with patronizing smiles wrapped around belittling questions about her life.

Where did you say you bought Eileen's shoes? I'm not sure they fit right.

Why was it you couldn't support the fundraiser? It's so important that parents be there for their children.

Do you want some suggestions on how to pack a healthy lunch that a child will actually eat?

I'd be happy to have Eileen over to our home after school one day a week, so she doesn't have to endure the afterschool care workers every single day. Those environments are so damaging, but I understand it's difficult when there's no father in the home.

As that child and Eileen drifted apart, Stephanie had a few months of freedom. Then, a woman named Sara had joined her Bible study group. She took it upon herself to advise Stephanie on how to live a life that wasn't so full of *complaining* and *self-centeredness*, a life focused on what *God* wanted for her, not what Stephanie wanted for *herself*.

After that, Alex swanned into her life. Despite Stephanie's horribly expensive makeover and new clothes, despite her opportunity to become a photographer, Alex was able to undermine her almost every day. She was just like Tom and others before him, as well as those after—a long line of emotional abusers stretching back to childhood.

The subway slowed. She stood and grabbed the pole, then began moving toward the doors so she'd be ready when they opened. She walked quickly through the crowded, steamy station and up the stairs to street level, turning right for the five-block walk home.

It was dark, as always, when she walked home from work during the winter months. Normally, she moved quickly, out of habit, not because she felt threatened. The neighborhood was decent—apartment buildings and a few bistros and markets along her route. There were often people around, so she was only nervous during the last block and a half, past well-lit but deserted building lobbies and equally deserted, unlit alleys.

Occasionally she'd see a man, or several, who ratcheted up her anxiety, his demeanor and attention to her urging her to walk even faster, worried her fear was leaking out around her.

Tonight, the alleys looked darker, and the few cars parked along the curb had an abandoned quality, although she realized this was her imagination. As she passed the alley two buildings before hers, she saw movement from the corner of her eye. She took a deep breath, but it emerged with an accompanying noise she hadn't intended, making it sound like she'd gasped in fear.

It was always a bad idea to let anyone know you were afraid, but Stephanie couldn't seem to help it. Her fears consumed every cell of her body. So the slightest unexpected occurrence caused the fear to rise to the surface, announcing to everyone she was someone to be picked on. She hated that about herself. At times, she felt that even her daughter sensed that weakness and took advantage of it.

The movement she'd seen in the alley turned out to be nothing but a discarded brochure pushed around by a gust of wind that had entered the narrow opening at the right moment. She slowed her pace to something less frantic.

"Hey." A man's voice shot a jolt of terror through her, and she felt her body convulse in response. She tugged her purse closer, moving it around to the front of her hip.

"What's the hurry, bitch?"

"I'm not—"

The laugh was loud. Finally, she saw him standing between

two cars. He was drinking beer from a can and holding an unlit cigarette.

"Got a light?"

"No." She walked faster again. She didn't want to run in her new boots because they were somewhat likely to slip, even on dry pavement.

"Liar."

She shouldn't respond. Don't engage.

"Hey bitch. I'm not gonna rape you. I just want a light for my fucking cigarette."

Her stomach heaved over the disgusting language. She desperately wanted to scream at him, but he might start following her, might actually attack her if she made him angry. She broke into a run, risking the unreliable soles of her boots. Her lobby door was only fifteen or twenty feet away now, if she could just make it… she looked over her shoulder. He would know where she lived! She couldn't fling herself into the safety of a locked building after all.

As she hurried around the corner, she heard him laughing. His voice sounded farther away, and she took several deep breaths as she slowed her frantic pace. He hadn't followed. He'd only wanted to terrorize her. Like Tom. Like Alex.

The world was so unfair! God was supposed to protect His people like little lambs. Why didn't He? Had she done something awful to make Him turn His back on her? Maybe a gun *was* worth thinking about. It would give her confidence, take away this sense that everyone was more powerful than she was. She would never have to use it. Just knowing it was there would make her feel in control. It would make her feel like she had a secret and that if something terrible *did* happen, she was ready.

CHAPTER 10

*T*rystan was frankly tired of the animosity between Alexandra and Stephanie. He didn't understand how it had started or why they had dug in their heels, but the attitude of both women was childish. He'd known Stephanie had neurotic tendencies and that she carried around a great deal of anxiety, but Alex's sullen attitude had shocked him.

From the moment he'd met Alexandra, she struck him as a woman who didn't get caught up in petty disagreements. She was confident and had a positive outlook. She didn't seem to care much what others thought of her. He'd thought that, alongside those qualities, she wouldn't be hyper-critical. Especially with someone who so obviously had less to offer. Why did she care so much? Why did she seem to *need* to put Stephanie in her place?

He supposed some of it was normal competition, both of them wanting to be the lead photographer, the sole photographer, really. That was the part that annoyed him. They'd been hired to work for his organization. Refusing to function as a team in a service that required more than one person was almost sabotage in his mind.

This wasn't a place for prima donnas. That role was reserved for their clients.

He sat in his office, staring out the window, watching rain splatter lightly against the glass. The fine drops of water were soothing and distracting. He was finding it hard to concentrate on anything else because he felt compelled to understand the dynamic between the two women. Keeping his attention on the water patterns should have helped him think clearly. It hadn't.

Maybe once Stephanie completed her classes and Alex saw that she did good work, once they had more in common, the tension would ease.

He pushed his chair back and stood. He stretched his arms, picked up his phone, and slid it into his pocket. He went to Stephanie's door. It was closed, as it often was lately. He knocked.

"Who is it?"

"Trystan."

The door opened almost instantly. "Hi. Sorry."

"No worries, but unless you're on a call, it's better to keep the door open as often as possible."

"It doesn't give much privacy," she said.

"We aren't here for privacy. This is a collaborative environment."

She shrugged one shoulder. "Sorry."

"How is the class going?"

"It's great! I love it. Do you want to sit down and I can tell you about it?" She gestured toward the chair across from her desk.

He stepped into the office, settled in the chair, and pulled his ankle up, resting it on his right knee. "Are you feeling comfortable with the camera?"

"Yes. We've mostly learned about lighting and some composition."

"Good."

"Which is harder with people. He...Leon...mostly talks about photographing objects. Portrait photography is a separate class."

49

"That class is in the mentoring plan, so you know it's already approved."

"Did Alex take that class?"

"I don't recall."

Stephanie gave a single shake of her head. "I don't think she did."

"You're not Alex."

Her face shifted into a glazed expression. A film of tears covered her eyes.

"I didn't intend that to sound so harsh, as if she's the standard of comparison," he said.

"I didn't take it that way."

He was quite sure she *had* taken it that way, and he regretted that he hadn't thought before he opened his mouth. He studied her face. In some ways, she gave the impression of being very exposed and vulnerable, but he realized, not for the first time, that wasn't reality. She was those things, but she also hid quite a lot. He knew very little about her beyond the fact that she had an adult daughter, she was divorced, and she'd worked for a recruiting firm before he'd hired her.

"Do you have any work from the class you can show me?" he asked.

She grinned. "I'd love to. You can critique me." Her skin turned pale pink then grew increasingly red. She swallowed and looked down at her keyboard. She grabbed the mouse and moved it around.

As she clicked through her files, he tried to recall what his first impression of her had been. He'd hired her to manage the office before he even brought Diana on board. Stephanie had come across as efficient and warm, highly ethical, and kind to everyone she met. She'd seemed even-tempered and easy to get along with. He'd since learned that, in addition to being neurotic, she was sneaky to the point that he occasionally had the irrational fear that she had the potential to destroy what he'd built.

It was difficult to figure out how he'd misjudged her so completely.

But had he? Those attractive qualities were still there. It wasn't as if she'd put on an act. He still saw that side of her, but it seemed her insecurity and the resulting tendency to lash out had swallowed most of her good traits. Had she changed under the influence of Alex, or had those facets of her personality already been emerging before Alex arrived on the scene? He couldn't be sure. Had he aggravated the situation by shoving her aside and offering the photographer position to Alex?

He wasn't going to lie to himself. He'd betrayed her. She'd been the one to suggest they make photography a core part of what they offered their clients, and he'd lapped up the idea. Then, when he met Alex and thought about her ability to entice people to let go of their inhibitions, he'd known she was perfect for the job. She presented a smooth, professional image which impressed their clients. She was articulate and witty. She wooed them with her camera, which made them feel special, opening them up to his guidance because they first trusted her so completely.

Shunting Stephanie to the side was wrong, but it was a choice between doing what was best to grow his consulting business and looking out for her easily wounded feelings. Building a business was tough. Surely Stephanie understood that. You didn't always get what you wanted just because you deserved it. There were other factors.

Their client list had grown significantly since Alex started taking photographs, and now was his opportunity to fix the situation. He was certain that if Alex would show a little generosity, she could mold Stephanie into someone stronger and more capable. The bottom line was, they needed at least two photographers, or they couldn't continue to expand.

While his thoughts ran over his views of the two women, Stephanie was rapidly clicking through photographs from her class.

"You're not saying anything," she said. "What do you think?"

"They're good."

"That's all? I know you expect perfection...I think if you look at them from the first ones to what you see here..." she clicked down the screen and began moving through the most recent set. "...you can see how they get so much better."

"They do draw the viewer in. I can see how much you're enjoying this. It shows in the work."

"I think that matters," she said. "Passion."

"I agree."

"I took a few shots of people in the park. I didn't get their permission, but it was just to experiment, so I figured it was okay." She opened the next folder and clicked to arrange the photos into a slideshow. The images moved in a graceful, gliding fashion, one fading to the next. It was clear she'd set this up carefully, hoping for an opportunity to impress him with what she'd done. The pictures were—

"I think I really captured the soul of each person," she said.

"They're good." He wasn't being genuine. They were interesting photos, it was clear she'd chosen her subjects carefully, looking for those who wore unusual clothing or had unique hairstyles. She'd gone out of her way to photograph the elderly and children and people with different racial mixes. But they were candid shots in a park. It wasn't the same as studying an individual and revealing the person beneath their appearance. Her images relied on the external traits to make them interesting, that and the scenery of the park.

"Knowing that God loves each person deeply and completely helps me bring out who they really are."

She hadn't done that at all, but clearly, she had no doubts that what she'd accomplished was exactly what he was looking for.

"You don't seem very excited about them. I put a lot of work into this."

"And it shows." He had to build up her confidence. He was

committed to this choice, and he had to give her a chance. If her confidence grew, surely her skill would develop alongside of it. "You're doing a terrific job. It shows a lot of initiative that you spent your weekend time working on this."

He could feel the shift in her body, a relaxing of the tension he'd noticed earlier, the tension that found its way easily into the words she spoke and most of her gestures. He felt disingenuous telling her the photographs were good when they were not at all what she would be expected to do with their clients.

"Do you think they're any good?"

He nodded. "I do." Her craving for praise was like a gaping hole beside him, needing to be filled with more words, more enthusiasm in his tone. But it could easily backfire if she didn't accept Alex's coaching on how the photography work for their clients differed from candid shots on a Saturday afternoon against the stark emptiness of winter.

"You have a lot of potential, Stephanie."

"I know. I told you that. I want your consulting work to be hugely successful."

He was touched. Despite his hesitations about her work, it felt good to have someone care about his success in such a personal way. "Thank you. I feel like this is almost a calling for me and—"

"Oh, I agree. That makes all the difference when you're called to something."

"It's not just about the money and building a reputation. I really do want to help people achieve the success they're dreaming of."

"You have a good heart," she said.

"It's great to see you putting so much into this. Once you get working with Alex, I think things will..."

He felt her stiffen again. He sighed. Why couldn't she, why couldn't *both* of them, be more professional? Women could be so petty, so competitive. It exhausted him. "Great work." He stood.

"Please do take that class in portraiture. If you're enjoying learn-ing, you should make the most of it."

When he left her office, he felt physically ill. He'd lied. And with that, he'd surely set himself up for more difficult challenges down the road.

CHAPTER 11

 *ortland, Oregon*

* * *

EVEN THOUGH I'D seen Brady Jackson around campus nearly every day for almost three years of high school, he'd never looked my way, and I'd never really looked carefully at him. He was a jock, and those guys were mostly boring, in my experience. There were enough of them at church for me to know what they were like, although I suppose a religious jock might be more boring than a secular one.

When he'd opened his front door to hear me explain why I was returning the money I'd skimmed from the church candy sales, I knew he was a guy I wouldn't mind hanging around with. It was just an awareness, nothing specific. Maybe it was mostly his smile and his very nice shoulders. And, he had a car.

So far, I'd kissed a lot of guys—seven or eight by the time I was sixteen. I'd let a few of them slide their warm hands up my shirt and fiddle around inside my bra. The last guy, partially because he was very smooth about it, managed to get his hand into my pants and had enticed mine into his.

Brady seemed like a guy I might want to have sex with. It wasn't as if I'd been planning this out, scouting for the perfect candidate, but all the little pieces came together in that single moment.

I liked kissing. I liked being touched, especially by guys who weren't afraid of my body, especially my tongue—its words, not its feel. I was getting tired of not knowing what was so awesome about sex. And I actually didn't know a lot about the awesome side. I mostly had been told my body belonged to god and my future husband. People talked as if some invisible spirit had made notes on all the guys my age that lived in my general area and decided which one I would marry. Someday. I definitely knew I wasn't waiting for *someday*. I wasn't even sure I *wanted* someday.

I was tired of hearing how I had to guard my feelings, how I had to be careful of boys that didn't honor the purity of girls, how I had to make sure they didn't put their hands, or anything else, where they didn't belong. I was tired of hearing that I would destroy my soul and tarnish my value. I would disappoint god and, most likely, end up with a child I hadn't planned on if I had sex when I was young and single.

All of those dire warnings made me think sex must be pretty remarkable. The adults sure were worried about it happening with the wrong person at the wrong time. My parents didn't address it much, they expected the church teachers who were trained in that sort of thing to take care of warning me. My parents' job, in their view, was to make sure I stayed around the house at night, that I wasn't out anywhere alone, that I didn't associate with the wrong people and other aspects of guarding my purity.

But a teenager, and even a little girl, learns about a lot more things at school than some parents seemed to realize. At least mine didn't. They tried to make sure I was primarily friends with kids I met at church or kids they knew in our neighborhood, but it didn't occur to them that during recess and PE and lunch and before class started and walking from class to class, there was a lot of time for kids to share important information. And sex was one of the most important topics there was. Our church leaders had made that clear.

So I knew it could be fun and exciting, and somewhat addictive.

I couldn't wait to try it out. But I didn't want some guy who bored me or a guy I kissed just because the circumstances happened to be right. I wanted it to be worth my while. I wanted it to be memorable, although I also knew enough to realize the odds of it being memorable in a good way were not in my favor.

Looking at Brady's smile as I stood on his front porch had changed my entire day. I realized that the miserable, disappointing chore of returning the money I'd skimmed, forced upon me by my mother, had opened the door, literally, to something I never saw coming. I had no idea I'd be talking to a very hot guy, no idea I would feel his interest drawn to me, and no idea that giving back the money would get me something else that I wanted.

As I gazed at him, I was also thinking about whether he owned a car. Until that moment, the worst thing in my life was that my father had refused to buy me a car, and my plan to earn money to buy my own had taken a spectacular nose dive into the pavement.

Here was a guy who interested me, and as a side benefit, might give me the transportation out of my parents' line of sight that I was longing for.

The following Tuesday, Brady was standing outside the girls' locker room after my PE class. The base of my neck was still damp with sweat because there was no time for more than a very quick shower after PE, basically hosing ourselves off, trying to keep our hair out of the stream of water because there certainly wasn't time to blow it dry.

"My mom said thanks for returning the money," Brady said as he began walking beside me. "She thinks you must be a very sweet girl."

"Because I lied about the price of the candy bars? That's pretty cool, to give it back and get credit for doing something good when you did something bad first. It's like extra credit to make up for getting a C on your Algebra test."

He laughed. "You're funny."

"Thanks."

"You don't get to take that as a compliment. You're either born funny, or you're not."

"You said it like it was a compliment."

"Fair enough. What's your next class?"

I told him I was headed to U.S. History, and he said his next class was in the same building. "English, with Crowley."

"Lucky you," I said.

"I know, right? Have you ever had her?"

"Nope. I've just heard the stories."

We talked about the English teacher who tore up papers right in front of the class if she found a grammatical error or a typo. The teacher who made kids explain why they didn't know the answer to one of her questions about the classic novels we were required to read. Then, we talked about our favorite classes—history and art for me, Algebra and PE for him.

"How are you doing in U.S. History?" he asked.

"3.9 average."

"I'm 4.1 in Algebra," he said.

"Brainy."

"I guess. Want to cut?"

"Sure."

He looked surprised.

"Where should we go?" I asked.

"Uh...I don't know. I didn't think you'd say yes so fast. Most girls don't want to get in trouble for cutting class."

"We could hang out in your car," I said.

"Sure. Why not. Do you want to smoke some weed?"

"No. Just talk."

We turned the corner and walked casually down the hallway toward the side exit of the humanities building. It wasn't hard to leave the building. The difficult part came when they called roll and marked you absent and then demanded a note from an adult and then handed you detention if you didn't have one. After three cuts, parents were notified. That was never good for me, but I'd only had one cut that year. Brady was worth it.

In the parking lot, he led me through the maze of cars to the Honda that belonged to him. It looked almost new, and I wondered if his parents had bought it for him. I doubted he had a part-time job because of all his time spent playing football. He unlocked it, and we climbed inside. He turned it on to roll down the windows and left the engine on so we could listen to CDs.

We talked about school, and he talked about football. He wanted to know if I ever went to the games. I did, but I never watched. I had no idea what position he played, and that seemed to disappoint him. It was impossible to concentrate on the games because the drama happening in the stands was much more interesting than a bunch of guys struggling to keep control of a ball that looked like a chocolate egg.

He asked me about TV shows I liked, and of course, I couldn't answer because the Mallory kids weren't allowed to watch any normal TV shows. I was always at a disadvantage when other kids talked about shows they liked. It was the same for movies and music. Still, I managed to bluff my way through most of the time, mostly by acting fascinated by what others thought of each show and actor and musician and song they mentioned.

Brady didn't fall for that quite as easily. He kept pushing.

I sighed. "My family goes to Pure Truth Tabernacle. Normal entertainment isn't their thing."

He laughed. "What kind of entertainment do you have?"

"Classic movies. Books. Classical music. Religious music."

"Shit. How can you even deal with it?"

I shrugged. "I'll catch up once I graduate and get out of the house."

He laughed. "See, you're very funny."

I didn't think my comment was that hilarious. I think he meant that I didn't get all wound up about it like most kids would. I didn't rant and rave about how my parents sucked and how deprived I was. There was no point. I did my best to get around the things I could with them or battled it out until I lost. Otherwise, I bided my time.

After a while, Brady and I stopped talking. He leaned toward me, put his hand on the back of my head, and drew my face close to his. He closed his eyes and kissed me. He kissed me softly at first, and then with so much intensity, it felt like I was kissing for the first time, which was exactly what I'd wanted, and what I'd hoped for.

CHAPTER 12

$\mathcal{N}$ew York

* * *

I'D MANAGED to put my mind to rest over Kent's questions without succumbing to my recently abandoned smoking habit, but the questions continued to bubble up in my mind when I least expected them. Kent and his curiosity hovered at the edges of my awareness, waiting to pounce. I could feel his need for answers simmering. The questions I'd shoved under the rug were inside his head, rattling around, craving resolution.

The human brain hates a question it can't answer and will expend all its energy trying to latch onto something, anything, to satisfy that unrelenting discomfort. Some people say that's what draws people to conspiracy theories. When no answer is forthcoming, like during the aftermath of a presidential assassination, neatly packaged theories provide comfort and understanding and some level of certainty. Conspiracy theories scratch that itch.

I shoved Kent and his questions out of my head. They

returned, and I shoved them away again. It was nothing to worry about. Nothing but casual curiosity. He didn't suspect me of being involved. He simply didn't like that Rafe's death was sudden, shocking, and unexplained. He didn't like that Victoria had disappeared so smoothly and quickly. And he wanted to know what had happened.

I'd hoped he would get busy with work, turn his attention back to lifting weights and having sex, and the questions would dissolve. But a text message on Tuesday afternoon brought him back to center stage inside my head.

Kent: *Dinner? I was thinking street tacos. And martinis.*

Alex: *Do those go together?*

Kent: *I think so.*

Alex: *When?*

Kent: *Tonight, obviously.*

I sent a thumbs up. There was a chance he just wanted tacos and martinis, catching up and sex. There was also a chance that taking his clothes off instead of answering his questions the last time I'd seen him had fed his curiosity. It seemed the easy solution at the time, but I'd known it might circle back around. And here we were. Maybe.

I closed the browser window where I'd been reading goal-setting essays and personality test summaries for a new client. I got up and closed my office door. I opened a private browser window and typed *apartments for rent.*

It was impulsive, but it was time to get started. Suddenly moving out of the building, leaving behind the ghosts of Victoria and Rafe, would double Kent's interest in *my* lack of interest. It would make the questions seem larger, more important, and critical to find answers to.

But, if I found a nice apartment and suggested we move in together, I could play the oppressive girlfriend, and he would probably back away. If it turned out he liked the idea of living together, my backup plan was to let him see the home decor I was searching for and bookmarking on my phone. The thought of a house filled with an abundance of furniture, tabletops littered with decorative figures and bowls, bookcases and game shelves, the thought of watching his minimalist lifestyle sink under the weight of my purchases, swallowed alive by a female's possessions, would change the dynamic between us. I expected he would shove me out of his life as firmly as I'd tried to shove his insistent questions out of my head.

The apartments I found were expensive. Of course. They were nicer and more modern than the one I was living in, and they were in neighborhoods that had more restaurants and shops, fewer alleys, and liquor stores. Although the prices made my eyes widen, I was making a great salary with Trystan—more than I'd ever earned in my life. I'd never wanted to spend too much on rent because I was saving all that I possibly could, but maybe I needed to find a way to get a whole lot more coming in rather than scrimping and saving my way to my dreams.

I was tired of freezing in the winter, and already I felt the thick, wet heat of summer creeping toward me. It seemed like the right time to consider a nicer home, even if it meant delaying my ultimately perfect home by a year or three.

By the end of the afternoon, I had a list of ten apartments that looked appealing to me. All of them were manageable on my income, even though it would take quite a large bite out of what I saved every month. At the same time, maybe watching cash flow through my fingers would put my attention on seriously finding some way to accelerate my income.

I told Trystan I had a dentist appointment and left early after arranging a time to see three of the apartments.

* * *

"YOU'LL HAVE to fill out a financial qualification form." These were the first words out of the real estate agent's mouth as I stood in an empty living room on the tenth floor, looking at other high-rise buildings at the edge of the Upper West Side. It was absolutely breathtaking. I could see myself with a small couch or a comfy armchair a few feet from that enormous window, gazing from above at the city, considering its occupants—the interesting and the bland, as well as the occasional person who deserved to die.

I knew I would pass the agent's financial test, but I also knew that her urgent need to tell me about it meant she had doubts about my solvency. She wondered whether and maybe assumed, I was wasting her time. Maybe it was my super high heels, and my hair scooped into a ponytail. Maybe it was just my relaxed attitude. I said nothing and left her to worry that I would drag out the afternoon when she could have been meeting with serious candidates.

When I was finished exploring the vacant rooms, touching granite countertops and silken stainless steel appliances, standing for several minutes in front of each window, wanting to make the view permanently mine, I thanked her.

She handed me a packet. "The financial application is on the left side," she said as if I would be incapable of finding it in the thin packet without her direction. "You can also find it online, which would be faster."

"Thanks." I gave her a charming smile.

"I have four other interested parties, so I'll need it back before the end of the week if you want to be considered."

"I'm just getting started with my search. I'm not ready to fill out forms yet."

Her already limp smile disappeared entirely. "I have to respect your honesty, telling me you just wasted an hour of my time."

"I need to see what's out there in my price range."

She nodded crisply. "That's fine, but it would have been more appropriate for you to attend an open house."

"I had time today."

She walked to the door, heels clicking, and wrenched it open. "The market is not in the renter's favor, so I suggest you learn the rules and follow them."

"Is it a *rule* that I can't look at an apartment if I'm not ready to make a deposit the same day?"

"It's unspoken."

"Good to know." I went out.

She hung back, then closed the door. I heard the lock turn. I went to the elevator and rode to the first floor. She wouldn't be welcoming next time, but I was sure if she saw my salary, money would triumph over the unwritten rules of New York real estate, if they even existed outside of her own head.

That evening I handed the brochure to Kent while I mixed our second round of martinis.

He opened the folder. As he removed the sheet showing the floor plan, I poured vodka and vermouth into the shaker, sealed the top, and began rattling liquid and ice to drown out the silence of him studying the layout, then glancing at a sheet showing an exterior photo of the building and shots of the rooms.

He studied the luscious photographs for several minutes, and it crossed my mind that Stephanie would be better suited to taking real estate photos than trying to get human beings to respond to her camera. She could be the photographer she longed to be, and she wouldn't deflate Trystan's business by making the clients squirm like bugs under a microscope.

I poured alcohol into the glasses.

"Are you moving?" Kent placed the folder, pages tucked securely back inside, on the counter.

I stabbed a stir stick into three olives, lining them up and placing them gently into the first glass. "I'm thinking about it."

"What started you thinking about that?"

I stabbed and sunk the olives into the other glass and handed it to him. "Cheers." Before he could speak, I took a sip of mine. I thought about toasting new experiences but decided that might close off the conversation before I had a chance to see how he was going to respond.

As it turned out, we went to bed after our martinis. We didn't discuss murder or previous neighbors, or new apartments.

CHAPTER 13

*T*he sound of voices seeped through Stephanie's closed office door. She heard Trystan's soothing tenor and Alexandra's clear, sharp words, but it was impossible to tell what they were saying. She couldn't even distinguish scattered words. She longed to open her door and listen to the conversation, but she was pretty sure it wasn't possible to do so without them noticing.

She moved away from her keyboard and stretched her hands.

The warmth of Trystan's words from the day before had stayed with her, comforting her through a quick dinner of salad with a bit of tuna, a cup of tea, and then early to bed. The words had rocked her to sleep as she recalled his voice and his obvious hesitation before gushing over the pictures she'd taken. It almost seemed as if he'd been embarrassed, afraid to share his feelings about how her work had touched him.

That morning, she'd woken early and taken extra care doing her makeup and styling her new haircut so that she looked as good as she had during that first week after the remake of her appearance. For a while, the effort of makeup and styling her hair hadn't seemed worth it. She'd begun to think Eileen had wasted money on the makeover, and Stephanie was wasting hours of her life putting effort into her appearance that wasn't paying off. It was hard to explain how she'd thought it *might* pay off, but she'd definitely expected some sort of obvious change in her life. So far, there had been none.

She touched her hair, then ran her fingers through the sides, lifting it off her face. The minute she pulled her hand away, the hair fell across her cheek again. It felt elegant and luxurious. She stood and walked to the door.

The voices were still indistinguishable. She pressed her ear against the door. If anything, the conversation was more muffled than before. She closed her eyes. Were they talking about her? Was Trystan telling Alexandra how sensitive and evocative Stephanie's photographs were? If he was, she had no doubt Alex was smirking and making vicious negative comments. She might even roll her eyes in a subtle way that Trystan would barely notice but still absorb.

Stephanie pushed the handle down and opened the door. She walked to the break room and opened the fridge. Staring inside, she strained to hear. The hum of the fridge prevented her from getting any more clarity than she'd had in her office. The world was conspiring to keep her from knowing what was going on. They had no right to talk about her as if she were a child, someone in need of guidance, too incompetent to do a simple job without their help. Trystan had implied that but then managed to recognize how wrong he was. Alex was probably talking him right back around to that insulting point of view.

She grabbed a bottle of berry-flavored water and closed the fridge, slamming the door a bit too hard. She twisted off the cap, took a swallow, and then coughed as the carbonation ran across the tender skin of her esophagus. She walked down the hallway, tossing her hair away from her face. She had a right to know what was going on.

Through the doorway of Trystan's office, she saw Alex seated across from him. She had arranged her hair so it fell over the back of the chair in thick waves. When she moved, her hair moved like it was performing a dance.

"I don't think she's ready to meet with a client," Alex said. "I mean, she could tag along, but she isn't ready to take photographs. Even as a backup."

"Don't make this more complicated than it is," Trystan said. "Anyone can take photographs, and hers will be better than most. Once you see them, you can give a few pointers, but this isn't brain surgery."

She moved into the doorway. "Talking about me?" She felt a smile creep across her face. It was something Alex might say—bold and almost embarrassing, but turning the embarrassment around to the others. She was proud of her sudden show of strength. Where had that come from?

"Actually, yes," Trystan said. "Come on in." He stood and grabbed the other chair, pulling it toward the desk.

Alex didn't bother to turn around. She acted as if Stephanie hadn't even entered the room. It was not surprising, but it still irritated Stephanie to the point that she wanted to deliberately bump her hip against Alex's chair as she passed by.

Stephanie settled in the chair Trystan had provided and turned so that Alex was at the very edge of her vision. She put her full attention on Trystan's kind, handsome face.

"We were discussing your readiness to start photographing clients."

"I think I should start now," Stephanie said. "I should have started ages ago. My class is finished next week."

"According to the plan, you're supposed to take a class in portraits," Alex said.

"I am, but that shouldn't stop me from getting started. That class is on top of everything else I've done. You started taking photographs before you even took the portrait class," Stephanie said.

"I didn't take it."

The room was silent. Stephanie kept her gaze locked on Trystan's face. He was staring at something she couldn't identify, meeting no one's eyes.

"Trystan loved my photographs."

He smiled but didn't look at her. "I think she's ready. It's good to dive in headfirst."

"May I see them?" Alex said.

"I don't know why we're even talking about this. Trystan thinks they're great, my class is almost complete, I need to start meeting with clients." Once again, she was proud of her strength. Maybe her makeover had helped after all, it had just taken time for her new hair and chic clothes to be woven into her personality. Or maybe she was just fed up with Alex. It wasn't Alex's job to decide when Stephanie was *ready*.

"I think it's a good idea for Stephanie to go with you and get the flow of what you do in each situation. We probably should have done that sooner," Trystan said.

Stephanie tried to keep the smile inside of herself. She was winning! For once, she was winning.

Alex shifted in her chair, crossing her legs slowly, moving her shoulders as if she were settling in for the afternoon. "You know best." The tone in her voice had changed—it was lower, softer.

Was Alex *flirting* with him? It sure looked and sounded that way. The thought made her furious. In one swallow, all her pride in her bold statements and her assurance that her photography was admired by Trystan was devoured by rage. Trystan was a wonderful boss, and she was starting to see what an amazing man he was as well. Alex would destroy him. Besides, if he was interested in anyone, it should be Stephanie. She'd been beside him from the start. She understood him and offered him quiet strength. Alex was a monster.

Stephanie leaned forward, trying to force Trystan to turn his attention back to her. "I can't wait to get started."

"We'll need to coordinate, so we don't trip all over each other." Alex placed the tips of her fingers on the edge of Trystan's desk. She laughed softly. "Remember that time with Jim—"

"Why don't you two go into the conference room and go over the upcoming photography sessions and figure out a game plan so—"

"Won't I be going with you and Alexandra when you have the first meetings to introduce the photographers?" Stephanie asked

"Too many people," Alex said. "They'll feel ambushed."

"That's ridiculous," Stephanie said. "Three people is not an ambush."

"I agree with Alex," Trystan said. "It's too much for an initial meeting. Eventually, you'll go with me when you're handling clients one-on-one, but for now..." He crossed his arms. He looked first at Alex, then Stephanie. "We're talking this to death. Go work out a plan." He stood.

Stephanie and Alex remained rooted to their chairs as if standing admitted defeat in their battle to the death. To the death of what, Stephanie wasn't sure, but it definitely felt like that's what was happening between them. Until one of them resigned? Until Trystan fired one or both of them? Surely he wouldn't do that to Stephanie after the absolute loyalty she'd shown him over the years. But he was smitten with Alex, and Stephanie couldn't imagine him telling her to leave. He seemed to think their recent success was purely a result of Alex's flair for photography. The idea was absurd. She smirked.

"Is this a joke to you?" Alex's tone was condescending. She was putting on an act for Trystan, trying to manipulate the situation so that she and Trystan were on the same side, making Stephanie out to be the failed protégé.

"No."

"Good," Alex said.

Trystan sighed. He walked out of the room, and a moment later, the main door to their suite of offices opened and closed.

"I see what you're up to," Stephanie said.

"You do? Why don't you let me in on the secret."

"You aren't going to sabotage me."

Alex laughed. "I wouldn't dream of it." She stood and walked out of the room. Stephanie followed her. Alex didn't go into the conference room as Trystan had told them to. Instead, Stephanie found her settled in her own office.

"Come here, and I'll show you the schedule," Alex said.

Stephanie walked into the office, feeling as if she'd been forced into enemy territory, lost the skirmish. Her skin was hot with rage.

* * *

THAT EVENING, she brought home sushi, wanting to make sure Eileen felt some obligation to linger over dinner, which she might not if they simply nibbled salads or heated the leftover chicken. She put a candle in the center of the table. She took the elegant rolls out of the cardboard containers and arranged them on plates. Beside each pair of wooden chopsticks provided by the restaurant, she folded a pale blue cloth napkin.

"This is fancy," Eileen said.

"A midweek treat." Stephanie poured water over several bags of green tea in the small pot her Bible study leader had given to her for Christmas. She placed it on the table and got out thin, china teacups.

"And it gets fancier." Eileen seated herself and began placing slices of the spider roll onto her plate.

They ate, dipping their rice and seaweed wrapped rolls into soy sauce. Eileen smeared wasabi on her pieces while Stephanie put the barest amount possible, terrified of the extreme heat burning her mouth.

First, she let Eileen talk about her day, the details of the photo-shoot, and the new guy she was seeing, although she continued to be vague about him. Any other night, Stephanie would have pumped her daughter for details, but she needed to get the stress of the day out of her head. She needed to talk, to complain if she was honest. Eileen could be a good listener when she felt like it.

"I have a problem," Stephanie said.

"What's that?" Eileen popped a California roll into her mouth.

"Alexandra is going to sabotage my chance to become a photographer."

Eileen smirked. She finished chewing and took a sip of tea. "She's not going to *sabotage* you."

"She told you about it?"

"No. I just know she won't do that."

"How do you know?"

"Normal people don't go around *sabotaging* their co-workers."

"She's not normal."

Eileen took another sip of tea. "Can we talk about something else?"

"I don't know what to do."

"Do your job and quit looking for evil intentions in every corner."

"I'm not doing that."

"I think you are." Then, Eileen began talking about her plans for the weekend, including dinner with the mystery man.

Eileen didn't believe her. The women in her Bible study group would tell her to trust God to take care of it. Stephanie felt very alone as if Eileen wasn't even in the room.

There was no way she was *looking* for evil intentions as if it were an Easter egg hunt. Evil was staring her right in the face.

CHAPTER 14

Once I had the idea of a new apartment in my head, I became obsessed with it. I spent Thursday evening searching online for more apartments. I compared floor plans side-by-side, I read about building amenities, I calculated deposits and the utility costs required for a larger place. I even started looking at furniture.

I'd lived like a college student for too long. Now that I was solidly in my thirties, it was time to find a place where I really liked hanging out, instead of just a place to sleep and store my clothes and makeup. I'd lived in beautiful homes—in Australia, and quite a few weekends in upstate New York, but other people controlled those spaces. In Australia, only my bedroom belonged to me; and in upstate New York, I was living precariously in someone else's suite of rooms. The beautiful spaces in those palatial houses might as well not have even existed a lot of the time.

Getting into the kind of place I imagined—a penthouse, an estate, something magnificent that's only seen in movies—was a long way off. I wanted to be living in this mythical home by the time I was forty or so, but at the rate I was going, that was not looking good. Maybe I would figure out how to make astronomical amounts of money if I had a place where I could stretch out, offering more space for my thoughts to roam, spreading my wings, so to speak.

It would be nice to have more satisfying views. Now that I no longer smoked, what good was a dingy roof garden that was too hot during the summer and icy cold in winter?

I wanted to enjoy a pleasant, comfortable home while I was young, not put off half my living until I was middle-aged. There was also the getting-away-from-Kent aspect. And I also liked the idea that I'd no longer be reminded of Victoria and Rafe every time I stepped out my front door, half-expecting Victoria to pop into the hallway, all ready to start a confusing conversation with me.

Most of the apartments I found had two or three bedrooms. A single bedroom was harder to come by. I definitely did not want a studio, no matter how spacious it claimed to be. I wanted to entertain without my guests tossing their coats onto my bed. I wanted a second bathroom, so I wasn't compelled to clean every time someone used it.

The more I thought about it, there were quite a lot of things I wanted.

Observing Arlinda, one of our recent clients, had shown me that the way to a more lucrative income was to have something of your own. The certainty was growing inside me—maybe if I had a home that really felt like a home, I could figure out what career I wanted to own.

When I walked into the Cuban restaurant where I was meeting Eileen for dinner, I had my messenger bag stuffed with brochures and floor plans. It was amazing that even in the digital age, every single real estate agent shoved business cards and folders stuffed with papers and sheets of glossy, colorful card stock into my hand.

We ordered drinks and opened our menus. I grabbed a tortilla chip from the stone dish, scooped it through the pico de gallo, and

CATHRYN GRANT

felt the satisfying crunch and tang in my mouth. Eileen talked while I ran my gaze up and down the menu.

She mostly wanted to complain about Stephanie. She alternated between that and praising her new boyfriend. But talking about her boyfriend caused her thoughts to circle right back around to Stephanie because Eileen was convinced her mother was not going to like this guy. I couldn't imagine Stephanie liking any guy her daughter was interested in, so it seemed sort of obvious to me that she wouldn't like this one.

When our drinks came, Eileen kept on about her mother.

"I feel like I can't breathe sometimes. I think Ned has a lot to do with how I'm feeling because some of my feelings seem like they popped up out of nowhere. She and I were pretty close when she was getting her new clothes and all of that. It was fun, but I think she took it that our shopping and salon visits meant we were girlfriends, that we were going to hang out. I love her but—"

"You want to be with people your age."

"Not that, exactly. Just people I choose...maybe, or people that didn't change my diaper." She laughed. "I like seeing her and doing things together, but we're not *girlfriends*. I feel sad for her. So that makes it hard."

"Why?"

"She needs me."

"She's your mother. She should have her own friends. It's not your job to be friends with your mother."

"Lots of women are close with their mothers."

"Maybe." I knew my situation was not the norm, but neither was Eileen's. Stephanie wouldn't know what a fun evening was if it bit her on the nose.

"Are you close with your mother?" she asked.

I shook my head.

Our food arrived. I hoped it would distract Eileen from asking more about my mother. I could easily change the subject myself, but then she might bring it up again. It wasn't that I was hiding

76

anything from her, I just didn't feel like talking about it. My mother was confusing and complicated. Every time I'd tried to explain her to people, they'd walked away with the impression there was something wrong with me. They thought my mother sounded perfectly wonderful, and I sounded stubborn and critical. Of *course* there was something wrong with me, but I didn't feel the need to make that obvious to everyone I knew.

We started eating our masitas and rice. Eileen returned to talking about her mother as if that was the meal we'd been served, and that was the topic we were stuck with.

"I can't choose what I want for dinner, or even if I don't want to eat dinner at all. Or maybe I want to eat at ten at night. Sometimes I have early calls, but most of the time, my jobs start in the afternoon. I like to go to the gym in the evening, and I don't want to go to bed at nine-thirty." She laughed. "I want some freedom. I don't want to have to tell her where I'm going every single day. I feel like I'm ten years old."

"Why are you still living with her?"

She sighed. She scooped up a forkful of rice and ate it. "To be honest, I'm not sure how we got to this point. I guess I felt sorry for her. I moved home after college to save money, and then I just felt too guilty leaving."

"Why would you feel guilty? Don't most parents want their kids to grow up and be on their own?"

"It's hard to explain."

"Try."

"I think it's partly her religion."

Maybe that was why Eileen and I connected—some unspoken awareness of mothers inclined to fanaticism. It was possible she would understand more about my mother than I'd realized. It surprised me I'd never thought much about it before. "Why do you think it's about religion?"

"I think she feels like she's not finished raising me because I don't go to church. I'm pretty sure she thinks if she keeps me around, she'll be able to convince me to start getting involved with all of that."

"Oh."

"It's not so bad. It means a lot to her. It seems to make her feel like her life has purpose. She has a lot of friends at church, so that's good."

"Then why are you still living there? If she wants to convert you and you don't want to be converted? It seems kind of...not relaxing. You always wonder when the next little religious bullet is going to get fired at your head."

She laughed. "That is the strangest thing I've ever heard someone say about religion."

"Is it?"

She took a sip of her drink and looked around the restaurant. "I should bring Ned here."

"You should. Does he like a lot of different kinds of food?"

"Everyone who lives in New York City likes a wide variety of food."

"Not your mother."

"Okay, true. Most people who live here." She sipped her drink. "I should move out. You're right."

"I didn't say you *should*."

"But I should. I don't want to make her sad, though. It's really hard."

"If you stay, you're making yourself sad. And people should be responsible for their own sadness. It's not your job to keep her company."

The conversation finally drifted to other topics, with Eileen looking more and more agitated the longer we sat there. We ordered a second round of drinks. I could tell her thoughts were on Stephanie and the idea of moving out of her apartment. I wondered if she was at the point with Ned that they wanted to live together. Maybe that's what had her thinking in that direction. Stephanie would go ballistic over that.

CHAPTER 15

 *ortland, Oregon*

* * *

AFTER THAT FIRST KISS, Brady's car became my home away from home.

I manufactured a study partner, complete with photographs of Brady's older sister, to show my mother the person with whom I was working on my history project. I created less detailed fake partners for my science project. These projects were real, so that part wasn't difficult. They were also group projects, for real. What wasn't real was the amount of after-school hours required. The teachers gave us most of the time necessary to meet with our partners in the classroom, to discuss what we were planning before we did solitary work at home.

Providing extensively detailed, daily progress reports on what happened at these school meetings dulled my mother's normally sharp radar over how I was spending my time. Well, mostly dulled. She didn't understand why we never chose to study at our home. I explained that the other kids in the group lived closer to one another, and even though I invited them, they always chose the house within walking distance of the school.

Another benefit of these after-school projects was that my parents didn't expect me to hang out in the living room with them on school nights. They knew I had other homework. I could spend the time in my room, learning about history and science. I could dig into assigned novels, even though some of them were so boring I thought my brain might curl into a tiny ball and become a hard shell without any visible signs of life, like a roly-poly bug.

When the final bell rang each day, I bolted out of school with a smile on my face, my books zipped inside my backpack where they would remain until after dinner. After we escaped the school grounds, Brady drove to a park that offered lots of undeveloped open space. We parked under a thick oak tree and got into the backseat.

For hours, we kissed and talked. The only thing I wanted was the feel of Brady's mouth on mine. Kissing was a transcendent experience, and I wondered if any of the people at my church who talked on about their experiences of god were describing the same kind of thing. My mind felt like a bowl that had tipped over, and all the liquid had run out. I thought about nothing but the smell and taste and sensation of that boy.

For the first few weeks we were together, we mostly kissed. Sometimes we stopped and talked about life and what we wanted. We talked about how stupid the school administrators were with their arbitrary rules. Sometimes we talked about football. He told me about camping trips with his parents and two sisters. I told him about church services and youth group lectures, and camps. We laughed at the ideas my church believed were deadly serious. Truly deadly. I told him Bible stories. He'd never heard most of them. I entertained myself at the same time, hearing my voice tell those familiar stories with my own spin. I felt the intensity of Brady listening as if I were telling the latest superhero story.

I had to admit, the stories I'd grown up with were interesting. My editorial comments that advised god how he could have handled the situation a bit better or gave biblical characters a more rebellious streak as if I were inhabiting each one of them, did make them seem like stories for the ages.

I suppose there's a reason those stories survived a few thousand years. I suppose there's a reason children like going to Sunday School—it's entertaining. I actually did like it, at first. It wasn't until I got older that the problems began. The teachers started hammering, with increasing force, on what I was supposed to *learn* from these stories and how I was supposed to live my life based on the hidden messages. They weren't problems to me, of course, only to the adults surrounding me. I had questions that no one wanted to answer.

When I came home from seeing Brady and my mother commented on my raw, bright red lips, I said the air in my classroom was dry, and I'd developed a bad habit of licking my lips too often. She bought me lip balm, which actually helped.

She also seemed to observe the mixture of desire and satisfaction in my eyes because she asked constantly whether I was feeling okay. After she finished picking at her dinner, she came around the table and touched the back of her hand to my forehead. The medium-sized diamond on her left ring finger scraped my brow, but she didn't seem to notice.

"You don't feel warm," she said. "Are you sure everything is okay?"

I nodded. I pushed out my chair and began picking up plates, stacking them to carry to the kitchen.

"Go upstairs and lie down," she said. "I'm worried about you."

"I'm fine."

"You don't look well."

"I feel great."

"Then why do you have those red spots on your cheeks? Why are your pupils dilated? There's plenty of light in here."

I shrugged.

She took the plates out of my hands. "Go lie down."

"I have homework."

"It can wait."

Obediently, I walked slowly out of the room, possibly dragging my feet for the dramatic effect. If there *was* a dramatic effect, it was lost on my father, and my mother already believed I needed extra rest.

One afternoon, as Brady and I wrapped our arms and legs around each other on his narrow back seat, he placed his hand over my breast. It felt as if he was testing the thickness of it, but possibly what I sensed was his lack of certainty about whether I would be okay with this.

I said nothing, and he continued moving his hand around.

Within a week, we were enjoying the simultaneous chill and heat of taking our shirts off, feeling the skin of the other, and wondering why anyone ever did anything else in life besides this.

In the back of my mind, the words of our preacher, my father, my mother, my Sunday School teachers, camp leaders, and older kids who were brought in to tell the high school kids where they'd gone off track so we wouldn't make the same mistakes, echoed in my mind. Not constantly. Not while Brady's hands were on my breasts, or I felt the gentle brush of his chest hair against my skin, but occasionally as we drove home.

All the things that I'd been told were so displeasing to god, things that would make him weep for me, danced across my thoughts. None of those remembered words brought up the guilt that was supposed to crush me, the guilt and restraint that was supposed to be strong enough to override the desires in my body.

Instead, I wondered why all those adults cared so very much. I wondered why they thought they had any right to decide how I should spend my time and what parts of me I should let this awesome boy touch. I didn't understand why they believed I should view myself as some sort of object—a prize to be won, a prize that I had to look after to make sure the guy who *did* win it got what he deserved, what he was owed.

CHAPTER 16

*N*ew York City

* * *

IT SEEMED to Stephanie that the guy who had crept up on her to ask for a light to his cigarette had waited all week, giving her time to feel safe, to let down her guard, before he pounced again. On Friday night, two blocks from her apartment, he appeared, as if out of nowhere.

He stood about ten feet to her right, leaning against the post of an awning. "Hey. Long time no see." His voice was giddy, most likely because he was high on some dangerous illegal substance.

She veered toward the curb and quickened her pace, tightening her grip on her purse and pressing it hard against her hip. She feared it might swing wildly away from her, giving him a chance to grab the strap, throw her to the ground, and escape with the purse in one swift move. The scenario racing through her mind made her step awkwardly on the outside edge of her foot. She stumbled, suppressed a cry of pain, and righted herself.

"Need help?" he asked.

She turned her face toward the street. There didn't seem to be anyone else around. It was Friday night. Yes, it was cold, but there should have been at least a few other pedestrians. It was only seven-fifteen. Thanks to Alex, Stephanie had been at her computer long after everyone else left, sorting again through the photographs she'd taken in the park, trying to find the best ones to send to Alex. It was a waste of time. Alex had asked for them, but she would *never* actually review them or offer any positive comments.

"Don't treat me like I don't exist," the man said, his voice rising to a near-screech. "I'm trying to be nice." He was walking behind her now, drawing closer. It felt as if his voice was drilling into her ear from just a few inches away. Somehow, he managed to make his voice both soft and deep, with the hint of a growl.

Tears rushed to her eyes. She shouldn't be afraid. Everything was fine. God was right there. Her King ruled over her life. He would not allow her to suffer an attack, to be hurt badly, or even killed—stabbed right there on the street, her blood pouring over the curb and into the gutter.

A sob pushed its way out of her chest, and she began jogging slowly, as much as her high-heeled shoes allowed. It was stupid to wear shoes like this when she had to walk to and from the subway. Stupid even to wear them around the office where they spent most of the day hidden beneath her desk.

He was right behind her. "Why do you have to be such a bitch? I'm not going to hurt you. I was being friendly. We live in the same neighborhood, you know."

She shook her head violently and said nothing. Speaking was the last thing you should do in these situations. It encouraged them.

He was right. He wouldn't risk hurting her. Not with cars passing by.

But the drivers and passengers weren't looking at her. They

were oblivious to his threatening proximity. He could shove her to the ground, and they wouldn't even notice as they zipped past.

She was moving faster now, using an awkward sideways gait, trying to dig inside her purse, furious that her phone eluded her fingertips. Slowing to look inside would make her more vulnerable. She was gasping for air, half-crying.

It was possible she was over-reacting. She tried praying, but her brain frantically circled around a desperate cry—*Don't let him hurt me!* It seemed as if she was simply talking to herself. Could God even hear what was inside of her head? Why had she ever believed that?

She broke into a run, trying to breathe and scream at the same time. But what was the point of a scream? With apartment windows closed, most occupants eating dinner or out for the evening, and car windows equally air-tight, no one would hear. What was the tagline from that movie? Something about no one hearing your screams, although it was a film about aliens, so it didn't really apply...*in space, no one can hear you scream.*

As a shiver convulsed her body, she slowed, still trying to get air inside her lungs, but it didn't seem to want to go.

He grabbed the back of her coat. "What are you so worked up about?"

"Leave me alone."

"I haven't done anything to you."

"You're following me. You're..." She couldn't tell him he was scaring her. It was stupid to give him that kind of power. What did he want? How had this *happened*? Maybe her expensive-looking clothes, her beautiful hair were attracting attention she'd never experienced. In the past, she slunk down the streets, invisible. Now, she felt like a target.

"Women want a guy to flirt and come on to them, and when we do—the shit hits the fan. *Harassment.* Pepper spray. What the hell?"

"I don't know you. I've never seen you before and—"

"I asked you for a light just a few days ago. Don't give me that *never seen me* bullshit."

"Before that. I'd never seen you before that."

"Oh. *Before* that. Sure. Before *that*." He turned his face to the sky, rotating his head as if he'd made a stupid mistake. Then he looked back at her. She couldn't tell his eye color, it was too dark, and the lone streetlight cast its circle of light away from the sidewalk.

"Let go of me," she whispered.

"I'm not hurting you."

"I want you to let go of me." She imagined that was something Alex or Diana, Eileen even, would say in this situation. Younger women were so much better at that, about expressing their feelings, about being firm, about demanding what they wanted.

"Or what?" He laughed, a goofy, cackling sound.

"Maybe I'll shoot you."

He let go of her coat and punched her large purse. "Hiding a .45 in there?" He laughed harder, still cackling.

She tried to think what to say. If she lied, he could easily force her hand. If she told the truth, he would laugh so loud some of those apartment windows might open after all. Why *didn't* she have a gun? Tamara was right—a woman alone in New York City should consider that a necessity.

"I mean it," she said.

He moved away from her. "You can't stand here on a public street and shoot me just for trying to talk to you."

She turned and started walking quickly. She headed in the direction of Times Square. It was blocks away, but there would be people there. Lights. She could wander around until he lost interest, and then she would call a cab to take her home. It was worth the expense. The critical thing was to make sure she didn't return home right now. He couldn't see her entering her building. Although, he probably knew she lived fairly close by, now that he'd seen her twice.

A moment later, she heard brakes screech, followed by someone cursing through a partially opened car window. She turned. The guy was jogging across the street. He flipped off the driver of the car that had stopped for him, wove between parked cars on the opposite side of the street, and headed back toward the Starbucks shop. A minute later, he disappeared inside.

She let out a whimpering sigh, feeling as if she were melting into the sidewalk as her body relaxed and the fear ran off her shoulders. She hurried to her building, entered the code, and flung herself into the tiny lobby. A moment later, she was unlocking the door to her apartment.

The place was dark. Eileen was gone. Probably out with her new boyfriend.

She went to the refrigerator, emptied the bottle of white wine into a glass, and took a sip. She grabbed two of the oatmeal cookies she'd made the previous weekend and went into her bedroom, where she fired up her computer. She spent the next hour researching guns, ownership laws, prices, and shooting ranges that offered lessons. As soon as the photography class was over, she would turn her attention to learning how to keep herself safe. Maybe she'd also take up karate or judo. Even kick-boxing.

Later in bed, Eileen still not home, she closed her eyes and conjured up a mental rerun of the evening's events. This time, she pulled a small gun from her purse and sent the guy running for his life.

When she was tired of imagining that situation, she turned her thoughts to Alex, who would not get off as easily as the creep who'd grabbed her. Simply pointing a gun wouldn't scare Alex. And pulling the trigger would be *so* satisfying! She could imagine the shocked look on Alex's face when she realized that Stephanie was going to win after all.

CHAPTER 17

When I'd first met Diana and asked her to go out for a drink, she declined for that evening and every evening thereafter because she didn't drink alcohol, suggesting ice cream instead. She'd also asked whether I wanted to go for a hike sometime. I'd laughed because it sounded like such a strange thing to do in a large, concrete-covered city. She'd laughed with me and said obviously we would go somewhere outside of Manhattan.

We'd never gotten around to it because it involved too much driving on either side of the hike. But we'd talked about it quite a lot. Then winter came, and we talked about doing it in the spring. Now, there were only a few weeks left until the equinox, but it felt like it should already be spring because there were more daylight hours. At the same time, it felt like the depth of winter with freezing winds and a fair amount of rain.

Then, right in the middle of all that chilly rain, they started forecasting mild weekend weather. Diana suggested we meet somewhere closer, even if it meant nothing more than a walk in Central Park. I mentioned the rustic park on Long Island where I'd gone running the day I made my decision to cut smoking out of my life. She agreed it was a perfect spot.

So on Saturday morning, she picked me up. When I settled into the front passenger seat of her Honda, it gave me a flood of memories from Brady's car. Diana's car was a different color, different model, different age, but there was something about the shape of the seat and the arrangement of the displays on the dashboard that made me feel like I'd been yanked back to high school, driving to a park to discover the dangers of sex for myself.

Diana put the car into gear and pulled away from the curb.

She had her hair styled into her usual braids, woven across the top of her head and hanging down her back. Her skin was free of her workweek makeup except for a bit of lip balm that glistened in the morning sun streaming through the windshield. Also missing were the bangles that usually covered her wrists. Instead, she wore a pale pink fitness band, looking like a strip of pink taffy across her dark skin. It matched the pink frames of her sunglasses.

We talked about New York. She told me again how she'd experienced an almost mystical connection with New York City before she'd even moved there, and it had felt like home ever since. We talked about work. It wasn't gossip, just a conversation about our clients and how we'd helped some of them achieve quite a lot of success. We talked about the unique service provided by our little organization. We talked about TV and movies and working out.

When we arrived at the park, we pulled on sweatshirts. There was no need for hats or gloves. The sun was out, slightly blurred from a thin covering of cloud that was like watery milk. We looked at the maps displayed near the parking lot and chose a two-mile route that had some slight inclines to make it feel more like a hike than a stroll through a park.

Diana led the way as we started. Because the trail was too narrow to walk side-by-side, I followed behind her. At first, she didn't talk so I followed her lead in that as well. It was very peaceful. The sounds of children's voices and a men's soccer game came from the sports field, but they weren't loud enough to disturb the birds hopping about in branches that had sprouted quite a few buds. The songbirds chirped and flapped and made a cheerful soundtrack for our hiking.

After about half a mile, the trail widened, and we began walking beside each other, the length of our strides evenly matched.

"Do you think you'll stay in New York permanently?" she asked.

I shrugged. "I'm not much of a planner. I don't think about my future very often, not the details, anyway."

"That sounds nice. I think it's in my DNA to map out every step of my life." She laughed softly. "Even though your approach sounds like a fun way to live, if I tried that, I'd probably end up making a plan about not planning."

"I guess you'll stay here forever?" I said.

She laughed. "'Til I'm an old lady. I'm hoping I'll find a way to be buried at Marble Cemetery."

When I asked why that was so special about that place, she told me I should visit it sometime. It had been built in the early 1800s in the East Village. The guy who established it was quite an entrepreneur—because of yellow fever, earthen burials had been outlawed. This guy jumped on the market opportunity and began providing underground vaults for burial. Of course, it turned out that only prominent families had vaults there, and descendants of the original owners could still be buried in those spots. "But never say never," Diana said.

I thought about her strange goal for a moment, then changed the subject. "Do you have a boyfriend?"

"Yes. A soon-to-be fiancé. Kids, in about four years—two of them."

"That is a lot of planning."

"How about you?"

"Nope."

"Nope to what? A future with Kent?"

"Definitely not."

"Why?"

"He's fine for now, but I need someone more challenging...if I was going to be with anyone for a long time."

"You don't think you'll ever get married?"

"I never thought about it."

She stopped walking. She turned to look at me. "You never *thought* about it? How is that possible? Not even for a few minutes? It never crossed your mind?" She wrinkled her brow, staring hard at me as if she was trying to decide whether she could believe me. What I'd said was incomprehensible to her, therefore I must be lying, and she was looking for the sign of that lie in the shape of my lips, in the faint movement of my brow, my eyelids, my eyes themselves.

"Are you trying to read my microexpressions?"

"Maybe." She laughed. "I just can't get my head around never having given a minute of thought to such a major life decision."

I shrugged.

The trail narrowed again, but as we continued, we stayed side-by-side. We started up a slight incline. The stretch in my muscles felt good. Our footsteps crunched on pebbles and twigs that littered parts of the path, tossed there by the recent wind.

"Are you keeping all your focus on your career?" she asked.

"Not really. I like what I'm doing, I like working with Trystan...and you, but I don't think of it as a career. Like I said, I'm not overly focused on what's ahead."

"It doesn't seem as if you're focused on it at all."

The sound of our breathing filled the air around us, and the sound of blood pumping filled my ears.

She inhaled deeply before speaking again. "So you don't like working with Stephanie, obviously. She was missing from the list of what you like about work."

"You know we don't get along."

"Yes, but I'm curious. Is it enough to make you look for another job?"

"Not yet."

"How is the mentoring going?"

"Not very well."

"That's not very fair to her."

It fascinated me that Diana could say those words yet remain so detached. They didn't come across as an accusation or criticism or like she was telling me what to do. Those words would have sounded like an attack coming out of most people's mouths. I wondered why that was. There was something unusual about her, but I couldn't figure out what made her different from anyone I'd known.

"She's not thrilled about me being her mentor," I said. "What she wants is to be rid of me so she can be the only photographer."

"It was her idea—making photography a bigger part of our client assessment. So she feels like it should belong to her," Diana said.

"Was it?"

"She suggested to Trystan that she could take over from the contractor we used before."

"I guess he only liked half of her idea." I was smiling, but I wasn't sure she heard that in my voice.

A moment later, she took a deep breath and shoved it out quickly. "You know I'm not much of a fan of hers either, but I try to just let her be."

"I'm not very good at letting people be," I said.

"I've noticed. Which is kind of ironic since that's what you expect from everyone else."

I laughed. "You're right."

"Once she settles into taking photographs, she'll probably calm down."

I doubted that would happen. Stephanie's hatred of me wasn't only about photography. It was about Eileen and Trystan and her belief that I was some kind of threat. Those beliefs don't disappear easily. Especially regarding her daughter.

"Maybe she senses you don't respect her religious beliefs," Diana said.

"She's right."

"Why is that?"

"Are you analyzing me?"

The trail turned sharply to the left and started downhill. I guessed we'd covered nearly a mile, and I wondered what would happen to the conversation once we'd circled back to the parking area.

"Just making an observation," she said.

"Isn't that what analysis is?"

She laughed. "So what do you have against her religion?"

"You said you're not religious, so I thought you felt the same way."

"Not in the traditional sense, but I don't care what other people want to believe."

"Neither do I, as long as it doesn't interfere with my life."

"Agreed. But how do her beliefs interfere with your life?"

"She acts as if taking my job is her divine right."

"Maybe you've misinterpreted her."

I knew I hadn't, but I didn't want to debate it with Diana. Neither did I want to explain the way I was raised, which gave me a pretty good idea of how Stephanie's mind worked. It wasn't because I read her micro-expressions, but because I'd been around people like her most of my life, and I knew the hive mind they inhabited.

Diana put her hand on my shoulder and gave it a light pat. "I get it though, she makes religion into something ugly. I don't like it either."

It sounded like she was the one doing the misinterpreting if that's what she'd taken away from the things I'd said, but I didn't mention that either. I was more interested in what she was think-ing. "So you are religious?"

"I think we're all connected somehow. I've...experienced things, I guess is the best way to put it. I meditate and try to sepa-rate myself from the world's chaos."

Part of me wanted to know what things she'd *experienced*, but another part did not. "That sounds...interesting."

She laughed. "You really mean it sounds disturbing. Don't worry, I'm not going to recruit you into a cult or anything."

"It never crossed my mind."

"Because you don't think of the future?"

"No, because you seem sane. Maybe meditation works after all if it makes people as calm as you are."

"A black woman in this world has to find something to help her detach, otherwise I don't see how I could deal with the way things are."

"I can understand that. But religion?"

"It's not religion. It's just life. Existence."

"If you say so."

"How did we get onto all of this?" She laughed. "Conversations take on a life of their own, don't you think?"

"Yes."

As if our conversation had decided to end the life it had taken on, we didn't speak any more about Stephanie or religion. We didn't talk at all until we were about a quarter-mile from the parking lot and could see people milling around, studying the trail maps, possibly looking for an experience that would help them detach from whatever was plaguing them.

CHAPTER 18

*T*he muscles in the backs of my calves were sore from my hike with Diana. For the past few weeks, since I'd quit smoking, I'd gotten back to a regular running schedule and had done more intense weight-lifting. I was looking for every possible way I could think of to give my body lots of oxygen and clean blood and keeping my mind on taking care of those things instead of letting my cells drift back to their state of craving.

The hike, even though the uphill portions were gentle, must have called out some muscles I didn't use regularly. Or maybe the tightness was the counter to wearing high heels too often, and hiking had located muscles that were distorted from those beautiful but dangerous shoes. This meant that walking into Bloomingdales, where I was meeting Eileen, made me realize the last thing I wanted to do was try on shoes. Maybe I would settle for watching Eileen and providing the opinions she'd asked for. I had no urgent need for new shoes, and trying them on with sore legs would not be the fun experience it usually was.

Yet, the minute I reached the low tables that formed the edges of the shoe department, I saw a pair of high-heeled sandals, some red leather ankle boots, and a pair of ballet-slipper flats that I knew I would adore. Maybe the lure of shoe-shopping needed to be approached like weight-training—push past the discomfort and pain to get your body what it needed. And what I needed was to save money, not buy more shoes. But new shoes always made me feel like all kinds of new things might happen to me. They made me walk differently, and they transformed clothes that had grown too familiar into something absolutely fantastic again.

Eileen was already there, seated in an armchair, four boxes of shoes stacked beside her. She was pointing her toes, admiring a pair of silver shoes with extremely high gold heels.

As if she felt my gaze on her feet, she looked up, waved, then turned her attention back to the shoes. She stood and walked to one of the floor mirrors, moving her foot from side to side to see how the shoes looked from every angle.

I settled in the chair beside hers.

She walked back and stopped a few feet from me. "What do you think?"

"What's the occasion?"

"A wedding."

"Yours?"

She laughed. "No. A friend of Ned's."

"What does your dress look like?"

"I haven't bought it yet."

"Then those are perfect."

She sat and removed the shoes and opened the next box, which held a pair of flat sandals. As she went through the boxes beside her, we talked about shoes. When the last pair was on her feet, we wound our way through the tables, plucking single shoes like flowers. As soon as we each had an armful, we handed them over, and the woman helping us left to find our sizes.

Settled back in our chairs, stockinged feet resting on the soft carpet, waiting for more, Eileen talked a bit about Ned—about his job and his family in New Jersey.

"He's made me realize I absolutely need to get out of my mother's apartment. I feel ridiculous even having to say that. I'm too old to be living with my mother, and I can't believe I've let it go on for such a long time. It's not good for either one of us."

"I suppose Ned doesn't want to spend the night with your mother on the other side of the bedroom wall."

She laughed. "I'm sure that's part of it, although he didn't mention it specifically."

"He just wants to tell you what to do, how to live your life?"

"It's not like that. Not at all." She slipped off her shoes and eased her left foot back into one of the silver and gold shoes. "He's a little older than I am. Well, quite a bit older…"

I waited. I really didn't care if the guy was sixty. Why should that matter to anyone? I suppose if you're thinking long term, you don't want to be left a widow when you're forty, but that seems a rather calculated decision that ignores the possibility of simply clicking with someone. Isn't it better to have a few great years than it is to pick someone just because your demographic profiles line up?

"Aren't you going to ask how old he is?" she said.

"No."

The saleswoman returned with several boxes of shoes. "This isn't all of them, but start with these, and I'll be back in a few minutes." She left, and we began opening boxes, admiring the contents as if it were Christmas morning.

Eileen pulled out another pair of sandals. She kicked off the lone silver shoe and slipped the sandals onto her feet. She stood and wiggled her toes. "He didn't tell me to do anything at all. It's just that spending time with him, I've realized I need some space. I need to feel like I can live my life without explaining or worrying about what time I come home. I need to be an adult." She laughed, the sound carrying over to another group of chairs with such force, the woman trying on eight different pairs of black leather pumps turned to stare at her.

Eileen looked down at me. "I need to buy my own furniture

and linens and dishes. Do you know I don't even possess my own set of sheets? It's ridiculous."

She walked toward the mirror, looking at her feet. While she turned in front of it, I realized the solution to my own housing problem. With a roommate, I could afford a much nicer place with a softer impact on my income. The apartments I'd looked at could easily be mine, every single one of them. In fact, that icy realtor would take one look at Eileen's assets and never give me a lecture about wasting her time again.

While we tried on the rest of the shoes, I turned the idea over in my mind. Eileen was easy to be around. We liked the same kinds of food, drank about the same amount of alcohol, and she'd already said she needed some mental space. I didn't think she would be the kind of person who would want to plan all our meals together and ask me where I was going every time I picked up my messenger bag.

The biggest problem would be my side gig. The next time someone turned up who needed to be removed from the planet, I'd have an extra layer of complexity. I'd be required to explain an overnight absence and hide my supplies.

But maybe she wouldn't care if I disappeared for a night. If Ned remained in the picture for a while, surely she would often spend the night at his place. There was no doubt it would make my life more complicated, but it seemed like it would be worth the tradeoff—one or two nights of complications versus weeks of living in a nice place, without roaches, with a decent heating and AC system, with modern construction and design. I'd have space. And I wouldn't have to crack my beautiful nest egg to do it.

I wouldn't mind having a few nice things—dishes and glass-ware. A real place to settle down instead of feeling like a nomad or someone biding her time, waiting for nothing in particular. And for what? I'd boasted to Diana that I didn't think about the future, but the result was a sort of limbo state. That condition was nice most of the time but left some of the edges of my life a bit ragged. It made me feel like a ghost, drifting from city to city, job to job.

Eileen ended up buying the silver and gold shoes but decided to defer the dress choice to another time. She bought a pair of sandals, and I bought the red boots. I didn't need them, wasn't sure what I would wear them with, and didn't think they were the best way to spend money if I was poised to buy home furnishings and increase my rent, but they were so seductive I couldn't take my eyes off them.

We went to a coffee shop and ordered frothy caffeinated beverages that were more like desserts than coffee. When we were settled in a small booth, I tasted the whipped cream then waited for Eileen to meet my gaze. "How fast are you planning this escape from your mother's nest?"

She laughed but looked anxious. "Don't say it like that."

"Which part did you object to?"

"Escape."

"It is, though."

She sighed. "I don't like hearing it, but I guess I need to think realistically if I'm going to finally act like an adult. And to be truthful, it does feel like planning an escape. I hate that."

"What area of the city do you think you'd want to live in?"

She shrugged.

"You could buy a place with the money from your windfall."

"I could. I need to do something with all that cash, and I've been talking to a financial planner, but I haven't made any decisions yet."

"I'm actually planning to move also."

"Why?"

I took a sip of my drink. "It's not an entirely different reason than yours—it's time to grow up."

"Grow up?"

"I'm living like a college student. I want a real home, with decent furniture. I've always tried to save as much as I can, but I think I over-steered in that direction."

"Your apartment is cute."

"It is. But it's cold in the winter and almost unbearable when it gets hot. And the roaches."

"Every building in New York has roaches, to some extent."

"I think nicer places do a better job of keeping them in their place."

"Have you looked at apartments?"

"Some." I sipped my drink and studied her long, slender fingers wrapped around her cup, the nails painted a nude color and filed short, which made them look aristocratic. Sometimes, I couldn't figure out how this woman had emerged from Stephanie's womb, grown up under Stephanie's oppressive view of the world, and turned out to be quite pulled together, even if she was still sharing an apartment with her mother when she was in her late twenties. I suppose most people would say she was kind-hearted, a good person. And she was, not that I tended to focus on those traits in anyone.

"What do you think about finding a place together?" I asked.

I thought she would look shocked. I thought she would hesi-tate. Surely she had negative thoughts about me that had been influenced by her mother. Surely she had become more cautious toward people in general after the things she'd been through.

"That would be fabulous." She smiled. "When should we start looking?"

We talked about our dream apartment and made a date for the following weekend. We picked up our shopping bags and walked to the door, placing our cups and saucers on the busing station before we stepped out into the cold night air.

CHAPTER 19

*M*eeting alone with Stephanie after her first client visit would be challenging. Trystan was not looking forward to it. She'd pestered him constantly until he'd finally agreed to let her join him and Alex. It was a mistake.

Now, he'd invited her to breakfast so they could talk without interruption and without being overheard. He also hoped the public setting would inspire Stephanie to keep a lid on her feelings. She seemed to be brimming with them all the time, constantly stirring her thoughts, turning up the flame, allowing complicated emotions to boil over.

The client they'd met with the previous afternoon was an artist who wanted exposure for her work to grow outside of the United States. She painted whimsical, mystical scenes of the night sky, adding figures that looked as if they'd been formed in another world—half bird, half human, with the intricate feather designs of tropical birds. Her work was extremely popular, and she was represented by a gallery that featured only two other artists.

What she wanted from Trystan was an understanding of why she was suddenly bored with her work. She wasn't sure if it was related to fear, or some kind of self-rejection, or a simple desire for change. She'd just turned forty and wanted to do a re-set for what she called the second half of her life.

During their visit to Eliza's studio, Stephanie had stayed in the background as he'd asked. Alex had been her usual charming and effective self, getting a great series of initial photographs after Trystan and Stephanie left the meeting. Waiting for Alex should have given him an opportunity to talk briefly to Stephanie, but he hadn't wanted to risk a conflict that Eliza might witness.

He glanced at his phone. Stephanie was ten minutes late. That wasn't like her.

The server came by and refilled his coffee cup, asking again if he wanted to order something while he waited. He shook his head.

It was nearly quarter past eight when he saw Stephanie walking toward his table. She settled across from him and unwound her scarf. She pulled off her gloves and placed them beside her on the bench. "I'm starved." She flipped open the menu and wriggled out of her coat as she read through the offerings.

They ordered—toast and bacon for him, along with a glass of orange juice to slow the river of coffee he was gulping down, and waffles with whipped cream and a side of bacon for Stephanie.

Stephanie smiled at him. "I thought last night went well," she said. "Eliza and I really clicked."

"Well, that's—"

"I could have handled it all myself. I'm not sure why you're being so slow to let me get going with this. We have appointments scheduled into April already because work is backing up."

He couldn't argue with that, but he still needed to move carefully. Stephanie had been decidedly awkward in her introduction to Eliza, and he was not looking forward to trying to explain that to her, trying to define exactly where and how her tone had been off. "It is backing up, but we need to get this right. It's critical to the ultimate success with each individual."

"I know that, Trystan. It was my idea, remember?"

He smiled, hoping it would soften his words, but he couldn't let her mischaracterization go unchallenged. "Handling photography in-house was certainly your idea, but the photography itself is one of my key differentiators. It has been since day one."

"Whatever."

"Excuse me?"

She gave him a smile that looked mocking, but maybe she was simply trying to put on a more aggressively friendly attitude and had missed the mark. Again.

"I meant I didn't want to waste time arguing about details," she said.

"Were we arguing?"

She gave him the same mocking grin.

"So…" He took several sips of coffee. "I wanted to do a small de-brief on how the meeting went."

"Okay."

While their food was delivered, Stephanie turned, surveying the other tables, seeming to lean away from him. She ignored the server until the coffee cups were refilled. Then, she looked up, waiting until the server met her gaze. "Thank you. This looks delicious."

"No worries." The server moved away from their table.

Stephanie sighed. She cut into her waffle and placed a small piece, thick with whipped cream, into her mouth.

"I appreciated that you followed the plan so that we didn't stumble over each other, that we each adhered to our roles," he said.

"You told me to just listen. I know how to follow orders."

"It wasn't an order."

She shrugged and ate another bite of the waffle, washing it down with coffee.

"I just have a few comments."

She laughed. "How can you have comments? I didn't do anything that you can comment on."

"I wanted to talk about your introduction."

She laughed again. "You're teasing, right?"

"Please take this seriously, Stephanie. These little things matter."

"Do you talk to Alex about her *introductions?*"

"I'm going to be blunt."

"I can handle it."

"Alex is confident. That attitude comes through in her interactions. She's not trying to make an impression, and that lack of effort puts other people at ease."

"You are totally deluded about who she is," Stephanie said.

He put down his fork. He closed his eyes for a moment. At times, his teenage daughter was more mature than Stephanie. Why did she have to make everything so difficult? Any other business owner would let her go and look for a replacement. But he felt bad doing that for too many reasons to think about right that minute. There was nothing wrong with her work, and to fire her based on nothing but the rough edges to her personality seemed wrong. Especially, when the entire purpose of his work was to help people develop, to learn to emphasize their strengths, and polish off those rough edges.

"I need you to stop making this personal with Alex," he said. "I need you to focus on where you need to grow. I need you to focus on how you can help our clients feel comfortable with us, to help cement their trust and their belief in what we do."

"Absolutely."

He sighed, managing to keep the exhale mild, so she wasn't aware.

"So what's wrong with my *intro?*" She giggled.

"A simple offering of your name and your role is sufficient. It's not necessary to mention how long we've worked together or your connection to the city, or that you have an adult child. Certainly not the name of your church."

"It's important to connect on a personal level. You've said that a hundred times."

"Yes, but there's a balance. You want things to be easy and light, especially at that first meeting. You want to keep the focus on our clients, not on yourself."

"That is the most hilarious thing I've ever heard you say."

"Why is that?" He picked up his orange juice and drained half the glass.

"Alex is always preening and strutting around, talking about herself, making everyone look at her. And you're annoyed that I mentioned I have a daughter? That's how most women connect if you didn't know. Talking about their children."

Despite all the coffee, he felt tired. Maybe it was impossible for someone to truly change if they lacked a certain level of self-awareness. The conversation was becoming pointless and rather foolish. You couldn't teach someone Stephanie's age how to properly introduce herself in a business setting. You couldn't teach someone how to recognize and respect the comfort of other people. You couldn't change someone who didn't have any social awareness. "Alex is very good at interacting with people."

"So you've said."

"She not only takes excellent photographs that capture aspects of our clients' personality that they themselves hadn't recognized, she understands how to make people feel at ease. She's good at her job, which is why I asked her to mentor you. I don't appreciate you bashing her every chance you get."

"I bet she does the same."

"We're not talking about her, but for the record, she doesn't. Not usually."

Stephanie laughed. "But she does, sometimes."

"We're not talking about her."

"You are."

"Just as a point of comparison."

"I'm never going to be Alex. So if that's what you're trying to do, forget it. I can't be someone else. And I would never, ever want to be her or anything like her. She's evil."

"Calm down."

Her eyes filled with tears. She pulled her napkin off her lap and patted it around the edges of her eyes. As she pulled it away from her face, she looked at it with an expression of horror. She shoved it back into her lap. "I'm perfectly calm. I don't like being compared to her. If you just want to clone her, then why did you even suggest I could be a photographer?"

"I don't want to clone her. I want you to learn from her. You're twisting my words. And you're missing my intent. Deliberately."

She shoved her plate toward the center of the table. She turned and caught the eye of their server. When he hurried to the table, she waved her hand over the plate, most of the waffle and all of the bacon still lying there, looking slightly limp now. "I've lost my appetite. I'm very sorry, but can you take this away, please?"

The server picked up the plate. "Can I bring you more coffee? Some juice?"

She shook her head, and he backed away, glancing briefly at Trystan.

"I'm not attacking you," Trystan said. "I'm trying to help get you up to speed so you can move forward."

"You make me sound like I'm totally inept, that I'm socially awkward, and that I can't do anything right. Maybe because she's young, or sexy, or both, you're dazzled by her. I'm not her, and I'm not ever going to be her. And I don't think it's right for you, who is supposed to be an expert at bringing out the best in people, to be telling me everything about me is wrong and comparing me to her."

"That's not what I'm doing."

"It's exactly what you're doing."

He was surprised by the force of her words. It was ironic that she was suddenly exhibiting the very confidence he was criticizing her for lacking. She'd introduced herself to Eliza as if she had to give her credentials, as if she needed Eliza to like her. The need clung to her like a wet coat, and he'd sensed Eliza pulling back.

"The way you're talking right now is exactly the kind of confidence that will put clients at ease. If you could draw on that more, tone it down of course, but use that energy, I think it will go a long way."

"Now you're calling me insecure?"

She was alarmingly insecure. She was a perplexing blend of insecurity and overly impressed with her own abilities. She was absolutely certain that everything she believed, every perception she had, was the indisputable truth. Maybe that certainty, which was a kind of blindness, also signaled insecurity, just dressed differently. "All I'm asking is that you put the client first. If you observe Alex's interactions, you can learn how she does it. We can all learn from other people."

"What can Miss Perfect Alexandra learn from *me?*"

He took a large bite of toast. He chewed and swallowed too quickly, knowing his answer was painfully slow in coming, but his mind was empty. "I—"

"I get it. Nothing."

"That's not true." He had to think of something. What a mess he'd stepped into. A mess of his own making. "She could learn humility." It was a flat-out lie, but it was all he had. In a weird, twisted way, Stephanie also lacked humility.

Stephanie smiled, nodding slowly.

An enormous feeling of relief washed over him. He'd avoided falling into a hole he couldn't climb out of. She finally got it. All it had taken was a little flattery and a little smoothing out of the playing field so that Stephanie didn't feel quite so inferior.

He shifted the conversation to Eliza's objectives, asking

Stephanie for her impressions of Eliza's career challenges, her stumbling blocks. She seemed to relax as she spoke. She relented enough to order a few slices of toast. The breakfast finished peacefully.

CHAPTER 20

Stephanie's day had started out awful. The moment she returned home from work and stepped into her living room, she knew it was going to get far worse.

The only good part of the day had been her decision to take the afternoon off. After eating street tacos at a taqueria near her office, she took a cab to the gun shop she'd identified online. The cab was necessary because she didn't want to be riding the subway into a sketchy part of the city. A cab ride was expensive. It was indulgent, and she felt as if people headed to the subways were staring at her like some entitled woman who believed herself too good for public transportation.

Inside the gun shop, she'd felt surprisingly comfortable. The owner had helped her choose a weapon that wasn't too heavy for her, that fit well into her grip, and, according to him, was easier to discharge. That was his word—*discharge*—as if he were describing getting rid of bodily fluids. She cringed but tried to keep her attention on the other things he was telling her.

He completed the transaction, guided her through the registration form, and signed her up for three shooting lessons. It sounded as if learning to fire a gun was more complicated than taking photographs. He'd said he would call her when she could pick up the gun after her background check was completed. It would only take about three days, he'd assured her.

Walking out of the gun shop, she'd been flooded with elation. She'd taken action to build her confidence, as Trystan had insisted she do, and as owning a gun would surely do.

Now, all of that powerful energy had washed out of her in a single breath. Eileen sat on the couch, holding a glass of red wine. Another glass stood on the coffee table, without a coaster.

Seated beside Eileen was a man who looked disturbingly like Eileen's father. And the worst of it was, much of that impression came from the fact that he was the same age as Eileen's father, maybe even two or three years *older*. He couldn't possibly be this Ned character that Stephanie was supposed to meet this evening. The Ned who was taking them to dinner. The Ned whom Eileen talked about non-stop.

Eileen stood. She took a sip of wine and handed her glass to the man, who placed it on the table beside his own. "Ned, this is my Mom—Stephanie Cook."

He stood and stepped around the coffee table, extending his hand. "Good to meet you."

"Ned?" Stephanie swallowed. How could Eileen's boyfriend be old enough to be her father? Who was this creep, dating a woman in her twenties? If he took them to dinner, everyone would think he and Stephanie were married, that Eileen was their daughter. It was embarrassing and upsetting. She had no idea what to say.

"Are you okay?" Eileen asked.

Stephanie nodded and tried to smile, knowing it didn't appear at all genuine.

Eileen gave her a strange look. "Do you want a glass of wine before we go to dinner? Ned made a reservation for seven-thirty."

Stephanie nodded. "Let me change my clothes." Her voice came out in a whisper.

"What you're wearing looks great," Ned said.

Stephanie stared at him. Was he *complimenting* her appearance? She shuddered and hurried out of the room. She stepped into the bathroom and closed the door. She leaned on the edge of the sink, gripping it for comfort, feeling the cold, unyielding porcelain hard against the bones and tendons of her fingers. It was soothing. She looked into the mirror. Staring back at her was a middle-aged woman. An attractive middle-aged woman, but there was no hiding her age. Just as there was no hiding the fact that Eileen's boyfriend was definitely older than Stephanie.

A wave of nausea passed through her. Why on earth had Eileen chosen a man so old? Was she going through some late-stage rebellion, doing this to upset her mother? She turned on the faucet and let the cold water run across her wrists. She held a washcloth under the flow. She wrung it out and placed it against her cheeks, then the back of her neck. She wanted to splash the stinging cold water across her entire face, plunge her face into a sink filled with it, but that would destroy her makeup. Even if she couldn't care less how her face looked for their dinner out, Eileen would notice and pester her with questions. She turned off the faucet.

She slipped out of the bathroom and hurried the few steps to her bedroom, closing the door and locking it. She leaned against it for a moment, then went to her closet. She wasn't in the mood for dressing up, and he'd said what she was wearing was okay. She kicked off her heels and slid out of her pants. After tugging on a pair of jeans and poking her feet into ankle boots, she ran her fingers through her hair and grabbed her purse off the bed. She went out of her room without checking the mirror.

Eileen was standing in the opening between the living room and dining area. She held a glass of wine in her hand. There was only the barest amount of liquid in the glass. She held it out to Stephanie. "So you can join us. I only gave you a little since I know you don't like to overdo it." Stephanie took the glass.

Ned stood. "A toast?"

"Yes." Eileen's voice was cheerful. She seemed oblivious to her mother's mood. Why didn't she see how upset Stephanie was?

"To the finest woman I've ever met." Ned clicked his glass against Eileen's and smiled.

In Stephanie's opinion, the toast was over the top for someone he'd only known for a few weeks. It looked as if his smile had a leering quality. Some old guy wanting to pretend he wasn't aging by wining and dining a young girl. It was disgusting.

Stephanie took a sip of wine. She settled into the armchair across from them. Eileen urged Ned to tell Stephanie about himself, and he didn't hold back. Stephanie learned he'd never been married but engaged once for two years. She learned that he'd grown up in New Jersey, that his mother was a schoolteacher, and his father was a journalist. She learned that Ned had gone to college in Massachusetts, where he'd earned an undergraduate and a graduate degree in urban planning, and that although he lived in New York, he worked as a city planner in Trenton, New Jersey.

It was far more than Stephanie cared to know. He had no problem going on about himself without expressing any interest in getting to know her. Maybe Eileen had already told him everything. Maybe he was full of himself. Maybe he was even more socially awkward than she apparently was, if you believed Trystan.

Ned ordered an Uber, and when the car arrived, they headed off to the restaurant.

Dinner was a painful affair, filled with more details of Ned's life—stories from college, from his childhood, from his travels. When he did finally ask about Stephanie, her mind went blank. She couldn't think of a single thing she wanted to tell him about her life.

Eileen tried to egg her on with prompts about work, relating stories from when Eileen was a child, and even issuing an invitation to talk about church, but there was still nothing she wanted to say to this man.

After a while, Eileen began giving her dirty looks, obviously upset that Stephanie was refusing to be a full participant in the conversation.

As she poked her fork at the pasta and sausage bits on her plate, Stephanie realized the reason she had nothing to say was because she wanted this guy out of Eileen's life so desperately, there was no point in telling him anything at all. Eileen needed to wake up and see that she was once again allowing herself to be used as a possession. And what about children? If this guy had any interest in children, he would already be married and have some.

All of his boasting about his world travels showed where his priorities were. And what about church? He hadn't said a thing about that. Not that it would make a difference if he were close to God. He was old, much too old for Eileen. She couldn't fathom what the attraction was on Eileen's part.

Then, during dessert, it struck her. It might have been Ned's comment that his parents were eager to meet Eileen. That statement terrified Stephanie, with its implication that this relationship was getting serious very fast. But the flash of insight came from the next words out of his mouth—*my Dad will adore you.*

Eileen had never experienced a father. He was gone before any memories could be formed and retained. He was simply a figure in a few photographs. When Eileen had been small, she'd asked about him. Stephanie had given the minimal amount of information necessary to answer her questions. She'd assured her little girl that having a Heavenly Father would do far, far more for her life than any flesh and blood man, especially one as hateful as the man who had impregnated her mother.

Only now did Stephanie realize how badly she'd mismanaged her life by marrying such a useless man. Her daughter had grown up without a father, and she was going to spend her twenties dating inappropriate men in her search for a father-replacement figure. Stephanie had read about this. She'd believed Eileen was grounded enough in her faith to not fall into that psychological trap, but she'd been wrong.

The need must have lain dormant, emerging suddenly and too late, when Stephanie mindlessly believed Eileen was a fully formed adult without any unmet psychological needs. But she wasn't. She was trying to fill that father-sized hole in her life, and Stephanie had no idea how she was going to stop it.

CHAPTER 21

ortland, Oregon

* * *

B<small>RADY</small> and I had managed to keep seeing each other for almost two months without my parents uncovering the slightest clue that I had a boyfriend. I never mentioned him, which wasn't difficult because all my conversations with my parents involved Q&A sessions, and they couldn't ask about what they didn't know.

They did ask about boys occasionally. Well, my mother asked, my father avoided the subject altogether. She asked whether there were any boys at church that I had a crush on. I wondered if she was starting to worry that I hadn't expressed any interest in boys. It never crossed her mind that I wouldn't tell her the details, or anything at all, about my interests.

It was funny how thoroughly I could answer their questions without ever revealing very much about me at all. Details, especially details about the minutia of schoolwork and church activities, the constant, low-level buzz of gossip, the logistics, the conflicts, made it sound as if I was pouring out information about my life. It was information about other lives, that was all. They didn't seem to recognize this. They heard what they wanted.

I think my mother realized I wasn't very forthcoming because she asked about my feelings from time to time. And they weren't just questions designed to find out if I'd changed my opinion of god, but honest, non-trick questions about how I was doing socially, about my dreams, about my feelings in general. When I had nothing to say, she assumed I was keeping my feelings private. It never occurred to her that I was deficient in the feelings category compared to her and compared to most people.

So, as far as she knew, I was too caught up in school and my love for learning and books, as well as exploring my addiction to running that had been sparked by my brother.

When Brady asked me if I wanted to go to a movie or a school dance, I told him I'd rather my parents not know I had a boyfriend. I explained how strict they were, how fixated they were on me keeping my social life connected to kids who were members of our church. He didn't seem to get it, but I don't think he understood at all what a different world they lived in. He couldn't comprehend not wanting your daughter to have friends at school, to go to school dances, to concerts and movies. I silenced him with a kiss.

Every week, as our hands went deeper into each other's clothing in the back seat of his car, as more clothes came off, I knew I did not want to have my first experience of sex in the back seat of a Honda. I knew that was a popular place, a common place, for the first time, but it wasn't for me. It was cramped back there. It was either slightly too hot or a little too cold. I usually went home with an ache in my side from twisting into awkward positions.

Brady didn't seem to feel the same way because each time we got together, he inched closer to the ultimate goal. I murmured that my back hurt. I mentioned that I was cold. He agreed and kept going. He put his mouth close to my ear. "I have a condom, you know. In case you're worried."

Worried wasn't the right word. It was his responsibility to have a condom, and I didn't like that he was acting as if he was doing me a big favor by providing it.

"I'm not ready for that," I said.

"Oh." He moved away from me. "I thought…"

I pulled my sweater around my bare shoulders. "I'm freezing."

"I can warm you up." He leaned into me again. "All the way."

His lips brushed my neck, and I shivered. I tugged my bra out from under his leg and put it on.

"What are you doing? I thought you wanted to do it?"

"I do."

He grinned.

"Not here."

"Why not?"

"It's uncomfortable. It's cramped, and I'm cold, and my neck is starting to hurt."

"I don't know where else we would go. I guess maybe my house, but I can't be sure…besides, that's kind of weird. To plan it out like that."

"Wasn't this planned?"

He looked at the window as if he was trying to figure out the answer to that question. "Not really."

"Why did we drive out here?"

"To get away and—"

"To fool around."

"Well, yeah." He grinned.

"Then it was planned."

He sighed. "Okay. What do you want to do?"

"I want you to take me home and then figure out a nicer place *with a bed.*"

He laughed. "What, you want a five-star hotel room or something?"

"It doesn't have to be five stars."

"You're crazy. No other girls want it all planned out in a hotel room."

I shrugged. I pulled my shirt over my head and slid my arms back into the sweater. I reached down and picked up my shoe, twisting away from him to shove my foot into it.

"Come on. Are you pissed now because I said that about other girls?"

"No."

"I shouldn't have said that. Now you probably want to know how many other girls."

"No, I don't."

"Why not?"

"Why does that matter?"

"Other girls always want to know."

"Well, I don't care."

He stared at me as if I'd sprouted a third eye in the center of my forehead. "Uhm, okay. Good." He pulled on his shirt. "I thought we would do it today."

"Why?"

"I thought that a lot of times."

"Then why didn't you think of a nicer place?"

He laughed. "You're a little entitled."

"I don't think I am. It's uncomfortable back here, and I want to enjoy myself. Don't you?"

"Yeah. But that's pretty easy to do." He laughed. When I didn't share his laugh, he stopped quickly. "I'm not sure where we can go. I—"

"Any place with a bed."

He nodded. "So it doesn't have to be a hotel?"

"That would be the nicest, but I don't think it's required."

We drove back to school and hung out in the library until it was time for me to get my carpool home. It was arranged by some mothers at the church, and they planned it for six on Tuesdays and Thursdays so kids could study in the library or go to after-school sports or clubs. It was very convenient for me to hang out with Brady without making up a story about a study group every single day.

That was on a Tuesday. On Thursday, right after we got out of homeroom, Brady came to my locker. He stood close and whispered. "We can go to my house," he said.

I liked it that I knew exactly what he meant, that he didn't feel the need to explain, and I didn't need him to.

"What about your mother?"

"Anna's gymnastics class got changed from Saturday mornings to Thursday afternoons. My mom always stays and watches the class."

"Nice."

"I thought you'd like it." He leaned toward me.

I backed away and put my head partially into my locker, digging in the back for a tube of lip gloss. "So I'll meet you at your car."

"Oh, and since she's not home, I can put the car in the garage, and no one will know I'm home."

"Sounds like a plan."

After school, when we got into his car, the air felt full of electricity. Both of us were breathing differently, and neither of us said a word. We were both thinking about what was going to happen and also trying not to think about it. At least I was because I didn't want to spoil it with overthinking.

We went into his house, and he locked the front door. We climbed the stairs, Brady in front, and he led me down the hallway and turned left into his bedroom. It faced the street. Mine was better. I loved looking out on the sloping lawn of our backyard, the huge tree just outside my window—

"I got the best room," he said. "Because I can see everyone who's coming over and what's going down on our street."

I nodded.

He pulled the comforter off his bed. "I washed the sheets."

"That's nice." Hearing him say that told me I'd picked the right guy for this. It wasn't that I'd doubted it, but he just confirmed it. He wanted things to be nice as much as I did, even if it didn't occur to him that a bed was much nicer than a Honda, even a single bed.

"It was a lot of work because I had to wash the sheets so my mom wouldn't notice I was changing them on the wrong day."

"I appreciate that. A lot." I smiled and pulled my shirt over my head.

We started kissing, then getting undressed while we were kissing. Finally, we collapsed onto the bed, and it felt perfect. I didn't have any stiff muscles, and I was warm and comfortable.

And when we were holding each other after it was over, he said there weren't any other girls. He'd just never heard of a girl who wanted to be in a bedroom, and also, he'd heard that girls always wanted to know how many others. *So even if you don't care, the answer is—no other girls. You're number one.*

I smiled when he said that. It's nice to be number one. Everyone wants to be.

CHAPTER 22

 ew York

* * *

STEPHANIE HAD CALLED to tell us she would be late. *A pounding headache*, she'd claimed. The minute the words describing her pain were out of Trystan's mouth, I sent a text to Diana, even though she'd probably heard him from her office across the hall.

Alex: *Breakfast?*

Diana: *Sure.*

Once Trystan was in his office, the door closed, starting a video call that would last at least an hour, I grabbed my coat and met Diana in our tiny lobby.

We rode the elevator to the first floor, hurried across the main lobby as if Trystan might be right on our heels, and out the doors onto the pavement. We walked to the diner where everyone from our office went when they wanted a real breakfast instead of the yogurt or piece of fruit or bowl of oatmeal or slice of toast or bagel we usually gobbled before starting the day.

Both of us ordered a Mexican omelette, bacon, and toast.

Diana ordered hot chocolate, I asked for coffee. While we sipped our drinks, I told Diana about my apartment-hunting plans. Just as the food arrived, she asked to see pictures. I pulled up one of the websites on my phone and handed it to her.

She scrolled through floor plans and interior shots. I cut off a piece of omelette and ate it, letting the cheese melt across my tongue.

She handed the phone back. "They all look expensive."

"More than I'm paying now."

She smiled but looked a little uncertain. "Did you get a raise?"

"No. But I've been saving a lot for a long time."

"I don't think it's a good idea to pay rent out of your savings."

"I just meant that I could scale back the savings and spend a little more."

She nodded. "Or a lot more." She put her lips over the whipped cream, letting it ease its way into her mouth, and gently swallowed it.

"Also, I have a roommate."

She nodded. "I don't mind being in a studio. Someday I'd like something bigger, but for now, I like living alone."

"I think it should work out with Eileen. She's not in my face."

"You don't know until you live with someone."

"Probably true."

"Just like you don't know what people are like until you work with them for a while."

I laughed, although I'd known what Stephanie would be like the moment the glint of that huge gold cross she used to wear caught my eye. And, from the start, there'd been something about Diana, a vibe, if you believe in that sort of thing, that I was going to like her. It might have been that she held herself back and also that it was clear early on that she was smart. "If you're always thinking about your future, tell me what else you're imagining about it."

"It's not imagining. It's planning." She took a bite of toast and chewed it slowly.

I thought about the blurry image of a magnificent house that was always drifting at the back of my thoughts, luring me into the future. Maybe I'd been wrong, saying I never thought about the future. I didn't lay out all the steps I wanted to take, I didn't think about getting married or a career path or anything like that, but I did think about where I wanted to be. I imagined it. Diana planned it.

"I suppose that means you'll get there faster," I said. "Since it's all planned out."

"It's the *only* way you'll get there."

"So what are you planning? Are you going to stay in this job forever?"

"Probably not. I love the microexpression analysis, and I believe in what Trystan's doing. It feels good to help people, but I definitely want to own something. I want a business that belongs to me."

"What kind of business?"

She shrugged. "That's one part of my plan that needs some work."

I laughed. "Do you have any ideas at all, or you just want to be in charge?"

She winked. "It's not about being in charge. I want to know that I created something, made it work, offered something valuable to people, and managed things in the way that seemed best to me."

"It sounds like your obituary."

"That's not a bad idea."

"It's a terrible idea. I'll leave mine to someone else—not my problem."

"Yes, but it's a good way to look at your life, don't you think?"

"I don't think that at all."

She smiled, and it seemed as if her eyes were peering into

mine, looking for a previously undetected fear of death, a desire to avoid reality, a persona that might be tempted to buy whole-heartedly into the idea of a being in the sky who would take away that fear of things coming to an end.

"It's healthy to face the reality of your death," she said. "It's healthy to think about the course of your entire life, to recognize that you'll age. In fact, I think if we don't do that, we're blindsided by old age. People who are blindsided find it difficult to cope. They turn angry and bitter and destroy the final years of their lives."

It was quite a speech, and I wasn't sure what to say at first. I ate a strip of bacon, chewing it carefully, letting the salty pork flavor fill my mouth. "I think it's a little early for you and me to think about old age."

She shrugged. She gave me another inscrutable smile.

We ate in silence for a few minutes, then I spoke. "You said you want to manage things in the way that seems best to you—"

"Of course. Don't you?"

"I'm not allowed to, right now. Trystan is deciding how things should be managed."

She nodded. "Yes."

"Does that mean there are things he's doing that you think could be better managed?"

"Maybe. But don't ask me to tell you what those are. I try to keep my mind on my own work. Since I'm not in charge, I'll leave the managing to him."

"But you think it could be better," I said.

"I think he could be more successful, yes."

"How?"

She looked at me with a cool, steady gaze. "There's no point in talking about it. He has his vision, and we're here to line up with how he sees things."

From there, she changed the conversation to the coming summer and vacation plans. I reminded her I'd spent New Year's in Australia and didn't see myself taking a vacation again so soon. What I didn't say was that I had a lot of things to work out—finding a new apartment, arranging things with Eileen, moving, getting myself out from under Kent's scrutiny, and figuring out how I was going to keep the upper hand as a photographer.

Maybe it was that planning thing again. Summer was too far away for me to be considering any kind of trip. It was almost too far away to think about hot weather and the desire to escape the oppressive humidity of Manhattan. After I was settled in a new place, I would think about those things.

I would never think about my obituary or old age, but I supposed at some point I would start doing more than dreaming about the future.

CHAPTER 23

*S*tephanie was not going to accept Eileen's new boyfriend lying down. And what a laugh—*boy*-friend. That man hadn't seen boyhood in more than thirty years.

She put the chain on the front door. Eileen wasn't due home until after eleven, and it was only eight now, but she needed to be absolutely sure Eileen didn't walk in on her. She lit a lavender-scented candle, placed it on the coffee table, and turned off the living room lights. She fell to her knees in front of the candle, ignoring the sharp pain that bolted through the back of both kneecaps. Kneeling was more difficult than it used to be, but just because there was a slight ache didn't mean she should give up true prayer. And part of true prayer was demonstrating with your body the reverence and humility and submission you felt in your heart. God would protect her knees from serious damage. She pressed the palms of her hands together and closed her eyes.

Speaking out loud, she poured out her complaints about Ned and her fears for Eileen's soul, not to mention her life on earth. It was okay to complain to God. A lot of unbelievers took a dismissive attitude toward complaining these days, telling people they shouldn't be so *negative*, they shouldn't be *whiny*. But God invited

His people to complain. He welcomed knowing the depth of the pain His people felt. It was all over the Bible.

She let her mind roam over all the things she'd done wrong in marrying when she did and in failing to provide her little girl with a step-father. She'd been so badly hurt by what Eileen's father had done to her, having another man around was the last thing she'd wanted back then. She'd thought God would fulfill all of her needs.

All of them.

But He hadn't. Not entirely. It wasn't too late—He could step up now. Surely He recognized all the years she'd been faithful to Him and the depth of her devotion. Surely He would step in to save Eileen, and most of all, kick that *boy*-friend to the curb. It sickened her to think of that middle-aged man touching her daughter's beautiful skin, to consider him kissing her little girl— those soft, sweet lips. Surely Eileen didn't enjoy that, did she? The image in her mind and the imagined sensation of it was revolting.

She took several long, deep breaths, letting her mind settle into an empty pool, using the pressure on her knees, the strain on her muscles from such a simple pose to muffle her disturbing thoughts. She begged God to speak to her. He needed to show Stephanie what her role was in making sure Eileen didn't get caught in another terrible mistake with a man who didn't deserve her, another man who would surely break her heart. A man who was too old.

Remaining silent, keeping her thoughts quiet, feeling the ache in her knees begin to overwhelm her, she held on until her eyes were filled with tears from the discomfort. When the candle sputtered, she opened her eyes and lowered herself carefully to the floor.

The candle sputtered again, then went out.

Was that her message? The sudden extinguishing of the candle? What did it mean?

There hadn't been any clear thoughts or suggestions that

popped into her mind out of nowhere, the kind of sudden thoughts she'd come to know as the voice of God. Where was He? Hadn't He appreciated her effort?

The tears that had been pooling in her eyes trickled down her cheeks. She felt like a fool, curled up on the carpet, breathing the scent of lavender, and surrounded by darkness except for the light from outside poking its way through the slim space between the curtains.

Where *was* He?

If she'd ever needed His help, it was now. Eileen was in terrible trouble.

She pulled herself up and leaned against the couch, hugging her knees to her chest. She kicked off her shoes, which she should have done before kneeling. She'd felt driven to immediately enter God's presence. She hadn't stopped to think about how to make it more comfortable, which would have allowed her to remain in that position for an extended period of time—a cushion under her knees, for example.

She closed her eyes and tried to think. There had to be something she could do to help her daughter. She had plenty of experience from previous situations that told her trying to talk to Eileen would get her nowhere. Eileen would dig in her heels, pout, and act like an angry, put-upon teenager, bent on rebelling for the sheer pleasure of it. Trying to convince Eileen that Ned was not the man she belonged with would drive her right into his arms.

How long had she been seeing him?

Stephanie tried to recall the first mention of his name. No clear recollection came to her. Had this been going on for longer than she'd realized? They certainly acted like they knew each other quite well. They almost seemed married, or at least engaged, the way they spoke to each other, the comfortable and casual way they touched each other.

Think, she told herself. *Think back.*

Had Ned been the cause of Eileen's sudden change from her

near-starvation diet to eating like a somewhat normal, healthy adult? Stephanie had attributed that change to Alex. The return to eating like a normal person had coincided with Alex's entrance into Eileen's life. For all she knew, Alex had introduced Eileen to Ned. Or set Eileen up with him, just to upset Stephanie. She should never have opened up to Alexandra all those months ago, telling her about the concerns she had for her daughter.

She sighed and rested her forehead on her knees.

Changes in Eileen's behavior flooded her mind. These memories must be from God because she'd never considered it all in a timeline before. She stood suddenly, then had to move toward the wall and press her hand against it until the dizziness passed.

What about all that money Eileen had spent on makeup and a haircut and highlights and clothing for Stephanie? Had all of her new-found money come from that man? She gasped at the thought. A rush of pleasure flooded her body, knowing that God was revealing things to her. But it was accompanied by a cold fear and a rage that was equally icy. What, exactly, was going on? She had to know.

She hurried into Eileen's bedroom. The hunger that had started to gnaw at her while she was praying was gone. She felt like the Spirit of God had filled her belly and her heart and her mind, all at once.

She started with the top dresser drawer, yanking it open and sifting through the odds and ends Eileen kept in the narrow drawer. There were a few credit cards, some coins and loose bills, receipts, and two buttons. A small box held some of her jewelry. There were two inspirational books, but they looked like they spouted New Age, humans-as-gods nonsense.

What was she even looking for? Evidence that man had given Eileen money. But it was a lot of money, and there wouldn't necessarily be a receipt just lying around. She'd hoped she would find a bank deposit receipt or evidence of a newly opened account.

People would say she was wrong for going through her adult daughter's things. She'd done it before—that's how she'd found out just how much Eileen had spent on her mother's new look. But this was okay because she wasn't looking for evidence with which to punish her daughter. She was trying to *help*. And when someone you cared about was in trouble, the rules were different. Eileen didn't even seem to be aware she needed help. She was blinded by the void created by her father.

Stephanie shut the drawer and looked around the room.

The laptop was closed, tossed on the bed like a discarded pair of socks. These new thin, elegant laptops were almost like beautiful articles of clothing, a fashion accessory to your career. Stephanie still used a desktop computer. If she required a computer more often, she might want one of these beautiful devices, but it wasn't worth it for the few Bible study forums she was involved with and the occasional bill paying and income tax preparation.

She sat on the bed and pulled the laptop toward her. She stroked the silky metal enclosure. It was cool and soothing. The color looked as if it had been designed to reduce anxiety, a color she couldn't stop gazing at. She guessed they'd conducted a focus group to determine which color elicited a sense of calm in the users. She opened it, knowing what she would find. Sure enough, the screen was locked, demanding a password. She closed it, wondering why Eileen felt she needed to go to such extreme lengths in order to hide her life from her mother.

How much did Stephanie even know about the girl? Her own daughter? There could be a thousand secrets hidden behind Eileen's clear, artfully made-up eyes.

She stood and looked around the room a second time, moving toward the closet.

Opening the doors, pushing the clothes to the side, she methodically went through every shoebox and every storage container. The only way to find what she wanted was to be thorough. Assuming a particular storage spot couldn't possibly contain useful information was a mistake. When the closet was put back together, she returned to the dresser. She went carefully through each drawer, sliding her hands beneath silky lingerie and soft sweaters, leggings and cashmere scarves, feeling for a texture that didn't belong.

In the very last drawer, as she knelt on the floor, she found it.

Her fingertips touched a thick envelope. She pulled it out and undid the clasp. Still on her knees, she removed the papers and read them, understanding immediately what they were telling her. Upon the death of Eileen's disastrous, emotionally abusive former fiancé, Jim Kohn, her daughter had been given four million dollars.

She gasped. She wasn't even sure if the sudden intake of air was simple shock, if it was fury at how that man had manipulated Eileen from beyond the grave, disgust that he'd effectively paid for Stephanie's makeover, or a hurt so deep she could hardly take a second breath. Her daughter had hidden all of this from her. Why? Why would she do that?

CHAPTER 24

*E*ileen and I met for brunch. While we sipped champagne and ate from the lavish buffet, we strategized about our apartment search. We clicked through websites on our phones, sharing the places we found that looked promising. We'd agreed the apartments we would consider needed the right blend of price, layout, building amenities, and location. Although real estate agents are notorious for proclaiming that only three things matter in real estate—location, location, location—I was not fixated on the location. If we spent enough, I knew we'd end up in a nice enough area. I didn't need prestige. Neither did Eileen, and that confirmed my thought that she and I saw the world the same way in enough aspects that we could share our possessions and our lives without driving each other to murder.

The server refilled our champagne glasses, and we studied the list of addresses Eileen had been compiling in a notebook. "We have ten. I think that's more than enough for today. By the time we go from one to the next, it will take most of the day."

"I was thinking of using cabs," I said.

"Okay. It sounds kind of pricey for apartment hunting, but it would be more efficient."

"What else can you do? If we take the subway, like you said, we'll see three apartments, and it will be almost dark. We can't make a decision at night."

"Although seeing it at night is important too," she said.

"When we narrow down the list, we can ask for second appointments in the evening."

We finished our food, swallowed the cool, frothing champagne, and settled our bill.

Outside, Eileen buttoned her coat. "I'll pay for the cabs."

"No. We'll split it."

"It's no big deal—"

"It's not how we should start out," I said.

"Do you think I'm waving my money in your face?"

"No. But we should have a plan for sharing expenses. Food and—"

"Later," she said.

"Yes, after we have the specifics."

She lifted her hand overhead, and a cab pulled to the curb. We climbed in and gave the driver the address for the first apartment on the list. By four o'clock, we'd seen six apartments. We loved every single one of them.

"Should we stop for today?" Eileen massaged her left temple with her index finger.

"Headache?"

"No." She moved her hand. "But I'm tired, and we won't be able to decide if we keep finding more that we like."

"One of the ones we haven't seen might blow our minds."

"Really? On our budget?"

I laughed.

"Let's get a drink," she said. She patted her purse. "We can write down what we liked best about each one."

We found a bar with a small interior garden. It was ringed with heaters. The windows of the restaurant rose to nearly the height of a two-story building, protecting the area from the wind.

I ordered a martini, and Eileen asked for a glass of Chardon-nay. She pulled out her notebook, opened it to a blank page, and began writing the street names, one at the top of each page.

"This seems like a lot of work," I said.

"It's to prevent buyer's remorse."

"If you say so."

She placed her pen in the center along the book's spine. She closed her eyes and rubbed her temple again, a single finger grinding into the side of her head. It was a strange gesture. Usually, a headache has people pressing on the painful spots with several fingers. They don't drive a single fingertip into the area that is already hurting. But she'd said it wasn't a headache.

"Are you okay?"

She opened her eyes. "Why?"

"You keep stabbing at your head."

"I'm not stabbing."

"Whatever that is."

"Just trying to relieve the pressure. Worrying about my Mom."

"Worried about what?"

"Leaving her alone."

"I thought you'd already made that decision?"

"I have, I guess."

"So you haven't."

She smiled.

The drinks came, and we leaned back in our chairs to give the server plenty of room to maneuver my martini without any of the liquid sliding over the edge of the glass. When our server was gone, Eileen lifted her drink toward me in a toast, eyeing my glass to let me know she realized I couldn't respond with a similar gesture. "To a change of scenery."

"Agreed." I carefully lifted my glass and took a deep sip. It was perfect, everything from the temperature to the balance of alcohol to the size of the olives waiting for me.

"I'm worried about her...my mother. She seems so..." She cut herself off, I assumed to keep herself from exposing more of Stephanie's private feelings and idiosyncrasies.

I was curious, but not too much. I had a pretty good idea how Stephanie would react to Eileen moving out. It wasn't about being lonely or anything like that. Stephanie wanted to keep Eileen where she could see her.

"She'll be fine," I said.

"It will be a blow."

"Nothing she can't handle."

She picked up her glass and took a sip.

While she finished jotting down short descriptions of the apartments we'd seen, I thought about my current apartment. I did love those French doors between the bedroom and living room. And I loved the staircase. Most of the buildings we'd looked at had elevators. One on the west side of the park had stairs to the first level but an elevator after that. I'd miss those things, but I would not miss my tiny bedroom and the roaches. I wouldn't miss the bizarre and slightly oppressive building manager. I would not miss the cold evenings that the radiator refused to warm. I couldn't wait to have a larger bedroom and a real kitchen that wasn't just a counter tacked on the side of the living room. I couldn't wait to have decent heating and cooling and huge windows that let you see the sky, not just the sidewalk below, a tiny sliver of sky available only if you stand at the perfect angle to look out and up to the left.

Eileen asked me to tell her the one thing I liked best about each apartment. As I spoke, she wrote down my comments, then added her favorite feature beneath where she'd written mine. Our drinks were gone by the time we completed our list since sometimes we had to discuss four or five different features before we could identify the best one. Then she told me I had to pick a second item, then a third, going through each apartment in its turn instead of making a list for one before moving on.

We ordered a second round of drinks and narrowed our favorites down to three apartments.

"This one is the most expensive." She tapped the end of her pen on the notebook. "Maybe cross that off the list because why spend more when there are plenty of places we love at a lower cost. We don't need to pay for more for love."

I laughed, loud enough that the two guys at the tables about four away from us glanced in my direction, offering cautious smiles.

Eileen grinned. "So *yes* to crossing it off?"

I nodded.

"Should we go back and look at both of these tomorrow?" she asked.

I shrugged. "I could decide right now."

"Then why did we make these complicated lists?"

"It seemed like you wanted to do it that way," I said.

"It was to help us make a decision we wouldn't regret. I told you that."

"I didn't need help. But I think you had fun sorting it out. Plus, we had two very nice drinks." What I didn't say was that it had also turned her thoughts away from worrying about how her mother would get along without her.

We talked about furniture and dates for moving. We talked about ground rules for guests, especially men. And, we talked about money. I had plenty to take care of myself, and I wanted our bills to be split evenly. I didn't want to nickel and dime every carrot and every bottle of wine we purchased. She agreed, although I could see how, inevitably, expenses would get tangled, especially with the visiting men we'd discussed.

If I was honest with myself, which I am, most of the time, I felt like her large cushion of cash was a bit of an insurance policy. Of course, I wanted to pay my own way, keeping our contributions equal. But if my job went upside down, she had the ability to string a safety net below me. Not that I would take her money, not that I would fail to pay her back, but with money, it's always nice just knowing it's there. And if something happened to my job, it was a good possibility that such a catastrophe would be caused by her mother.

After a while, we ordered sparkling water and appetizers. Then, as her wineglass was swept off the table, the cloud of anxiety filled Eileen's eyes. She returned to worrying out loud about her mother and her ability to cope on her own. It seemed to me that moving out of her mother's apartment would be the best decision Eileen had made in a very long time. You can't spend your whole life making sure your mother isn't lonely. She has to put forth a little effort. And if Eileen stayed with Stephanie, she would never have a life of her own. I wondered what was wrong with Stephanie, that she seemed to be okay with that possibility. For all the things my mother had done to make my life difficult, she never tried to keep me from becoming an adult, from launching out on my own. My mother never wanted to be room-mates with me.

CHAPTER 25

*S*tephanie sat in her bedroom. Waiting. Eileen hadn't mentioned going out with that man again, her so-called boyfriend, so where was she? She rarely worked on Saturdays.

It was nearly dinnertime when she heard Eileen's key in the front door. She stood and ran her fingers through her hair, lifting it away from her face, smoothing away the static electricity from leaning against the pillows on her bed. Before she could move, she heard Eileen's bedroom door open and close.

She stepped into the hallway and tapped on Eileen's door. "Eileen. I'd like to speak to you."

"Sure." The door remained closed.

"Now, please." She rattled the doorknob. "Why is the door locked?"

"Because I'm changing my clothes."

"I know what your body looks like."

The lock clicked, and Eileen opened the door. "I like privacy when I'm getting dressed. Just like you do. What's the big rush?"

Stephanie looked past her, curious to see what Eileen had been up to.

"Are you okay?"

"No, I'm not okay," Stephanie said. "Please come into the living room." She turned and walked away from the doorway and Eileen's irritated expression. No one should look at her mother with that kind of expression—as if she considered Stephanie both an intrusion and a burden, someone to be managed.

Eileen trudged after her, stopping at the opening into the living room. She stood there, sipping water from a glass.

Stephanie settled on the couch. "Did you have any dinner?"

Eileen nodded.

"What did you have?"

"Alex and I went to a place in midtown. We had some wine and a few appetizers."

Because of the way Eileen's voice faded over the last few words, Stephanie sensed there was more to the story. "I didn't know you were with Alex."

Eileen said nothing.

Stephanie knew she needed to let it go, as everyone at church was always telling her. Talking about Alex would turn Eileen against her, it always did. Things would end in hard feelings and undermine their discussion of that horrific amount of money Eileen had taken as if she were some kind of a ghoul, a dead man's kept woman. "Will you come sit down," she said.

"What is this about?"

"I prefer to talk to you in here," Stephanie said.

"I don't want a long conversation. I'm a little tired, and I was planning to go to bed early."

"After you have phone sex with Ned?"

"God, Mom. Where did that come from?"

She didn't know. She honestly didn't. All her feelings were jumbled up and confused and angry. "I've heard of things like that. I'm not naïve, you know. And please don't take His name in vain."

"I didn't."

"You used it as a curse word."

"What do you want?" Eileen asked. "You sound angry."

"I want you to sit down. I have something extremely serious to discuss with you."

"Is everything okay at work?"

"I need you to sit down. Now."

"I'm not a child. You don't get to order me around."

"I'm not ordering you around. I want you to sit down so we can have a *very* serious conversation, hopefully as equals."

"Are we equals?" Eileen went into the kitchen and refilled her glass. She returned to the living room and perched on one of the armchairs facing her mother. She placed her glass on a coaster. "What's so dreadfully serious?"

"Don't mock this."

"Heaven forbid."

"I mean it, Eileen."

"What is this about?"

"I'm concerned about you. Very, very concerned. Extremely concerned."

"Wow. *Very-very* and *extremely*. That's something."

"Don't mock me. I'm your mother."

"I thought we were equals?"

Stephanie glared at her. She folded her hands in her lap and leaned back, straightening her neck. "I'm still your mother, and I deserve respect. And consideration."

"Just tell me what's going on."

Stephanie shifted her position and pulled a large white envelope out from under the seat cushion. She tossed it on the floor.

Eileen stared at the white rectangle.

"Do you know what that is?" Stephanie asked.

Eileen kept her gaze on the floor. She stood and took a few steps toward the envelope. She picked it up and held it to her ribs. She spoke softly. "You went through my things?"

"That pervert left you money? Four *million* dollars?" Stephanie's voice rose, much louder than she wanted it to, but she couldn't help it. The feelings rushed through her, demanding to be released. The questions festering inside screamed for an explanation.

"You went into my room and looked through my things?"

"I didn't think you had anything to hide. Obviously, I was wrong."

Finally, Eileen looked up. Her eyes were teary. "I thought we were *equals*. I thought we respected each other's privacy."

"You don't need to hide things from your mother."

"I'm an adult."

Stephanie sighed. "This isn't about privacy. It's about that man giving you money. Why? To atone for how he abused your body? Your dignity? He tried to pay you off, or something like that? And you *accepted* it?"

"What I decided to do is none of your business."

"You paid for my new clothes, my haircut, for everything, with that filthy money? It's disgusting. You make me feel like a, like a—"

"Don't be so dramatic," Eileen snapped. "It's just money. I'm not going to say no to that kind of money. So get over yourself."

"Don't talk to me like that!" Stephanie rose to her feet, her voice echoing around the room like a screech of terror in the confined space.

"I am so disappointed that you went through my things, that you think you can interfere in my life, that you don't trust me to make good decisions. You don't even seem to *realize* I'm an adult."

Stephanie didn't like the tone in Eileen's voice. There was a suggestion of finality, a hint that she'd given up. She wasn't going to have a tantrum like those fits she'd thrown when she was two, and twelve, and eighteen. She would do something worse.

Eileen walked toward the hallway.

"We're still talking," Stephanie said.

"No, we're not. You're talking. And there's nothing to talk about. You don't respect me. I'm not sure you ever have."

"You lied to me."

Eileen kept walking. Stephanie lunged toward her. "Wait. It's not right to just walk out of a room because you don't like what someone is saying. You paid for my clothes with his money, and now I feel disgusted even looking at them."

"That's your choice."

"You should have told me."

"I tried to do something to make you happy. But I'm finally getting it—that might not ever be possible."

"What's not possible?"

"It's impossible to do anything to please you. I think you like being miserable, and no matter what I do, you're going to stay that way."

Stephanie sobbed out her words. "I love you, Eileen. I'm your mother. You're everything to me."

"That's not how it's supposed to be. You need your own life. I have my own life now."

"You'll understand when you have children."

"What I understand is that children become adults, and you have to let them live their own lives. You don't sneak into their rooms, go through their things, or treat them like they're stupid."

"Please don't talk to me like this." She felt a sharp pain shoot through her chest. "You're breaking my heart."

Eileen sighed. She tucked the envelope under her arm and moved toward her bedroom door. It stood open, revealing a room with a single pale blue wall behind the bed, framed photographs on the adjacent walls, simple furniture with clean lines. It was a beautiful room, and it made Stephanie happy that Eileen had put so much effort into decorating it. The trouble was, Stephanie rarely saw it. The door was closed most of the time, shutting her out, as if Eileen wanted to send a message to Stephanie that she wasn't wanted.

It didn't have to be this way. Lots of mothers and daughters became close friends as adults. When she and Eileen had gone to the hair salon together, eaten a sumptuous lunch, shopped for chic clothing, Stephanie had felt that was finally happening for the two of them. Had she spoiled it all? But it wasn't her fault! Eileen had lied to her. Hiding something like this—four *million* dollars—was the same as a lie. Worse, maybe.

"We need to talk this out," Stephanie said. She took a deep breath. "We can decide together how you should handle the money."

Eileen laughed. "Decide *together*? It's my money."

"I don't think—"

"It's my money. And the decision has already been made."

"You should give it back."

"Who would I even give it to? No. Wait." She held up her hand in Stephanie's face.

Stephanie hated it when people did that. It was so disrespectful.

"I don't even want to hear the answer," Eileen said. "This is over."

"I can't wear clothes that man paid for!" Stephanie grabbed fistfuls of her hair and pulled it away from her face. "And what about this? I can't even look in the mirror."

"You're losing it," Eileen said.

"Don't you see what you're doing?"

"I see that I have financial security. I was engaged to him, remember?"

"It's degrading."

Eileen shrugged. "Not in my opinion."

"Does *he* know about this?"

"Who?"

"Your *boy*friend!"

"Ned?" She smiled.

Stephanie wanted to smack her. That was another subject they needed to discuss, but one thing at a time. "Please come back into the living room. We can—"

"I'm done talking about this. The decision was made, and it has nothing to do with you."

"But the clothes. Can't you see how that makes me feel?"

"It's just money. It's not like there's blood on it." Eileen laughed. "If you don't like them, donate them."

"But I—"

Eileen laughed. "You don't want to."

"Of course not. And I can't return my hair."

"Then deal with it."

"You can't talk to me like this." A sob caught in her throat. She swallowed. "Please."

Eileen put her hand on Stephanie's arm. "Calm down. Jim had so much more than this, it was almost nothing to him. And I believe I earned it. If you think about it, you'll see that I'm right."

"*Earned* it? That's disgusting."

Eileen shrugged.

"I suppose your boyfriend is okay with all of this? He doesn't have any scruples, letting another man give you that kind of money?"

Eileen stepped inside her bedroom doorway. She tossed the envelope onto the bed.

"Ned seems to have quite a lot of money himself," Stephanie said.

Eileen shrugged.

"Does he?"

"I love him, it's not about money."

"You love him? You can't possibly...you don't even know what love is."

"That's condescending."

"You hardly know him," Stephanie said.

"I know him quite well."

"Maybe from sex, but that's not knowing a person. You can share a bed with a person for years and not know who he really is."

"I said, I'm done talking about this." Eileen nudged the door toward closing it.

"We just started."

"You're treating me like I'm ten years old, and I don't like it. I have a headache."

"You were never like this before."

"Like what?"

"So argumentative. So...so...rude. So arrogant and—"

"All I'm doing is telling you what I think. There's nothing rude about it."

"This is because of Alexandra."

"What?"

"You've changed since you started doing things with her. I don't like it."

"Too bad," Eileen said.

The bedroom door closed. Stephanie heard the click of the lock.

CHAPTER 26

The moment Eileen's lock turned, Stephanie knew she'd made a terrible mistake. Again. Why did she always say the wrong things? The words just boiled up inside her and spilled out as if they were scripted by someone she hardly knew. Wasn't the Spirit of God supposed to be living inside of her, taking control of her tongue and causing her to speak with grace and kindness? With love? What was *wrong* with her?

Silent tears poured out of her eyes. If Eileen heard her crying, she would be angry; she would accuse Stephanie of trying to manipulate her.

She turned and walked to her bedroom, opened the door, and slipped inside. She closed the door and collapsed onto her bed. It felt as if there was a poison in her apartment, knowing that money had purchased the beautiful clothing hanging in her closet and possibly quite a few other things that Eileen possessed that she hadn't mentioned. The poison was inside her body, evident in her hair. She wanted to grab the scissors out of the kitchen drawer and chop it off, rush to Duane Reade and buy a box of dye to obliterate all the expertly colored strands. Of course, that would do nothing to convince Eileen to return the money—filthy, degrading money that had no place in their lives. How was she going to manage to open Eileen's eyes to the truth? Why couldn't Eileen see it herself?

She thought about the gun, hidden deep beneath her bed. But of course, she couldn't kill the man who had degraded her daughter. He was already dead. The thought made her laugh. She took a deep breath and turned onto her back.

Laughing, even though it wasn't really that funny, cleared her head. The laughter dried her tears, and she could feel her brain begin to sort through the problem, placing it before the throne of Grace, knowing that she would receive clear guidance. She wasn't in charge of this, God held Eileen in His powerful hand. He loved her far more than Stephanie ever would, although that was honestly difficult to imagine and almost impossible to believe.

Crying about heartache never helped. There had to be a way to help Eileen see how the money she'd been given would rot her life from the inside out.

She sat up and leaned against the headboard. Once again, she blamed herself for Eileen's poor choices in men. Without a decent father or step-father, how could Eileen know what a real man was like, how a decent man behaved and treated women?

When had she made the decision never to remarry? She didn't remember it as a clear-cut choice, maybe just a series of miserable short-term relationships, followed by feeling more and more content living in a cozy world with only Eileen to share her meals, to sleep under her roof. They'd been devoted to each other— mother and daughter—*just us girls*—doing nearly everything together.

Then Eileen reached high school and started to peel herself away from her mother. Yes, she still talked about her life and her feelings, and it seemed as if everything was okay between them. Eileen had had a few boyfriends, and they'd all seemed nice enough. When she started modeling, Stephanie worried, but it seemed to go well. Eileen had been earning a good income, and she loved the chances to try on all kinds of different clothes, she loved being in front of the camera, selling a look.

It made Stephanie smile, remembering how Eileen had loved to dress up in Stephanie's clothes when she was a little girl. When Stephanie looked at it from that perspective, modeling seemed like a perfect fit for her daughter. She laughed at that mild pun, glad that her mood was improving. She could feel the Spirit of God gently holding her heart, lifting it up and making it stronger.

She couldn't go back and change what had been done. It wouldn't have helped anything to have the cruel and utterly selfish man who had fathered Eileen remain in her life. That might have given her even worse messages about men.

But now, Eileen was longing for that older, supposedly wiser, caring man. And so she was drawn to these guys—far too old for her, and all with more money than was good for a person.

Stephanie was fairly confident it wasn't the money that had attracted Eileen. Although maybe it was that too. Eileen was looking for security, a fatherly man to take charge, so she gravitated toward the financial aspects of security along with her desire for a man so much older, a man who would tell her what to do, who could look out for her.

Eileen would argue with all of that, but she was too young to know. She hadn't had nearly enough life experience to understand how human psychology sometimes took strange, distorted turns, especially when someone didn't have God intimately involved in her life and was left to the devices of her pagan brain and base instincts.

She closed her eyes and began to whisper her thoughts to God. She asked for help guiding Eileen in the right direction, for a more appropriate man to appear in Eileen's life...Then, her thoughts drifted to the past, to her own experiences with men.

It had happened about four years after her husband left Stephanie and Eileen to fend for themselves.

She'd met a man at church. He'd been warm and friendly,

eager to get involved in church activities. He'd spoken to Stephanie during the coffee hour following the morning worship service.

She could almost hear his voice now. "Hi. I'm Jacob." His voice was warm and deep, filled with kindness.

She'd held out her hand for him to shake and given him her name.

"I'm sure you've noticed," he said, "I'm new around here."

"I did notice," she said.

"How long have you been a member?"

"Close to twenty years now."

He'd asked her about the various mid-week Bible studies. "Is there a social group for singles?"

"Not really. Most of the single people are women."

He nodded. He didn't make any rude expressions or look terrified that he might be pursued more than he wanted.

They talked about the message from the morning service, and then he'd invited her out to lunch. After that, he'd asked her to visit the Museum of Natural History and then MOMA.

They saw each other two or three times a week for nearly two months. She thought she knew everything about him. He was open and talkative, told her stories about his past, and all about his job as a high school teacher. She thought she was falling in love. She admired his devotion to teaching, and she was thrilled and relieved she'd actually met him at church, so she had the solid assurance of knowing their beliefs were the same. She'd spent hours thanking God for bringing him into her life—the perfect man for her, a gift from her Heavenly Father who knew the deepest corners of her heart.

Then came that awful night. She and Jacob were attending a Bible study focused on how to follow your principles in your career.

Jacob had been strangely quiet the entire time they'd been in the study group. He was very talkative when the two of them were alone, but during the study time, he said only a few words, even when the group leader asked him a direct question.

Finally, at their sixth or seventh meeting, he'd spoken up. The flood of words that came out of him more than made up for his previous silence. "The things you're talking about really aren't very practical," he'd said. "We live in a post-religious world. These stories and myths were useful when people weren't educated, but now..." He laughed. It was a sharp, loud sound like a gunshot. It reverberated in the same way, filling the small room. It had a mocking tone, like the laughter of the Devil himself.

Stephanie felt her heart freeze and saw looks of shock on the others. A wave of nausea rode through her stomach, followed by a tremendous ache in her heart. He wasn't who he'd said he was at all. What was he doing here? And why had he been interested in Stephanie? It made no sense.

The study group had ended on a weak and deflated note that evening, without anyone saying much after their leader had argued for the Word of God, countering the blank, disbelieving face of Jacob.

Later, she and Jacob sat in a coffee shop over steaming cups of hot chocolate.

"Why do you have feelings for me if you don't believe any of the same things I do?" Stephanie said.

"I told you I'm a high school teacher. I told you I teach contemporary culture and philosophy. I felt I needed a first-hand experience with religion. There are a number of kids in my class who have strong religious backgrounds, and I felt I should understand their mindset to help facilitate our class discussions. You could call this a bit of a sociology experiment."

"I'm an *experiment*? I..." Her throat clogged with tears, and she couldn't say more. She wasn't even sure what she wanted to say. Her skin burned with the humiliation of it. She felt so hot, so uncomfortable, she wanted to sweep the hot drinks off the table and rush to the door into the cold night air. "I thought..." She coughed. "I thought you cared about me."

He looked genuinely confused. "Romantically? Why did you think that?"

"We've been dating."

"We have?" Now his face registered shock. "Why would you think that? We never slept together, never even kissed."

"But you told me all about yourself. You asked about my life. You lied. You—"

He held up his hand. "I'm sorry you perceive this as a lie, that you think I misrepresented—"

She laughed. "Don't pretend—"

"Let me finish." His voice was loud, smothering hers. Then he spoke in a more normal tone. "I suppose I should have mentioned what kind of information I was looking for, but I assumed we were simply friends and would have a good laugh when I told you."

"That's a lie."

"Not at all. God's honest truth." He laughed. "I suppose that wasn't the best way to put it."

She glared at him. "You made a fool out of me." She didn't tell him he'd hurt her so deeply she felt her lungs had been punctured, and she could no longer breathe. She wouldn't give him the satisfaction of knowing how badly she ached. But the shame...maybe she shouldn't have said that either. She was giving him too much room to hurt her further. She stood and shoved the small wooden chair away from her. It crashed to the floor. The other patrons turned to look at her, excited to witness the drama that was unfolding. All the other conversations stopped, forcing her to speak in a loud whisper. "You're the biggest jerk I've ever met in my life. And you'll be punished for this if you don't wind up in hell, which seems to be where you're headed. You're mocking God and infiltrating his people like an evil spirit."

He laughed. "Calm down."

People were still staring, still not talking. The temperature of her skin increased as if she'd stepped into the fires of hell. She turned and walked quickly to the door. She wanted to let it slam behind her, but it had a compressor on it that forced it to move slowly, closing with a whimper. Maybe that was more fitting.

After that, she never again looked at a man as a possible romantic partner. Eighty percent of them were creeps and liars and abusers, ungodly and filled with bad thoughts. The good ones, the ones who weren't like that, had all been grabbed up long ago.

She was too late to find love, but she was not going to let it ruin her life. She would pour all of her love into her daughter. She would raise a daughter that was admirable in every way, a daughter who felt cherished and wanted and special.

For many years, she'd thought she'd accomplished that.

CHAPTER 27

*E*ileen sent me a text message at six a.m—*Can we meet for breakfast? Brunch? A workout? Shopping? ANYTHING?*

My finger paused over my phone for a moment. I'd been looking forward to running by myself. I almost always ran alone, and with Eileen poised to become a roommate, I didn't want to set a precedent. Alex: *I'm headed out for a run. I'd rather go by myself.*

Eileen: *But you have to eat. After your run.*

Alex: *What's so urgent?*

I wondered if she was considering changing her plans. Maybe she didn't like any of the apartments. Maybe she wanted to sit on her entire nest egg and continue dealing with her mother in exchange for ridiculously below-market rent. Maybe she wanted to move in with Ned.

She sent a string of emojis with confusing and contradictory expressions, then another text—*I had a thing with my mother. I need to bitch and complain.*

I smiled. Everything was still moving forward. I didn't think there was anything new she could tell me about Stephanie, but roommates are supposed to talk to each other about what's going on in their lives. At least I was pretty sure that was how it worked.

Alex: *Absolutely. Brunch. Ten-thirty?*

Eileen had made a reservation, and we were ushered to our table almost the minute the doors closed behind us. We settled ourselves, Eileen on the banquette, me on the chair facing her. The white linen tablecloth draped across our legs, hiding the knee-high boots we'd both worn. It was March, but it felt like January. After that little whisper a week earlier, spring was not coming fast enough for me. As much as I loved those boots, I craved sandals and bare legs and skirts. I wanted to feel warm evening air on my skin at ten o'clock at night. Then I remembered I'd often felt those warm breezes when I sat in the roof garden and smoked. I shoved the thought out of my brain and focused on the champagne glasses our server was placing on the table.

We ordered eggs Benedict and bacon and small bowls of fruit, then settled back to toast each other.

"To my baggage-free roommate," Eileen said.

I laughed, and we clicked our glasses together.

As we sipped champagne, she told me in precise detail about how her mother had gone into her room, taken the documents related to Eileen's inheritance from Jim Kohn out of the dresser drawer, and then confronted Eileen as if she'd caught her stealing money red-handed.

By the time Eileen was finished talking about how upset she was, how difficult her mother was, how eager she was to move out, our food had arrived, and we were well into the eggs and the creamy delicious hollandaise.

I was mostly silent while she talked. I'm sure she thought, as most women would, that she was talking to someone who could feel what she was feeling, whose emotions rode up and down the same rollercoaster. I hoped she took my silence as shock. It wasn't. Nothing Stephanie did shocked me. The fact that Stephanie would work overtime to smother her daughter, prying into her private life, literally pushing her out the door when she claimed she wanted the opposite, was the only thing that shocked me.

That was the trouble with Stephanie. She got so caught up in what she wanted and what she thought god was directing her to do that she completely lost sight of her real goal. Every single time.

"I just feel so sad and so angry, at the same time," Eileen said.

I nodded.

"What's your mother like?"

The change in course was so sudden, I almost choked on my bacon. I swallowed and took a sip of champagne. My glass was now empty, and a moment later, the server appeared, offering a refill. When the glass was full again, I took another sip, feeling the light, newly released bubbles tap against my upper lip.

"You don't want to talk about her?" Eileen said. "It's that bad?"

"No."

"You never mention her."

"I don't think about the past much."

"That's probably a good policy. Where does she live? How often do you talk to her?"

I took another sip of champagne, considering what I would say to explain the situation and end this part of the conversation quickly.

"If I'm being too nosey, just tell me."

"It just doesn't really apply here."

"Because she lets you live your own life?"

"She does now."

She heaved a loud, dramatic sigh, but I didn't think it was put on. She really was tired of it all.

"Why did you want to talk about it?" I asked.

"Like I said, just complaining."

"I probably can't help very much."

"No, I know that. I just get so upset, and I need to get it out of me."

"I can understand that."

She looked at me as if she expected me to say more, but I wasn't sure what.

"I don't know what I'm supposed to do," she said.

"Are you supposed to do anything?"

"I don't know how to get her to back off." She ran the knife through her eggs and stabbed her fork into the small piece she'd separated from the rest. "I don't understand why she treats me like this."

I shrugged.

"She wants her fingers in every part of my life. She hates Ned, she thinks she can control my money, she doesn't like what I eat, or even that I hang out with you. She's going to lose it when she finds out we're moving in together."

"You still haven't told her?" I took a sip of champagne. I wondered if Eileen had agreed to move in with me deliberately to annoy her mother. It was possible. Some people do things like that. I think I've done a fair amount of that in my life, although mostly when I was younger and still living with my parents.

"I can't deal with her rage."

"Rage?" I knew Stephanie hated me, but rage? Hearing Eileen put it that way was very intense.

"I can feel it in her all the time. Rage at the world. Maybe she's angry at God, who knows."

"Could be. Well, just tell her and get it over with."

"I will. But I still don't know what to do."

"I'm not sure what you mean."

"To help her. To make her feel better."

"I don't think that's your job."

She sighed. "I know you're right. I know I need to just be out of there. The sooner, the better. To be honest, I'm a little scared."

"Of what?"

"It's hard to watch someone get as upset as she does. It's like she doesn't even hear what I'm saying. I don't want her to feel so bad."

"Isn't god supposed to do that for her? Maybe she doesn't really believe in him after all."

"Maybe not. I don't really know. I try not to talk to her about it. I thought things were getting better when we did all that clothes shopping together. But it seems like it was all a waste. The inside of her needs to change. You can't do that with a new haircut and some highlights."

We continued eating and didn't talk for a few minutes. The server offered a third glass of champagne, and we both said yes without even looking at each other. One more glass, and I was going to have to get an Uber home—riding partially day-drunk on the subway isn't a good thing.

"So what should I *do*?"

I thought I'd made it clear I wasn't going to be much help, but maybe her question was just her desperation. "Pack your things, tell her what day you're moving out, and let her scream and yell."

"It's not really screaming and yelling. It's hard to explain. It's the things she says, the way she twists every situation, and the way she acts as if her viewpoint is the truth and everything else is irrelevant."

I really had no idea what Eileen expected from me. I decided to stop pretending to be the sensitive person I would never be. "The longer you listen to her, the more it will mess up your head. Tell her you're moving out and if she loses her mind, call the police."

She laughed. "Are you serious?"

I sipped my champagne. I didn't know whether or not I was serious, it was just something to say. For a woman with four million dollars, she seemed oddly unaware of how much power she had.

CHAPTER 28

Talking to Eileen about her mother turned my thoughts toward my own mother. Most of the time, she was an occasional, faint shadow passing through my head. A ghost. A voice that had grown soft and difficult to hear in my mind. She was someone who almost didn't seem real anymore.

My mother had been diagnosed with ovarian cancer when I was in college. She died so fast that none of her children had been able to get home to see her. Part of this was because my parents didn't mention the cancer to us until the very last minute. They were praying for its eradication, and by the time they were willing to even consider the possibility that perhaps this prayer might not be answered, she was swept away to the hospital and died. Only my father was there.

When he called to tell me she was gone, he asked me to come home immediately. It would comfort him to have all of us together. He needed me, he said. He'd bought me a plane ticket. I told him I would be there for her funeral. Until that was arranged, I had nothing to offer him. His selfish decision to let no one but god in on her diagnosis, on what she was going through, didn't earn him much sympathy.

I needed time. I needed time alone to think about it, needed to get past the shock of something I'd never expected in a hundred years. I felt strangely lost and slightly empty. I didn't know what to think. I couldn't understand why I wasn't crying. That's what most people did when someone close to them died. But that's not how I am, and long before she died, I'd known I was fundamentally different from most people. I'd known that with increasing clarity for years, but my reaction to my mother's death made it definite.

That didn't mean I felt nothing. I felt a strange, floating away from the earth feeling—lost. As if I were a balloon that had slipped out of a child's hand and was drifting up into the clouds. Everything looked very far away. The world grew deathly silent around me.

The day after she died was the day I started smoking. I needed something. I couldn't talk to my roommates at the time because I knew they would expect tears. They would be afraid of me when they saw that I wasn't like them. I already knew this from many experiences. When tears don't flow for you the way they do for others, they are terrified of you, angry at you, turn away from you, and want you out of their lives.

So instead, I walked three blocks to the liquor store. I bought a pack of cigarettes and a cheap lighter. I had no idea then, and I still don't, why that was my inclination. I suppose I needed something to do with my hands, I needed something to give shape to my life. I needed to feel the burn of smoke to know I was alive. Nothing else made any sense.

Maybe I simply wanted to do something dangerous in the face of her death. Maybe I wanted to damage myself to defy that mysterious being she believed in who had definitely abandoned her this time, the one time it really mattered. All that praying and believing and singing and preaching and Bible reading and following god's path, and now she was dead.

The funeral was held at our church.

As my entire life had, and my mother's life had, the service also included lots of singing, prayers, and Bible readings. In between all of this were a lot of preachy words about how my mother was singing with the angels, blissful and pain-free. There was a strong undertone of—if those who hadn't repented like my mother had didn't turn around fast, cancer might strike them down without warning. Unlike my mother, they would end up in eternal suffering. Act now. It was like a high-pressure salesman—*Buy today to take advantage of this once-in-a-lifetime deal*.

My mother's suffering, on the other hand, was definitely over now. Or so the preacher said. Obviously, he couldn't know this at all. Believing something and having proof of it being true are two different things.

Later that day, my brothers and I escaped to a tiny park near our house. We were eager to avoid cleaning up from the sandwiches and salads that had been served on our dining room table to nearly a hundred people after the service and burial. We were eager to escape my father's grief, and the promises from my mother's friends and others at the church meant to reassure and comfort us. They all sounded like words that had been lifted out of the Bible and other religious books, memorized, and handed off to us like bandaids.

My father's grief was something so far outside of his usual behavior, all of us were a bit shocked, and even I didn't have a lot to say to him. He wandered around the house, touching things and telling random stories that he seemed to think were related to the objects he touched but were not. He appeared to look right through us, as if we were ghosts or as if he were seeing my mother in another dimension. Who knows, maybe he did. He didn't cry, but his eyes were swollen, so there was no doubt he'd done quite a lot of crying when no one else was around.

Eric brought two six-packs of beer to the park, and we settled on the benches that faced a secluded grove of oak trees. He popped open a beer, took a long swallow, and passed the pack to

Tom, who took one and passed it off to Jake and then to me. When we all had open cans, Eric raised his beer. "To Mom. She'd be pissed at what we're doing, but none of us will ever be sure she wouldn't have loved to drink a beer with her kids."

We all raised our cans.

"Except Mom wouldn't say pissed, she'd say she was disappointed," Jake said.

We laughed.

It was such a perfect toast. It summed up everything without griping about our strange and oppressive upbringing. It described our mother perfectly. All of us knew she was on our side most of the time, but she also willingly and cheerfully executed our father's wishes, which of course, came straight from the mouth of god.

For me, it was so awesome to be seeing my brothers again, my mother slipped to the back of my thoughts. We rarely saw each other now that Tom and I were in college, hundreds of miles apart, and the other two had actual jobs and apartments, which was stunning to me. Adults. I could hardly picture it. We exchanged emails and text messages a few times a week. We talked on the phone once in a while. But none of those things make up for seeing the flicker of someone's eyes as they catch your gaze, or the movement of their body as they change position on the hard bench, or the heat and life that emanated from their skin and bones.

It felt as if we were falling back in time. Except for the beer, which had now turned to two, and I had no doubt would soon be three, we could have been little kids. Laughing about stupid stuff, making fun of each other, telling wildly over-dramatized stories about family vacations and our church-going experiences.

My brothers all still went to a church of one kind or another, but they'd each found places that didn't tell them what to think. Eric was a Quaker. Jake was into meditation, which I suppose isn't technically church, but similar. Tom belonged to a group at his college that met weekly, like church, to talk about and plan social justice activities, counting on some vague god-like creature to ensure they were successful at it.

No one asked me about church. They already knew.

Two days later, we all went back to school and work, leaving my father to fend for himself.

Within six months, my father had a girlfriend. He'd met her at church, obviously. She doted on him and annoyed the hell out of me when I finally met her. They got married before my mother had been in the ground for a year.

So I kept smoking. It calmed me. It helped me think. It helped me keep people who bored me at arm's length, and it helped me meet lots of new people—most of them interesting.

CHAPTER 29

Stephanie and I were in a cab on the way home from a client's first photography session. We'd met with the client at her art studio in Park Slope in Brooklyn. Stephanie was smug with what a marvelous job she'd done, getting Mandy Miller to relax, to stop paying attention to the camera, to look natural. I was not looking forward to Stephanie's fit when I told her she had a long way to go.

At this point, we were both taking photographs, which was part of the reason Mandy had been overly self-conscious. I could imagine how it would be, having two rather large camera lenses following you around the room, the click of the shutter, the flash blinking at your peripheral vision. But until Stephanie was up to speed, it had to be that way. Otherwise, we'd have to take up another hour or more of Mandy's time while I re-shot the photos where Stephanie had missed the mark. That would make her even stiffer in front of the camera, repeating the stories she'd already told us.

"We have some great shots here." Stephanie patted her camera bag.

"You didn't take enough close-ups," I said.

"Well, didn't you take any?"

"That's not the point. You're supposed to be photographing our clients as if I'm not there."

"And when you quit following me around, I will."

"Trystan wants it this way."

"Because you whined to him about me." She edged farther away from me, pressing herself against the door of the cab.

I wasn't going to start arguing with her. No matter what I said, she would put the blame on someone else. It was a waste of breath and brain cells to try to argue with her about things that weren't directly related to my impossible task of mentoring her. "You need to follow the list he gave you."

"I did."

"You didn't. And you'll see that when we go through the shots and upload them to the database."

"Well, I thought it went great, and I don't see why you're so negative. Trystan doesn't like negativity. And negativity, in general, is very unattractive. It's not all about how you look on the outside, you know. Character matters."

Again, the argument wasn't worth it. She wore me out. I'd met plenty of neurotic people in my life, but no one like her. Usually, I like arguing with people, I like countering their incorrect statements, I like getting the verbal upper hand. But with Stephanie, she wandered along her own convoluted path of logic, and even when I pointed out where she was wrong, she somehow managed to believe that wasn't the case. She could stare right at reality and insist it wasn't real.

I settled back and closed my eyes for a moment. It was better to wait until we were sitting in front of the computer, reviewing the photos she'd taken. I knew what they would look like, but when they were staring her in the face, and there were no close-ups, it would be more difficult for her to argue...except for that *staring-at-reality-and-saying-it-wasn't-there* thing she had going.

Neither of us spoke.

For the remainder of the trip, the cab driver looked in the rearview mirror every few blocks as if he was worried we'd died back there. I suppose he wasn't used to two women riding in deathly silence. And since we'd started out talking with each other, he'd expected it to continue. Maybe he wanted to hear the outcome of what was clearly turning into an argument.

The elevator ride up to our suite was equally silent.

Stephanie went immediately to her office, and when I passed by her doorway on my way down the hall to give Trystan an update, she was plugging her camera into her computer. I knocked as softly as I could on the closed door in front of me. Trystan called out for me to come in, and I pressed down on the handle as gently as I could, trying to avoid a click that would bring Stephanie running. I stepped into his office. A moment later, as if she'd teleported to my side, Stephanie was beside me. I supposed it was unavoidable, given my knuckles on wood.

Before I could speak, she did. "Our session with Mandy was absolutely fantastic. She was totally relaxed. I asked her about her work and her vision, and she really got talking. She completely ignored the camera."

Proving he was familiar with her distorted view of herself and the world, Trystan said nothing. He looked at me, waiting to hear my assessment. When I didn't speak, he did. "Alex? How did it go from your perspective?"

"My opinion means nothing?" Stephanie turned to me, giving me a hard, angry stare that made me want to laugh. "You're setting me up to fail, aren't you?"

"Don't be ridiculous," Trystan said. "Alex is more experienced. I want her take on it."

"Because you don't believe me!"

His voice rose. "Stephanie. Calm down."

She made a sound, but I couldn't make out whether it was a whimper or something with more anger inside.

"She was clearly uncomfortable with two cameras," I said. "But anyone would be."

"That's because you kept moving in too close," Stephanie said.

"We need close-ups. That's the whole point."

"Yes," Trystan said.

"That's why you have a zoom lens," Stephanie said, her voice childish as she hoped to point out that I was stupid.

"Sometimes, you just need to be closer," I said.

"Well, it made her self-conscious," Stephanie said. "You were pushy if you want my *take* on it. And I think that made her close off quite a lot. Until I started asking her more questions."

This was going downhill fast. I looked at Trystan. I couldn't tell if he wanted to laugh or cry or fire both of us. I decided I was going to have to be the one to de-escalate, as they like to say, even though it wasn't my normal tendency. "You asked some good questions. She had to think about her answers, and it provided some interesting facial reactions."

Stephanie turned toward me. Her mouth was open. I suppose she didn't realize I was capable of saying something complimentary. She didn't get me at all. I will say whatever I have to in order to get what I want, to ultimately turn things in my favor.

I thought she might thank me, but that was too much to ask for.

"To be honest," I said. "I'm not sure it's going to work having Stephanie shadow me." I was tired of all of it. I wanted to go back to chatting with our clients and taking their photographs and having fun with them, trying to get them to say things they might regret later. I did not like having the dead weight of Stephanie on my back.

She could fail or not on her own. If she screwed up and chased away some of our clients, it was her problem. Of course, Trystan didn't want that, but I was tired of being around her, tired of telling her to do things that she felt compelled to argue with, tired of her always talking about how great she was at photography.

She wasn't as good as me. She would never understand that. But Trystan did.

Mostly, I was tired of being expected to teach her things that cannot be taught. Trystan should have realized—you can't teach someone to keep their mouth shut if they're a compulsive talker. You can't teach someone to ask casual questions if they're so wound up with anger and messages from god they don't even know how to have a normal conversation. And you definitely cannot teach someone to make others relax in your presence.

Trystan was glaring at me, angry that I was trying to abandon my mentorship and abandon it in front of Stephanie, where she was sure to leap at the chance. And she did.

"I agree," Stephanie said. "It's too clunky."

"If the two of you weren't having this highly unproductive power struggle, it wouldn't be so clunky," Trystan said. "You should be working out a joint strategy before you meet a client."

"We did," I said. "But Stephanie started the conversation without waiting for my cue."

"I'm not a child. I don't need you to tell me when I can talk," Stephanie said. "And, I *know* how to take photographs. It's not brain surgery."

"It requires finesse," Trystan said.

Stephanie moved toward his desk. She didn't stop until she'd nearly bumped into it. She put her hands on the surface, curling them into fists, her knuckles pressing against the wood. "You treat me like I'm a clueless hick. It's hurtful and unprofessional."

"I never—"

"You said I don't have finesse. And that's only the most recent derogatory thing you've said. There are a lot more."

"I didn't say you don't—"

"Telling me something *requires finesse* when you don't like how I'm doing it says you don't think I have finesse."

Trystan placed his elbows on the desk. He turned his hands upward and rested his forehead on his palms. I wondered if he was regretting allowing Stephanie to be a photographer. He should have been. I wondered why he didn't find a way to get rid of her. I wondered why he allowed her to be so dramatic and angry and, yes, clueless. He'd created a lot of trouble for himself. It was kind of fascinating, waiting to watch him work his way out of it. Like a large dog that's run into a tube and is now trying to back out, only then realizing there's no room to maneuver.

The room was quiet for several very long seconds. Stephanie was still leaning on the desk. Finally, she straightened and folded her arms. "This is unacceptable."

Trystan looked up. He stared at some point between the two of us. "Work it out." He turned his chair deliberately toward his computer and began typing.

Stephanie made a sound as if she planned to argue, but Trystan held up his hand like a traffic cop.

She and I retreated to our offices, closing the doors.

CHAPTER 30

The minute I saw the profile summary for our newest client, I was certain he would offer the worst possible scenario for a photography session run by both Stephanie and me. He was the minister at an average-sized evangelical church who wanted to develop the mindset he needed to see his flock grow to mega-church status.

Stephanie was not going to be able to sit in the background for this one.

I thought about telling Trystan I should handle it myself, but after all the arguing and hurt feelings and drama so far, I knew he would see it as another snide swipe at Stephanie. There was no way to protect myself or the client or even Stephanie herself from the impending disaster. So I decided to throw myself into it wholeheartedly and enjoy the fireworks.

We met Reverend Sherpa in the lobby of his church.

Trystan had introduced us to him two days earlier. It had been a quick shaking of hands. Trystan was so anxious about the dynamic between Stephanie and me that he'd hustled us in, shot off our names, and sent us on our way. It had been awkward, which didn't put us in the best position for this meeting. I wondered if Trystan was losing his equilibrium. There was an obvious solution, but he was blind to it.

I hoped the results of this doomed photography session might open his eyes.

Matt Sherpa was tall, easily six-three. He was slim and in good shape, somewhere in his mid-forties, with dark hair showing a few silver strands at the sides and one streak in the back that I wondered whether he was aware of.

"Hi Alex, Stephanie. I'm really excited about this." He laughed nervously, I thought. "I've never been photographed professionally before, so please forgive me if I'm a little awkward." He laughed again.

"It's my job to make sure you forget you're being photographed," I said.

"Both our jobs," Stephanie said.

I smiled. "Of course."

Matt nodded.

"Why don't we go into the sanctuary, Reverend Sherpa," Stephanie said.

And that's all it took. One slip of the tongue on my part, taking ownership without giving equal credit to Stephanie, and she was off-script. We'd agreed, and Trystan had been adamant that it was my job to take the lead. We would confuse the client if we both tried to give direction. Or rather, I'd thought, that for once in her life, Stephanie had agreed. But of course, the Reverend and the double doors, yawning open before us, the darkened sanctuary beyond, were too much for her.

"It's gratifying to photograph someone who's a child of God like I am," Stephanie said.

Matt nodded. "No need to call me Reverend, by the way. It's too formal." He turned and walked into the room filled with rows of cushioned metal chairs that were hooked together to make neatly arranged rows and aisles. At the front was a raised platform with two leafy green plants in large red pots on either side. There was a podium on the left side and several chairs behind it.

Matt turned on the lights, and the room became so bright I had to squint.

"Can you dim those a bit?" I asked.

"Don't we need the light?"

"Not that much. Unless you want us to snap you in sunglasses, which might be interesting."

"That's a terrible idea," Stephanie said. "Eyes are the windows to the soul. People need to see the fire of God in your eyes."

Matt smiled.

I tried to avoid a smirk. My effort to keep my expression neutral didn't matter because Stephanie was gazing at Matt. It sounded as if she was under the impression we were taking publicity photos. No one but the people on Trystan's team would ever see these, and none of us cared whether the fire of god was in his eyes. If he did have supernatural fire in his eyes, maybe the sunglasses would be useful to protect us all.

I suggested he sit on the steps leading to the platform. "What do you love about being a preacher? Is it intoxicating to have all those eyes staring at you every Sunday, waiting to hear what you'll say?"

He didn't blush, but the shock registered on his face. I could tell he thought I'd looked into his soul. It wasn't that hard.

Stephanie's faced turned red on his behalf. "Alexandra! Being a preacher is a calling from God. Preachers don't—"

"Alexandra is right," Matt said. "There is an ego-fed addiction to that attention. I have to fight it every single time. Very perceptive of you." He laughed, and I snapped several photographs, the lens focused tightly on his face so that even his hair was cut out of the frame.

"Why are you taking pictures?" Stephanie asked. "He's not ready."

I knew she lacked a real understanding of how the process

worked, but the most obvious, basic part of our job was to take candid shots. The last thing we wanted was the client feeling *ready*, which led to the instinct to begin posing. And now, she'd managed to make him aware of not only the camera but the dynamic between photographer and subject.

I said nothing, hoping she would shut up. But of course, hoping was hopeless.

"I've always had a huge amount of respect for ministers," Stephanie said. "It must feel so good to know you're doing the most important work there is. And it must feel so good to know you're helping people. I can't tell you how many times I've felt the minister at my church was speaking directly to me during a sermon. It's such a blessing to know that God gives him the right words, so I'm nourished and lifted up. So that everyone—"

"Stephanie," I hoped that gently speaking her name would wake her up. I immediately wondered why I'd hoped anything. Stephanie was going to do whatever popped into her head. In many ways, in that way especially, she and I were a lot alike. It's just that the things that popped into my head weren't about baring my soul when no one asked about it or even when they did. My impulsive words weren't aimed at focusing the spotlight on myself during a client meeting. "Why don't you go to the back and take some long shots while Matt and I chat?"

She glared at me. "What about the closeups?"

Matt glanced at her, then me. "What am I supposed to be doing? Should I—"

"Hey. Steph, let's step out to the lobby for a second and sort things out," I said.

"I'm sorry," Matt said. "Am I doing something wrong?" His nervous laugh erupted again. "I really don't know what I'm supposed to be doing. Sorry."

"Nothing at all," I said. "Just relax, and we'll be right back."

"There's nothing to sort out." Stephanie moved toward the steps where Matt was still seated. She placed herself in the chair closest to the center aisle in the front row. "How did you know God wanted you to be a preacher?"

It was actually a good question, but her face was right in his, and the camera was on her lap. A series of expressions flashed across his face. I raised my camera and caught the very end of them. Stephanie was not going to step out for a chat, and even if she'd agreed to that, she wouldn't have agreed with anything I suggested. It had all been said before.

"I was in my last year of college," Matt said. "I was studying to be a software engineer, which is supposed to be the career of the future, right?"

I snapped a few photos. Stephanie's camera remained in her lap.

"I felt a lot of anxiety, like something inside me was just... wrong. So I took a semester off and went to the Rockies to do some hiking and camping. Except I didn't plan very well and—"

"I've never been there," Stephanie said. "I hear it's breathtaking."

He nodded.

Stephanie raised her camera. "Look toward the pulpit," she said.

Matt obligingly turned his head, gazing up at the wooden podium with a cross carved into the front.

Stephanie snapped several photos. I wondered if we were going to have to do a second session. I wondered if Trystan would realize, when he saw her photos, that I would have to do it alone. So far, we weren't even close to getting what we needed.

"What's your first thought when you step up to the lectern each week?" I asked.

"He was telling us about his calling," Stephanie said. Her voice was too loud, echoing through the large empty space, rising to the rafters and booming back down at us.

While Matt stared at her, I snapped a few more pictures, but I was pretty sure his microexpressions were about his uncertainty around Stephanie, not the experiences he had when he was preaching that might be holding him back from delivering the kinds of messages that would bring an overflow crowd.

I found it mildly entertaining that he thought Trystan and the work we did would get him his megachurch, rather than thinking that was the job of his supernatural benefactor. I really did want to talk to him. For all my religious experiences, I'd never talked one-on-one with a preacher. When I was living with my parents, our preacher came to dinner quite often, but my father and the preacher did all the talking. The kids did all the listening.

There were a lot of questions I wanted to ask this guy, and many of them were just as self-serving as Stephanie's.

Matt turned toward us, he shifted his legs and rested his elbows on his knees. "I was camping. Alone. One night, I was in my tent, and I heard several bears prowling around my campsite. I knew that if I went out and confronted them, I might be their midnight snack. But I felt like a trapped bird with nothing but a sheet of nylon between me and them. And stupidly, I'd brought some beef jerky into the tent with me for a midnight snack of my own. I was stuffing it into my mouth before they smelled it, trying to chew..." he laughed. "It's not a very spiritual story, is it? Anyway...my mouth was full of stiff jerky, and I was trying to chew and listen for where the bears were, and suddenly I had this flash that the only thing that matters in this life is your spiritual journey. And I wanted to be a part of showing that to as many people as I could."

"You mean God wanted you to be part of that," Stephanie said.

"No. I said *I* did. I told you it wasn't very spiritual. And we're fooling no one if we pretend our motives are pure when there's human desire mixed into it. God isn't fooled. And, we end up misleading the people who trust us if we aren't honest with ourselves."

Stephanie glared at him.

I don't know why I did what I did next. I suppose it was that *being-like-Stephanie* thing, a bit of wanting the spotlight on myself because maybe I'd lied about that just a little. Maybe I wanted the photography session to end because it wasn't working anyway, and *maybe*, I wanted to sabotage Stephanie's career as a photographer. Probably all of those things.

I placed my camera on the chair behind where I was standing. I walked toward Matt, stopping a few feet away. I lifted my hair off my shoulders and let it fall back into place, sliding through my fingers. I arched my back for a moment, then straightened and lowed my head so that I was gazing up through my lashes. As he stared at me, I took a few more steps and sat beside him. I put my arm around his shoulders, my hand higher up so my fingers rested on the bare skin of his neck. I put my other hand on his leg and slid it up until I felt his muscle tense. I looked at him, holding my gaze steady. After a moment, he turned and looked at me.

Noises that sounded like someone being strangled were coming from Stephanie, but I didn't let them divert my attention.

When Matt had turned toward me, looking confused and a little upset, I smiled at him and said, "Take our picture, Stephanie."

"Alexandra!" Her voice was loud, angry, and shocked. I heard the suggestion of tears.

I still didn't look at her. I moved my face closer to Matt's, staring deep into his eyes, searching for the fire of heaven that Stephanie claimed was there. Although now that I thought about it, now that Stephanie was babbling in the background, hissing at me to get away from him, insisting she was not going to take our picture and that I was being horribly inappropriate, it struck me that usually, when people talked about fire, it came from a place that was decidedly not heaven.

"Stephanie. This is the purpose of what we do. You have a chance to catch Matt in an unguarded moment, in a situation that's likely to happen to the preacher of a megachurch. There are all kinds of wily, conniving, seductive women and men out there. Take our picture. Now."

176

It shocked me when I heard the click of the shutter. Then again, and again.

I imagined she was thinking that she could use this as evidence to show Trystan what an awful person I was, but I knew the words I'd spoken would ring true when I repeated them to Trystan. And I knew that I'd cut Stephanie off at the knees.

CHAPTER 31

*S*tephanie and I did not share a cab back to the office, even though Trystan asked us to use cabs rather than the subway when we met with clients. He wanted us to be comfortable, to be in a calm and enthusiastic state instead of drained from battling crowds. He wanted us to avoid carrying expensive cameras onto the subway. He also thought a cab gave a better impression to clients if they happened to observe our arrival. I'm not sure which was more important to him, but it didn't matter, I liked taking cabs. I liked chatting with the drivers, and I liked the relative comfort. I liked the efficiency of getting from point A to point B rather than the zig-zag feel of using the subway system.

Stephanie had marched out of the church after photographing Matt leaning into me. She hadn't even bothered to put her camera back into the case. When I'd hailed the cab, she turned and started walking toward the corner.

I called after her, telling her the cab was waiting.

She didn't respond, and a moment later, she rounded the corner. I assumed she was taking the subway. She defied the other guidelines, why not that one? I climbed into the backseat. As he pulled away from the curb, I asked the driver how his day was going. He told me his day was better than usual. I said mine was also going quite well.

When I returned, Stephanie's office was dark. Trystan heard me come in and stepped out into the hallway. "Where's Stephanie?"

"She took the subway, I think."

"You think?"

I shrugged.

He moved toward me. "What happened?"

I glanced at Diana's closed office door. "Should we go out for lunch? It's a long story, and—"

"If you want to debrief, it would be better if I met with you and Stephanie together."

"I don't think those joint meetings are very productive, do you?"

He glared at me. He glanced at his watch and closed his eyes for several moments.

I imagined his thoughts—worrying about the intensity of Stephanie's anger, trying to picture what awful thing had happened, worrying about his client and the reputation of his firm.

He opened his eyes. "Tell me what happened."

"Stephanie is very angry with me because she thought I behaved inappropriately. With Matt."

He frowned and shoved his hands into his pockets. He looked down at his feet. "What did you do?"

"I sat close to him and put my arm around him. I told Stephanie to take our picture."

"That's—"

"Why don't we go have lunch and talk about it?" I said. "I know it sounds possibly inappropriate—inserting myself into a client's world like that, but I can explain over lunch. And I don't think a shouting match will give you a clear picture."

He looked up. "I've never heard you shout."

I smiled, and I saw the point click home in his eyes.

"Let me get my jacket," he said.

When we were settled in a booth at a nice steak house, I ordered a martini. "Do you want one?"

He looked slightly tipsy already, undoubtedly from the tsunami of thoughts crashing through his mind.

"Sure, why not," he said.

When our drinks were in front of us and our lunch order was placed, I sipped the sharp, icy-cold liquid in my glass. I put down the glass and turned toward him. "I know what I did sounds shocking. But first, you need to know the session wasn't going well." I told him about the things Stephanie had said and about her refusal to take candid shots. "I was pretty sure we would have to do a re-shoot."

"That's not good."

I told him what I'd said to Matt about the challenges of managing a church with thousands of members.

Trystan nodded, and I could see he was starting to have a slender thread of respect for how I'd taken charge of a bad situation.

"In his profile, Matt said that he worried his church hadn't grown because he didn't have enough passion. I started thinking about how a lot of preachers from big churches are pretty ambitious, alpha-male types."

Trystan laughed. I wasn't exactly sure why, but I didn't ask. I didn't want to get de-railed.

"A lot of them fall prey to sexual harassment scandals. More than you see in other fields. They aren't very different from CEOs. And so it occurred to me that Matt's comment about passion came from his subconscious recognition of something that was holding him back—that he doesn't have that selfish drive, and that could mean he's afraid of his integrity getting challenged. One of the first things he admitted was that he's human, and he likes the ego-stroking of preaching and having everyone hang on his words. So I wanted to make him uncomfortable. If Stephanie managed to get the shots, I think they will show quite a lot in a much smaller number of photos than we usually have."

Trystan stared at me. He picked up his drink as if he wanted to take a sip, then put it back down.

Our meals arrived. We began eating, and he still hadn't spoken.

Finally, he placed his knife across the edge of his plate. "You know Alex, you really are an asset to my company. You have a gut instinct for this work."

"And Stephanie will never have that," I said.

He took several sips of his drink. He didn't agree or argue, but I knew he knew this.

We ate and talked about Matt and the things that had emerged in his profile. When my steak was half-gone, I ordered two more martinis without asking Trystan whether he wanted one. "The two-martini lunch, right?"

He smirked and swallowed the rest of his drink.

When we were nicely uninhibited from our drinks, I turned the conversation back to Stephanie. "I really do not think this is going to work. I know you believe I just don't like her and that I'm not giving her a chance, but you're wrong. She's too weird. There's no other word for it."

He sighed. He pushed his plate away and took a sip of his drink. It was clear he was never going to tell me why he was so insistent on letting her do something that was destined to hurt his business. It was clear he felt trapped and frustrated. And I realized his mood suggested he'd been feeling those things for a while. As a result, he'd tried to make me do his dirty work for him. Maybe he even thought Stephanie would quit if she were forced to be around me.

"I really need you to—"

"Come on, Trystan. What are you doing?" I swallowed the last of my drink. I ate the last olive. Part of me wanted to order a third drink. I ordered a cappuccino instead.

The server picked up our plates and turned away.

"It almost seems like you're sabotaging your business. I don't get it. I don't get why you're so afraid of upsetting her. Maybe you need some high-end coaching." I laughed, but when I looked at his face, it seemed as if he agreed with me. Maybe not, maybe I imagined it.

CHAPTER 32

*N*o matter what I'd thought was going through his mind during my lunch with Trystan, he caved again. Like a box of crackers left out in the rain. We returned to the office, and Stephanie was sitting in the waiting area of our suite. She stood when we walked in, her eyes on fire so that it was impossible to look away from her. She really looked quite beautiful with her expertly applied makeup and her new hair. It was almost frightening sometimes when I compared her new look to the being living inside.

"I see how it is. You lured him out of here so you could tell him your side. Why am I not surprised? You're trying to make sure I look like I'm failing, and I'm not going to put up with it. I'm not the kind of person who lets someone stab her in the back and spread slander." She turned toward Trystan. "You won't believe—"

Trystan stepped toward her, holding up his hand, which was probably like waving a red flag in front of a bull. "Calm down."

"You've been drinking!"

"I—"

She cut him off. "You reek. I hope you aren't letting her influence destroy who you really are."

"Stephanie. Relax," I said. "I told him what I told Matt. Maybe it was shocking to you but—"

"Just stop," Trystan said. "I want the two of you to go out for a cup of coffee right now. I want you to work this out between you once and for all. I want both of you on my staff as photographers. I will not be a nice person if this petty fighting and refusal to get along affects a single client, not to mention this entire enterprise."

So. He did have a backbone. It just wasn't shaped to my liking. I gave Stephanie a charming smile. "Where would you like to go?"

She glared at me. She turned to Trystan, "It's not—"

"I'm not discussing this again." He turned and walked down the hallway. When he got to his office, he slammed the door closed.

I wanted to laugh. He sounded like a pissed-off teenager. I looked at Stephanie. I had no idea how I was going to make this work. The first thing that flashed through my head was my fancy new apartment because I was thinking I might need to look for another job, and that would probably mean delaying my moving plans. But before that, I would do all I could to make sure Stephanie was the one looking for a job.

When she and I were settled at a coffee shop, drinks ordered, I looked at her, staring and waiting. She held my gaze without flinching. I had to admire that she never looked away when someone put their full attention on her when she was challenged or criticized.

"So, how are we going to make Trystan happy?" I asked.

She glared at me. Our drinks came, and she ordered a large chocolate chip cookie to go with her coffee.

"Any ideas?" I said.

"Nope." She took a sip of her coffee, recoiling as it burned her lips.

"Why won't you let me tell you some of the things I've learned about photography, about working with our clients?" As the words flowed off my tongue, it occurred to me that, for once, I was actually curious about how she would respond. I thought I knew her answers to those questions, but maybe I was wrong.

"Because you're a know-it-all. Because taking photographs isn't rocket science, and I do a great job. And because you think you're in charge when the whole idea for having a staff photographer was mine to begin with."

I let her words hang in the air, considering my next move as if I were a chess player. Responding to anything she'd said would put us back on the same circular racetrack. I took a sip of my cappuccino which was probably not going to help things as I was already feeling the earlier coffee drink pumping through my blood, sharpening my tongue.

Her cookie arrived, and I waited until she took a bite and started chewing before I spoke.

"I realize you probably won't listen to this, but I know some things about photography. Trystan is aware of that, which is why he made me mentor you."

She scrunched her face up when I said he *made* me, but it was time to change the dynamic, and arguing with her nonsense would never do that. She needed a verbal slap in the face. "What I know is that being a photographer is like being a voyeur."

She made another face. "That's disgusting. And sick."

"That's why Trystan loves my photographs."

"Because he's a voyeur? He is *not,* and he's going to be disgusted by you when I tell him you said that."

"I didn't say he's a voyeur. I'm telling you that's how you get the kind of photos that he and Diana find useful. You let the camera look for things the clients expose without realizing it, like someone watching through a window for their neighbor to take off her clothes."

"I'm not going to listen to this." She began wrapping her cookie in napkins, ready to place it in her purse, which I thought was far more disgusting than anything I'd said.

"I'm trying to help you. Trystan will love your photos if you approach it that way." Following my advice would have helped her, but of course, the very use of that word—voyeur—set her in the opposite direction. And I'd known that's what would happen.

She laughed. "Well, that's your first mistake. He loves my photographs al-*ready*." She pushed her coffee cup to the center of the table. "What do I owe you?"

"He told us to work this out. We have to work it out."

"I'm not going to think about sex when I'm doing my job. And the fact that you do sure explains a lot."

"What are you planning to tell Trystan?"

"That he needs to fire you. We can't work things out because I'm a child of God, and you're wicked." Forgetting that she'd asked what she owed for her coffee and cookie, she yanked her coat off the back of her chair, picked up her purse, and walked out the door without turning to look at me.

I sat back and finished my coffee. I wondered what Trystan would do. As I thought about the idea of being a voyeur and what he'd said to me over lunch, I knew he would be very upset if I found another job. At the same time, he was beholden to Stephanie. I realized now he felt this obligation because the photography had been her idea, and she believed that meant she should have the position.

He had a difficult choice to make. Because of that, I figured we still had a few more rounds before he finally built up his courage. He was still going to try to change the relationship between me and Stephanie, and I knew without a doubt, the directive for changing would fall on me.

CHAPTER 33

Since Alexandra had already gotten a head start in telling Trystan her side of the story, Stephanie decided it was better to take the opposite approach—she would wait. She needed to think about the disgusting things Alex had said to her. Then, she needed to figure out how to tell Trystan in a way that he wouldn't think she was being catty.

It was annoying that he viewed their mutual loathing as something petty. His dismissiveness was demeaning. This was important—it was about character and doing what was right, about following the path of righteousness. She knew ethics were important to him, and she couldn't understand why he didn't see how ethics were involved in this situation with Alexandra. Pointing out amoral or downright evil behavior was important. She'd thought he would understand that, but he had such a blindspot with Alexandra. For Stephanie, it was like trying to scratch her way through a brick wall with her fingernails.

She thought she might play on his guilt. It horrified her to have such manipulative thoughts, but this was war. It was a battle for her career and her self-respect and proper behavior in the workplace. Trystan should care about that if nothing else. This was his business, and he should want it to be the epitome of integrity.

She settled herself into the pillows propped against her headboard. She took a sip of wine from the glass on the nightstand. It made her feel guilty when she drank wine before bed, but she wondered if sometimes her church was too strict about drinking wine. It wasn't the same as hard liquor. The Bible talked about wine. Jesus had turned water into wine so people could enjoy it.

Right now, her life was incredibly stressful. She needed something to calm her enough so she could sleep. They said wine was good for your heart, so there was that. She took another sip.

Scrolling through the search results on her phone, she saw that once again, she'd had no luck. As she'd done many times over the past few months, she'd entered Alexandra's name into Google. There were never any results. It annoyed her. How could someone supposedly so hip not have any social media or have ever been in a group or club that dribbled her face and a few bits of information into the bottomless well of the internet?

She plugged in her phone, picked up her glass, and continued sipping until the glass was empty.

The next morning, she dressed in the most daring outfit she'd allowed Eileen to choose for her—skin-tight black leggings and a crisp white shirt with tails that hung to the middle of her thighs. She had a pair of black faux riding boots to finish off the look. If she wasn't being too delusional, and she didn't think she was, she looked just as good as Alex, who often wore wild, unconventional outfits.

At the time, she'd argued with Eileen's selection. But Eileen insisted, and the top and leggings had hung in the closet ever since, pricking her with guilt that money had been spent on them and she wasn't wearing them.

She was waiting outside Trystan's locked door when he arrived a few minutes before eight. She didn't care if Diana had seen her lurking there and given her a pitying look. She would not allow him to open a single email or return a phone call before he talked to her. If he hadn't locked his door, she would have been waiting in a chair across from his desk.

"Good morning, Stephanie." He gave her a puzzled look and unlocked the door.

She gave him a clipped *hi* and nothing more.

Without asking whether he had time for her, she followed him into the office, closing the door behind her. She pulled the chair from the corner of the room and settled herself across from him.

"Please don't start complaining about Alex," he said.

"Go into the photo repository. I uploaded the pictures I took of Reverend Sherpa." She didn't tell him that she'd moved Alex's photos to another folder so Trystan would only see the ones Stephanie had taken.

"We can look at them during our meeting at—"

"I want you to look now," she said. "You owe me that."

He sighed. His expression softened, slightly.

It struck her again what a good-looking man he was, and at heart, a kind person. A good person. He was supportive and interesting to talk to—all the things you wanted in a boss. Until Alex came on board.

She gave him a gentle smile. "I don't mean to sound so terse. I'm excited, actually. I respect you so much, Trystan. And I'm really looking forward to your reaction. I think you'll be stunned by how good they are."

He moved the mouse and began clicking.

"Should I come around the desk so we can look at them together?"

"That's not necessary," he said. "I can turn the screen."

Wishing she'd done so before suggesting it, she stood and walked around his desk anyway. She stopped about a foot behind him, then moved to wedge herself in the space between the arm of his chair and his desk. Her pictures came onto the screen, and as he clicked each one, she talked about what she'd captured in Reverend Sherpa's face.

Trystan nodded. "These are good," he said after several minutes. Although by the time he spoke, she wondered if the words were genuine.

"The next ones are a bit shocking," she said. "I don't know what Alexandra told you, but I was so upset...and embarrassed, mostly for Reverend Sherpa."

Trystan clicked on the photos of Alex hanging all over Matt. They were even worse than she'd remembered. Alex was gazing into his eyes as if she wanted to eat him. She was so close, there was no space between their bodies. Matt looked more delighted and excited than he did embarrassed. It made her want to cry, that Alex had done such a shameful thing to him. She wondered if Trystan saw the thrill in Matt's expression.

Trystan closed the file. He wheeled his chair away from her. "You can have a seat."

Hating to tear herself away from him, from that feeling of being close that had warmed her more than she'd ever experienced, she trudged back to her chair.

"Alex told me what her intention was," Trystan said.

"Trying to upset him!"

"To elicit some telling expressions."

"I didn't know we were supposed to throw our bodies at our clients to get a reaction. I thought it was all about talking?"

"Yes, but I think sometimes it's okay to step outside the lines... once you have more experience."

She scowled, but she wasn't going to get drawn into that. She wanted him to think well of her, and he was obviously tired of the complaining. She needed to be factual. "Well, I was concerned because Matt, I mean, Reverend Sherpa, looked very upset. And I don't think flinging yourself at a man is...did she tell you what she did before she sat down? I bet not. She did this little wiggly thing and was flipping her hair around like she was dancing for him."

Trystan laughed.

"It's not funny. You should be concerned. Do you know what she said to me when you sent us off to work things out? She said we're *voyeurs*! That you're a voyeur, and the photographs need to be taken like that's what we're doing."

"That's a good way of—"

"It's perverted. It's wrong. What kind of business do you want to have? I thought you wanted to be professional and respected. Elite."

"We also want to be provocative."

"Well, not like that."

"I'm sorry you're upset. You don't have to take her suggestion. That's how she works. You can find your own approach. Once you've learned more about getting the right shots and how to get clients talking naturally—"

"I don't want to hear any more about that. Not about her skills or how she's a better conversationalist or anything. After what I saw, I know who the most talented photographer is here. I don't need to pretend I'm watching people have *sex* to do a good job."

Trystan smiled, but he looked tired. "We all have our own value systems. Part of living in this world is accepting that. Of course, you don't want others to poison your own behavior, but you have to be tolerant, even when it's upsetting. Tolerance is a virtue."

As he spoke, she had to stifle a gasp.

At first, she'd wanted to fire back at him that ethics weren't something that shifted with the wind, but then it struck her what he was really saying! It was a revelation, but she shouldn't have been surprised. It was clear now that Trystan tolerated Alex even though she went against his own moral code. That's what he was really saying.

In the past, she'd wondered from time to time what his religious beliefs were. Now she realized that this was why he treated everyone with such respect and kindness. He was a child of God just as she was. He was quiet about it, but men often were. He must have realized that hiring Alex had been a mistake. The reason he wanted Stephanie to work with Alex and improve as a photographer was because once she had the skills he demanded, he would fire Alex.

Why had she never seen that until this moment?

The thrill of her new understanding made her heart pound so hard against her bones, she wondered if he heard the thudding, wondered if he could actually see it thumping beneath her crisp, white shirt. She'd completely misjudged him. She hadn't given him a chance to execute his plan. Of course he wanted them to work together. It was meant to ensure a smooth transition. It would be a terrible risk to fire Alex before Stephanie had hit her stride. She smiled.

He seemed to be studying her but didn't return the smile. After a moment, he spoke again. "Thank you for not reacting to that. I really need you to work with her."

"Of course. I'm so sorry I let her get under my skin. I really want to be an outstanding photographer. I want to come up to speed so that I can handle the full workload of clients you need from me."

"Good. You did a good job with these pictures. Of course, there's room for improvement, but you're still learning. Did you sign up for the portrait class yet?"

She shook her head. "No, but I will. Right away."

"Good. Anything else?"

She stood. "No. I just want to tell you how much I respect your judgement. And I want to exceed your expectations. It's really important to me."

"Good. The more experience you get under your belt, the more you'll get an instinctive feel for it."

"I know you're right." She dragged the chair back to the corner of the room, then turned to face him. "I hope you know how much I love working here. I feel invested...since I was with you from the very beginning."

He nodded. His face was suddenly pale. She must have touched a nerve.

When she was back in her office, she closed the door and went to the window. The sky was a soft blue, suggesting spring was ready to unfold across the city. How perfectly timed, since tomorrow was the first day of spring. She felt like the entire world had changed.

And she felt an overwhelming desire to make Trystan happy, to get to know him better instead of fighting with him all the time. He was such a wonderful man—a godly man! She was sure of that now. Maybe she also had a touch of spring fever.

CHAPTER 34

 ortland, Oregon

* * *

LUCKILY FOR BRADY AND ME, his sister continued to attend her gymnastics class on Thursdays after school. If I believed what my parents' church taught, I would have interpreted that as a sign that a superior being wanted us to have sex in a nice, comfortable bed, undisturbed.

But then his mom got the flu, and a friend's mother drove Anna to her class, and Brady and I were trapped, drooling over each other's bodies from a distance and thinking about nothing all through the school day, missing most of what our teachers were saying. Even running two miles around the track during P.E. didn't get it out of my system.

I didn't want to wait a whole week, which was really two weeks. I had become totally addicted to this thing I was not supposed to be doing, this thing that everyone said was so powerful. They were right about that. A week felt like a year.

I considered carefully whether my mother's schedule would allow us to hide out in my bedroom.

The problem was, my mother was unpredictable. She did a lot of volunteer work at church, but that wasn't like a job with set hours. I never knew when she would pop home to get supplies for the group that knitted baby hats and blankets or realize she'd forgotten some of the items she'd purchased for the church's food pantry.

If she came home and saw Brady's car, I might end up locked in the house for the rest of high school, literally. Even if Brady parked a few blocks away and walked to the house, I couldn't count on her not coming upstairs to my room to ask why I was at home when I was supposed to be at the after-school study group.

She would know. She had a sense for things as if there was still some invisible cord binding me to her. When I was in the house, she would just *know*. It sounded ridiculous and slightly paranoid, but it had happened enough times for me to believe she had this weird, invisible awareness of me.

I thought about the goofy things you see in movies where lovers hide in closets and under beds to avoid discovery. I could try sneaking Brady down the hall to one of my brothers' unoccupied bedrooms, but that still had some risk.

I didn't want to wait a week. Two weeks.

Then, once again, as if someone were watching out for us, my mother informed my father and me during dinner that she had to have some medical tests. The next day at school, I told Brady we were on. She couldn't show up and surprise us this time. We would park three blocks away to be sure no overly curious neighbors felt the need to tell my parents about an unfamiliar Honda sitting on our street.

It felt strange walking into my house with Brady. Everything looked different, as I imagined seeing each piece of furniture, framed photograph, and painting through his eyes. Not wanting to explain all the photographs of missionaries that occupied the walls in our hallway, I hurried him up the stairs and into my room. We wasted quite a bit of time while he checked out all my things.

He sat at my desk and admired the tree outside my window. I told him about the time I'd snuck out of the house by climbing onto a branch that grew too close. I told him how the tree received careful pruning every year after that. Then, I regretted telling him because I was wasting time. He continued poking through my belongings.

Finally, his curiosity was satisfied, and we were lying naked in my bed. That too felt strange, but soon, the thought passed out of my mind, and I lost myself in the smell and touch and taste of that awesome boy.

Everything worked perfectly. By four-thirty, we were dressed and out of the house, driving back to school for my carpool pickup. I knew my mother wasn't due home until after five because she'd asked me to get dinner started.

I felt quite victorious and satisfied. Going to sleep that night was a thrill, closing my eyes and remembering Brady in my bed. Since I was responsible for washing my own clothes, along with my sheets and bath towels, I wasn't worried about my mother picking up an unexpected and telling odor. As soon as I'd come home for the second time that day, I'd opened my bedroom window. I washed my sheets. I made a cup of cinnamon tea and left it sitting in the room with its semi-sweet aroma. Everything was under control.

Then, I found out Brady wasn't as careful as I was.

Two nights later, my mother came into my room while I was studying for my history exam.

"I need to talk to you."

"I'm kind of in the middle of—"

"Now."

I placed my highlighter pen in the spine and closed the book. I turned to face her.

"Please come sit beside me." She settled herself on the edge of my bed and waited.

I hated these bed-sitting confabs. I didn't like being so close, I didn't like the way she always wanted to touch my leg or hold my hand. She was invading my space even more than she had by walking into the room. It wasn't that I didn't care for her. I just didn't want her concern dripping all over me. I didn't want to constantly have to explain myself.

"What is this?" She opened her hand. Lying in the center of her palm, slightly curled from having her fist wrapped around it, was a square dark green package with the obvious rubber ring of a condom pressing against the foil from the inside.

Of course, she knew what it was. It said quite clearly in bold white print.

"A condom."

"Yes, I know." She paused for dramatic effect. "Why was it under your bed?"

"Why were you crawling around under my bed?"

"Answer the question." Her voice trembled, and I knew this was going to be a long *talk*. I worried I wouldn't get to study for my history exam at all. I glanced toward my desk. "Pay attention," she said. "This is more important than school. Are you having sex?" Her voice broke. "Are you planning to?"

"I—"

She dropped the condom onto the floor and wrapped her arms around me. A moment later, my shirt was wet with her silent tears. I leaned into her slightly and tried to think about the best way to shorten this conversation. "I'm sixteen. Most—"

"You're a child! If this was your choice, I've failed you in every way possible."

"I'm definitely not a child. I might not be an adult, but I'm not a little kid. It's normal to—"

She pulled away. "So you are? You have?"

I was annoyed that I hadn't anticipated she might eventually find out and taken time to plan what I wanted to say. I decided not to pull my punches. The punishment would be the same. "Yes."

"Oh, my baby. My sweet little girl. Haven't you listened to a word anyone has said? Your body belongs to your future husband, and before that, to God. Why would you toss it away like a piece of trash?!"

"I don't think I—"

"You can never get it back! Not ever!" She was sobbing now. "Why didn't you talk to me?"

"About what?"

She stared at me as if I were the most thick-headed person she'd ever seen. "About your feelings. I ask you all the time how you're feeling. I've tried to keep the doors of communication open. I've tried to let you know you could share anything with me. That I'm here to listen."

"But you would have said don't do it."

"Even if you don't care that you've spit in the face of God, there are reasons not to have sex before you're married. Your emotions aren't developed. You don't fully grasp that it means so much more to you than to whatever boy has talked you into this. You've given the most precious thing you have to a boy who..." She began crying again.

I was pretty sure she was wrong. I didn't think it meant more to me than it did to Brady. This was the weird thing about my parents, especially my mother. After all this time, she didn't seem to understand that I was very different from other people. She also didn't seem to grasp that I couldn't care less what some invisible, dictatorial, murderous being thought about my sex life. If this being even had a mind to think with, because that would assume it existed, and I wasn't sure about that because he hadn't bothered to offer any evidence of that.

"I'm so deeply disappointed, honey. This breaks my heart. I'm worried for you."

"I'll be fine."

We went on like this for another two hours. *Two hours.* I ended up staying awake until midnight to study for my test. She wanted to know who the boy was. I told her I couldn't say. I did not need her, or much, much worse, my father, calling Brady's parents and yelling at them because their son had spoiled the purity of their daughter.

I hated seeing my mother so upset. She cried almost non-stop during those two hours. Not heaving sobs, but water trickling and sometimes gushing out of her eyes. The things we said went in circles because she couldn't grasp what I thought about the situation. I wasn't interested in god or purity or some ghostly future husband.

Mostly, I was trying to figure out how Brady and I would get together after this because I was pretty sure the chains around me would tighten.

I also wondered if she planned to tell my father.

CHAPTER 35

 ew York

* * *

STEPHANIE'S OFFICE door had been closed all morning. I'd heard her come out of Trystan's office right after I arrived but hadn't heard a single human voice, including hers, for the past two hours. It was disturbing because usually, there were threads of conversation drifting about as my co-workers ran into each other in the break room or passed in the lobby area. Even with only four of us, it was amazing how often we bumped into each other as our bodies pursued their needs for coffee and snacks, water, and a few moments of escape from sitting. It was a small space, you really couldn't go anywhere without being observed by at least one of the others.

My door was open because it often was, and, with the situation between us, I didn't want Stephanie to do anything outside of my awareness.

It was just after eleven when I heard her door open, followed a moment later by the sounds of her lifting the coffee carafe off the burner, then putting it back. By that time of day, the remaining coffee was undrinkable. Apparently, she didn't want it badly enough to brew more.

I decided to stir the pot, but I almost lost my will when I saw her. For half a second, I thought it was Eileen standing there. Until that moment, I hadn't noticed how much they resembled each other. Stephanie looked thin and very unlike herself, wearing a tailored white men's-style shirt, leggings, and riding boots.

"Nice outfit," I said.

She smiled. There didn't appear to be even a hint of irritation in it. Something had changed.

"I'll make fresh coffee if you want a cup," I said.

"I changed my mind. Water is better." She opened the fridge and pulled out a bottle of sparkling orange-flavored water.

These words also did not carry any of her usual aggrieved tone, egging me to pick a fight with her.

"I looked at the photos of Matt," I said. "We'll probably need to take some more."

"*Reverend* Sherpa. And Trystan liked the ones I showed him."

"Did you talk to Diana about it? She's really the one who decides if there's enough range."

"Trystan said—"

"Let's ask Diana."

She shrugged and twisted the cap off her bottle. She took a long, gulping swallow.

"You seem like you're in a good mood," I said.

"I'm always in a good mood."

I laughed softly, it slid out of me too fast to stop it, but even that didn't bother her. It was quite strange. What had happened between her and Trystan? Obviously, she'd talked to him, and obviously, he'd calmed her down in some way.

"If we do need to go back and photograph Matt a second time, it might not be a bad thing," I said. "You can practice the voyeur approach I told you about."

"I'm not doing that."

"Your call. I think it would help."

"Trystan doesn't agree."

I wondered how she'd described my suggestion to him. I was pretty sure she'd either mischaracterized it or left it out altogether. I wondered whose version of the photography session he believed. He'd acted as if he'd accepted everything I'd said as straightforward and utterly truthful, which it was. Had he given Stephanie the same impression? Maybe he was playing us. Maybe he *liked* the competition, the drama.

Stephanie took another sip of water. Rather than glaring at me with undisguised hatred, which was her usual expression, she looked smug. She screwed the cap onto her bottle and took a step closer. She gave me a slow, lazy smile. I knew, like everything with her, it wasn't real. Maybe she was exactly like me, her nature had simply taken a different path.

"Trystan doesn't agree with your approach, and neither do I." She grinned.

"He said that?"

"It's disgusting. Honestly, it doesn't matter to me what he said about your perverted ideas. It matters that I have talent as a photographer, and I don't need to pretend people are having sex to take excellent photographs."

I laughed. I didn't plan to, and I knew it was gasoline on fire, but I couldn't help it.

"You think that's funny?"

"I think it's funny that you honestly believe you have talent."

"I do."

"Is that what Trystan told you?"

She took a step back. Whatever calm she'd manufactured at the beginning of our conversation was gone. "He didn't have to."

I laughed again. "You'll never be as good as me. Not with a camera, and not with people, because you're trying to force yourself into some archaic set of rules written by a bunch of men.

Rules that were shoved into a book that pretends to come from the mouth of an invisible creature—also a man. It's kind of sad. Maybe it's time to take a step back and think about who's really in charge of your life."

"I'm not sad. And God will have a few things to say about you when all of this is over."

I laughed again, and this time, it was too much for her.

"Stop laughing at me!" Her voice was loud, almost screeching.

"Please don't shout."

"Stop laughing at me. It's rude and unprofessional. You better watch out, or you're going to be in a lot of trouble. You think you're so smart...so..."

I turned and saw Trystan and Diana standing in the doorway.

"What the hell is going on?" Trystan scowled, moving toward us until he stood between Stephanie and me.

"She's laughing at me," Stephanie said.

He glared at me.

"You two need to get a grip," Diana said. "You're making this a horrible place to work, and you're going to destroy this company if you don't stop right now."

Everyone stared at her. Diana, who had never gotten involved in our conflict, Diana who had brilliant insights into human nature, Diana who spoke with such easy-going calm. Her utter calm made it sound as if she were the one in charge, as if this all belonged to her instead of Trystan.

Trystan turned. "Thank you, Diana." He looked at Stephanie, then me. "Both of you need to leave," Trystan said. "Immediately. Go home and spend some time thinking about whether you want to continue working here."

"Absolutely," Stephanie said. "I don't have to think about it."

"I need you to leave for the day. This is unacceptable."

Stephanie smiled. "But just so you know, I don't have to think about it at all. You know where I stand. I told you earlier, and nothing's changed."

"Go home, Stephanie." He turned and walked out of the room. She hurried out after him.

Diana looked at me. "You need to back off. You aren't going to win this."

I smiled. I was used to winning. I liked winning, but she was right. The voyeur thing might have gone a step too far. I kind of did use it myself, but I'd known it would get Stephanie in knots.

Later, waiting for the subway, it crossed my mind, not for the first time, that I might be rid of Stephanie in my usual way. But the situation made it too risky. And it didn't feel right. Yes, it would be ridding the world of someone who was determined to inflict her beliefs on everyone she could, force-feeding them to her daughter and co-workers, meeting with like-minded people, and plotting how they might bring more vulnerable minds into their group. Maybe if Eileen weren't able to escape from her mother's apartment, I would change my mind. But right now, the thing holding Eileen captive was her own thoughts, not her mother. Of course, her mother had planted those thoughts and watered them for years, but Eileen allowed them to continue growing.

For now, ridding the earth of Stephanie didn't seem like the right solution. But that left me with no solution.

CHAPTER 36

*F*riday night was not the night to be taking an employee to dinner, but dinner with an individual employee was always a borderline situation. Trystan was choosing not to think about the fact that it was technically the weekend, and he was now truly crossing a line between professional and personal.

There was no choice.

The situation between Alex and Stephanie was eating him alive. He had no doubt it was eating at the core of his top-shelf consulting business, and he had to find a way to get the firm functioning smoothly again. They needed to project class and style, not reality-TV-style brawls.

Alex had called in sick, and he hadn't spoken to her since witnessing that outburst of ego and emotion in the break room. He had to find a way to get through to Stephanie. If he couldn't, what did that say about his abilities as a coach? What did it say about his insight into human behavior and his fitness for managing a team of employees, no matter how small?

He'd chosen a Chinese restaurant, hoping the variety of dishes and the act of manipulating chopsticks and serving food would create a sense of ease between them. They walked there together after work, moving quickly along the crowded sidewalks. As they neared a small alley just before reaching the restaurant, a car bolted out of the single-lane street and turned right. The sudden motion and the closeness of the vehicle caused Stephanie to cry out. She stumbled slightly, the heel of her boot skidding along the pavement. She wobbled and fell against Trystan.

He grabbed her arm and steadied her, continuing to hold her elbow as they stepped off the curb and crossed the alley.

On the opposite side, she looked up at him and giggled. "Thank you for rescuing me."

"I don't think I'd call it a rescue." He let go of her arm and quickened his pace, reaching the restaurant before she did. He grabbed the elaborately curved iron handle and pulled open the door. As she entered the restaurant, Stephanie brushed against him, causing him to jerk back and slam his shoulder into the edge of the door.

When they were seated, she smiled at him. "You truly did rescue me back there. I would have fallen. I could have broken a bone."

He opened his menu and began talking about his favorite dishes, considering what they might order, asking what she liked. The server came to ask about their drinks. Stephanie asked for a gin and tonic, which threw him for a moment. He'd been under the impression she didn't drink. That had been the cause of the disaster at her apartment on Thanksgiving. Two glasses of wine had sent her straight over the edge.

"You're having a drink, aren't you, Trystan?"

He shrugged. "Since you are...I'll have a shot of Macallans. Neat."

The server disappeared. "I thought you didn't drink," he said.

"Sometimes I do."

It was a non-answer, but he didn't pursue it. The sole focus of this meal needed to be her behavior toward Alex, her extreme sensitivity. He had to make her understand once and for all that she needed to get guidance from Alex and that she couldn't allow her emotions to dictate her behavior. Ever. Framing the conversation in the context of her religious views might help him drive home that point.

As the dishes of food began to arrive, he knew they'd ordered too much. But again, it would help them to keep busy, which would allow the words to flow more smoothly. He hoped the companionship of it might soften her sharp resistance that was constantly on the lookout for ways to take offense.

Stephanie sipped her drink. "It's so great to see you outside of the office."

"I apologize for interfering with your weekend."

"It's not interfering at *all*. I enjoy your company." She smiled.

Her words confused him. Was she suggesting she was interested in him? It hardly seemed possible. The way she was looking at him was childlike if he were pressed to describe it. Her tone sounded off, the ambiguity of what she'd said was unsettling. There was just enough to tease, to open a door.

It was best to ignore it. Move on. Keep focused. He bit into an egg roll, chewed it quickly, and set it back on the plate. "I need to talk to you about what happened yesterday. I—"

"Oh." She put her hand over her mouth and widened her eyes in mock horror. "Am I in trouble?"

He glanced at her drink. She sounded giddy and on her way to intoxication, but her glass was still two-thirds full. "Let me give you my view of the situation. Then, we can brainstorm about how to approach it."

"I would *love* that." She smiled. "It's so stimulating to toss ideas around with you. You're such a creative person, it brings that out in me."

"Let's stay focused."

"But it is Friday night. And we have this delicious meal and our cocktails. We can't be *all* business." She tilted her head slightly.

"Let me be blunt. We're not going to survive if you and Alex can't learn to work together, if you can't share responsibility for the photography."

"That's a little dramatic, don't you think?" She twirled chow mien around her fork and put the wrap of noodles and strands of vegetable into her mouth.

"It's not dramatic. I'm deadly serious."

After a brief pause, she spoke. "What if that's not possible?"

"I believe it's entirely possible. There's a clear lack of professionalism here. If one of you takes the high road, if we remove the emotion from the situation, it won't be difficult."

"And you expect that to be me." The matter-of-fact petulance dripped from her tongue, making him think she might be right. It might not be possible. He refused to accept that. They were adults, and they needed to behave like professionals. Both of them.

"Doesn't the Bible advise you to turn the other cheek?" he asked.

She put down her fork. She pushed her drink to the side and leaned her forearms on the table. "It does. I'm so..." She sighed. "It's refreshing to hear someone mention the Bible without having a negative attitude toward it. How people can be so dismissive of the word of God is beyond me."

"There's a lot of wisdom in that book," he said.

"Yes. Straight from the lips of—"

"People are advised to turn the other cheek and to love their enemies."

"You think Alexandra and I qualify as enemies?"

"Let's not get sidetracked with semantics. The point is, I think there's very clear guidance in your religious beliefs for you to be the bigger person. And to be honest, blunt again, aren't you expected to follow that wisdom? Aren't you required to apply it to your life as much as possible? Isn't that the entire point?"

"You understand! You feel...I never realized until yesterday..."

She gave him a syrupy smile. "It touches me that you want to talk about this."

"What?"

She broadened her smile.

"What didn't you realize?" he asked.

"You don't let your personal side show much at work."

"Most of the time, it's not appropriate. That's what you and Alexandra need to learn."

"This is good, so refreshing, so different from what I expected."

He cleared his throat. He took a sip of his drink and tackled the spicy prawns. "I'm not sure what you're talking about."

"It's okay. I think we understand each other." She placed her hand on the table, stroking the cloth gently as if she were petting a cat.

"You understand that you have to tolerate Alex? You have to listen to her guidance. You have to treat her with respect and keep your frustrations to yourself. You need to stop reacting to things she says that you find disturbing. Can you do that?"

"It's really difficult."

"But according to your beliefs—"

"Yes. You're right. I know that's what God wants of me, and I'm not sure why I didn't recognize it until you laid it out for me."

"Please don't just agree with me. You've done that before and—"

"No, I haven't."

"Let's not waste time arguing." He took another sip of his drink. It was disappearing far too quickly. He should have ordered a glass of wine. Then he could have asked for a second.

She smiled, leaning forward even more, her hair falling over the plate, in danger of touching her food. Her hand was back on the table, stroking, stroking. "I don't like arguing either."

He said nothing more about it, and then, for a while, they talked about other things. He hoped that as they made small talk, his pointed words would penetrate her stubborn skull. He couldn't fire either woman, and the only way to get them to do what he needed done was to manipulate Stephanie. Attempting the same with Alex would surely backfire.

When most of the food was gone, and the server was clearing the rest for packing into takeout containers, Trystan allowed himself to pick up his scotch and take the final swallow. He looked forward to a second one at home. "What we talked about is critical, Stephanie. I'm deadly serious. We can't have any more issues. You need to treat this like you would a direct message from God, if I can put it in those terms. In a sense, it is. I'm asking you to follow what's written in the Bible, as if your eternal life depended upon it, which I think is your desire anyway, so it shouldn't be difficult."

She looked like she was going to cry. But when she spoke, her voice was clear and strong. "I know you're speaking truth. I know what I need to do. You can trust me. You can count on me."

He allowed himself a relaxed smile, but there was something about the set of her eyes that made him wonder if she'd comprehended a single word he'd said. He felt trapped and helpless. He'd only felt that way once before in his life, and for the most part, that incident was also connected to Stephanie. It seemed as if he were bound to her for life.

CHAPTER 37

On Saturday, I texted Trystan. After calling in sick on Friday, I'd planned to go into the office near the end of the day, grab some time alone with Trystan, and hopefully a martini with him after Diana and Stephanie were gone for the day. But as I watched the building from across the street, I saw him and Stephanie leave together. They were walking side-by-side, and she didn't turn toward the subway as she usually did.

Staying on the opposite side of the street, I followed them for six blocks. Just as they were ready to cross a narrow alley, Stephanie tripped. She looked up at Trystan, gazing into his eyes as if he were Mr. Darcy himself. In that moment, I realized she had a distorted perception of their relationship. I realized why she'd updated her look. I also realized that Trystan had no clue what was going on. So much for his marketable insight into the human psyche.

If Stephanie believed he felt the same, she might agree to do whatever he asked—meaning she would agree to play nicely with me. In that case, I didn't have a problem after all. But if he picked up on what she was thinking and drew a hard line, rejecting whatever feelings she had for him, she would transform into an even greater monster. I imagined her swelling to epic proportions like those witches and queens in Disney fairytales that become larger than life, terrifying small children.

I had to persuade him to see me as soon as possible.

Before I'd seen him going to dinner with Stephanie, I'd decided I was going to risk the job I loved because it was no longer that lovable. I wanted Stephanie out of there, or else I would find something else to do. I didn't care that I'd have to delay my new apartment because I didn't have a long-term employer to prove my stability. I didn't care about winding up in a tedious job tied to a computer all day long. It would be a brief detour.

Besides, I didn't truly think that would happen. Despite what Diana had said, I was going to win. There wasn't a shred of doubt in my mind. Unless there *was* a faint whisper of doubt, otherwise I wouldn't be thinking about losing my apartment and acquiring a boring job.

I sent my message just before lunchtime. I didn't hear back from him until four. I wondered whether that was a game or he'd been busy. My message asked him to meet me for a drink.

His reply informed me that it was *the weekend,* and therefore, *not appropriate.* He texted that we would *talk Monday.* He would *schedule time.*

I texted back: *You owe me.*

Trystan: *You're not starting off on the best foot with a comment like that. I asked you to think about how you were going to develop a more cooperative attitude—some team spirit.*

Alexandra: *I left a great job in Australia to move to this ridiculously expensive island.*

It was a lie that I felt my job in Sydney was great, but an easy, impossible to disprove lie.

Trystan: *I don't owe you anything.*

Alexandra: *Equal footing.*

Trystan: *??*

Alexandra: *I saw you heading out to a cozy dinner with Stephanie last night.*

Trystan: *And I've done the same with you. It needs to stop.*

Alexandra: *I have a proposition. You'll want the rest of the weekend to think about it, because I'll need an answer Monday morning.*

Trystan: *Don't give me ultimatums.*

Alexandra: *You know you can trust me. Besides, you'll have a good time. We always do.*

Trystan: *Email me your proposition.*

Alexandra: *I need to see you face-to-face. You'll be glad. I promise.*

Trystan: *One drink.*

I laughed when I saw that. There was no way he was getting away with one drink, and his curiosity had triumphed.

I was already seated at a table near the back when he arrived, two martinis waiting. Trystan was always prompt, so I knew the drinks would be icy fresh. I'd tipped the waiter ahead of time to keep an eye on me and serve the drinks the moment I signaled him.

As Trystan settled across from me, I moved the stick of olives slowly around the inside of the glass, eager to consume those luscious fruits. I was already planning how I would time my order of a second round in a way he couldn't avoid.

He grimaced and took a sip of his drink. "I really don't know why you're so in love with these things," he said.

"It's an acquired taste."

He looked at me over the rim of the glass, and I knew he got my meaning. "Sometimes, I prefer a smooth, warm scotch."

I smiled and ate an olive.

"So, what's your proposal?"

"My proposal is that you fire Stephanie."

He scowled. "That's not a proposal. I want to move this business forward, and for that, I need two photographers. I don't know how many times I have to repeat that before it sinks into your head."

"Then hire someone else. There are a thousand photographers in this city who would love to work with you, who have talent and skill, and who know how to function with other human beings."

"You know she would say the same about you."

"Did she?"

He took another sip of his drink. He put the glass on the table and moved it around slightly. Then he picked it up and took several more sips. "This is good."

"You were complaining about it before you even tasted it."

He laughed. "True. I have a love-hate relationship with martinis. And right now, I'm not feeling terribly sociable. This thing with the two of you is tearing apart what I've worked pretty damn hard to build."

"I don't think that's completely true."

He studied my face. I wondered what he was thinking. He didn't blink or change the shape of his mouth. He just stared. Finally, he took another sip of his drink. "So there is no proposal. You just wanted a drinking buddy."

"That's not what this is. I think..." I sipped my drink, making him wait to hear the rest. "I think you're in more trouble than you realize."

"I'm not in any trouble. I have a personnel issue with two women who are behaving in the most unprofessional way I've ever witnessed."

"Not me." I took a sip of my drink. We were downing them too fast, but without food, it was a natural reflex to keep picking up the glass, taking tiny and sometimes not-so-tiny sips.

He let out a deep sigh, something that sounded as if it came from the depths of the earth. For a guy with charming good looks and a fascinating career, and plenty of money, he sure looked like he was hanging by a thread. There had to be something going on here that he wasn't saying. There was no way he thought

Stephanie was even close to adequate as a photographer. There was no way he didn't have a significant concern that if he let her loose in front of clients, she would drive every single one of them away.

This wasn't just arrogance talking. He knew I was a valuable asset, and if he put Stephanie and me on a scale, I would far outweigh her. Not even in the same class. Why on earth couldn't he make a decision? Why didn't he give her an assignment, anything really, and tell her if she didn't meet expectations, she would be let go? It was so simple, but he clung to her as if the company would dissolve without her. Instead, the reverse was about to happen.

I picked up my glass and took several sips.

"You're sure guzzling that," he said.

"I'm not too far ahead of you." I ate the other two olives and signaled for the waiter. "I need something to eat." The server arrived almost immediately. I ordered stuffed mushrooms, arancini, and two more martinis.

"I don't want another," Trystan said. "This was supposed to be a quick drink, and you were going to present a proposal. You haven't, so..." He made a move to get his wallet.

I placed my hand in the center of the table, bending my fingers slightly so the light would cause my cherry red nails to glisten. "We have lots of debates, Trystan, but I know that deep down, you trust me. You trust my instincts. That's why you hired me, and that's why I'm good at what I do. My instinct is telling me that Stephanie is going to cause a lot of trouble. You know this, but you feel trapped for some reason I can't figure out. I know I have a difficult relationship with her, but I really want this company to work, more than I want to one-up her. If you tell me what's going on, I won't use a single word of it to make the situation worse. I promise." I truly meant it. Of course, I might change my mind later, but at that moment, I not only meant it, I meant that I would always mean it.

He pinched the bridge of his nose and looked down at the table. He picked up his drink and finished most of it, rejecting those delicious olives. It was all I could do not to ask if I could eat them. When our glasses were swept away a moment later, I felt a physical ache in my throat, thinking of those lovely olives going to waste.

"There's something going on with her," I said. "With you. If you tell me, maybe I can help."

He shook his head. "Your instincts are wrong."

I knew they weren't. Any rational business owner would have fired her a long time ago. I ate a mushroom, letting the savory filling melt across my tongue, chewing the firm flesh, and then popping another into my mouth the minute the first one was gone. They were amazing.

"Stephanie has a crush on you," I said.

He stared at me. If I wasn't imagining it, tears were filling his eyes. "That's ridiculous."

I ate another mushroom. He hadn't touched the food. I wondered if the arancini would be enough to satisfy me for dinner. I could see them taking off the edge when I got home, but then I would wind up craving pizza or a burger and fries just as I was getting ready for bed.

"If you don't get this resolved, you're right—your consulting firm is dead in the water."

"I already spoke to Stephanie, and I think things will work out," he said. "She's going to stop taking everything so personally."

"Not when you tell her you don't want to be her lover."

"Don't be absurd."

"Why else did she spend thousands of dollars on new clothes and makeup and getting her hair colored?"

"She—"

"You have no idea, do you. She either did it to get promoted, which maybe that worked, or she wants more. You treat her nicely, and I imagine most people don't because she's so difficult.

You value her work. You listen to her. It wouldn't take much for any woman to fall for you. Have you checked a mirror?"

He laughed, but he looked like he was going to vomit the martini all over the table.

"Have an arancino," I said.

He plucked one off the plate and took a bite.

"If you don't put everything on the table, this is going to blow up. Or, I could resign. I initially planned to tell you I'm leaving if you don't let her go, but then..." I didn't often leave sentences unfinished but decided he didn't need to know my change in direction had come after observing him and Stephanie together.

He took a few sips of his fresh drink, which seemed to revive him. He looked angry. "Okay. Maybe you're right. If I can't sort this out, I'll be forced to watch everything I've worked for fall apart." He sighed. "You can't tell anyone. Ever."

"I won't."

"If you do, I'll fire you on the spot, and I will not give you a good reference."

He sure had his bases covered. He wasn't trusting me. He wanted an opinion, but he was going to make our casual agreement as air-tight as possible. I smiled, and he took that as acceptance of his terms.

"In normal circumstances, it wouldn't probably be such an issue, but you know what Stephanie is like."

I did know. I nodded.

"What happened is...I had a one-time thing with her daughter."

I stared at him.

"It was a weird series of events. I ran into Eileen in the lobby after she'd had lunch with her mom..." Once again, that look of nausea washed across his face.

"I don't need to tell you the whole story, but she and I were talking. I happened to mention a movie she was obsessed with. We started discussing it and ended up going for a drink and..."

I nodded. I didn't want to hear the details. The problem was absolutely clear. He felt guilty and indebted. He shouldn't have, but it was all over his face. It hadn't been nausea at all. It was guilt. And fear. He was probably terrified of what Stephanie would do if she found out, and firing her might upset Eileen enough that she would tell her mother what had happened.

CHAPTER 38

The buzzer rang, telling Stephanie someone was downstairs at the lobby doors. She went to the intercom and pressed the button to speak. "Who is it?"

"Hey, Stephanie. It's Ned."

"Eileen isn't here."

"She said she might be a few minutes late. We're going to dinner. Mind if I wait?"

Of course she didn't mind, although she did mind that she hadn't known they were going to dinner. And she knew he didn't mean wait outside by the entrance. He meant she should release the lock and welcome him into her apartment, disrupting her quiet Sunday afternoon. Eileen had gone shopping. Stephanie had hinted around, hoping to be asked to join her, but Eileen let the hints fly by without flinching as if she'd missed the suggestions entirely. Now, Stephanie would be stuck entertaining Eileen's *boy*friend because if she left him standing outside, Eileen would be angry at *her*.

"Fine." She pressed the button to release the door handle. Several minutes later, he was knocking on her apartment door. She let him in and returned to her spot on the couch. She picked up her open Bible and placed it back in her lap. "Have a seat. Let me know if you want tea or anything."

He smiled. "Leeny and I are going out to dinner, so I don't need anything."

"*Leeny?*"

He gave her a sappy smile. "My pet name for her."

It was a ridiculous bastardization of Eileen's name. Demeaning. It shredded her beautiful, unique name and made it sound juvenile. Eileen wasn't his pet. But Stephanie knew her place— bite her tongue, show respect to Eileen's boyfriend. For now. If things started to slip toward an engagement, she would be forced to speak out. Eileen had already shut her down when she expressed concern, though. Maybe waiting was a bad idea. The more entrenched Eileen became in this relationship, the harder it would be to show her how wrong, how doomed, it was.

In fact, maybe God had dropped this opportunity right into her lap. She had Ned all to herself. She could find out a few things, possibly speak to him as a peer and get him to see how ridiculous he looked dating a girl so young.

She closed her Bible and placed it on the end table. "I was praying and listening to God. I like to do that on Sundays when I have so much free time."

He nodded. "Sundays are great."

"Do you belong to a church?"

He shook his head.

"A spiritual foundation in a relationship is important. Both people need to see the world the same way for a marriage to work."

"I agree," he said.

"But you don't go to church. Did you as a child?"

"No. My parents wanted me to—"

"Eileen was raised going to church. She still believes in God. That seems like a big gap between the two of you. Almost as big as the gap in—"

"No. It's all good. We're pretty much on the same page."

She smiled. "Women can be complex."

He gave her a puzzled look as if he failed to see the connection between Eileen downplaying her faith to him and the truth about women. "I guess you know that about women," she said. "You probably have a lot of experience."

He laughed. "Not as much as you'd think, given my age."

So, he was going to address the elephant in the room head-on. She had to admire that. "You're so much older than Eileen. It must feel uncomfortable for you."

"I go with the flow. How else can you approach life? It's going to flow no matter what you do." He laughed. "Nothing much makes me feel uncomfortable."

"But you must get uncomfortable when you think about the future—you'll be ready to retire just when Eileen starts to think about having a child."

He laughed. "How old do you think I am?"

"A few years older than I am."

"Good guess."

It wasn't a guess at all. It was glaringly obvious, proving the man did have some delusions about his age, even if he pretended otherwise.

"So you're planning your retirement *already?*" he asked. "I think we both have quite a few very productive working years left. In fact, most people would say we haven't reached the pinnacles of our careers."

She didn't like how he was taking control of the conversation. He was more aggressive than she'd realized during that dinner a few weeks ago. He must have been trying to win her over, but now, the gloves were off. "Raising children is very demanding."

"You could look at it that way. It's also satisfying and fun and—"

"Fun?" She laughed. "It's not all trips to the park and ice cream." She would never describe raising a child as *fun*. It was the most serious work God entrusted to his creatures, and it wasn't supposed to be playtime. That was an increasing problem—parents thinking they were friends with their children. It was fine once the child was an adult, but not when they were growing up—you needed to guide and mold them.

"I guess we have different ideas of parenting." He settled back in the chair.

He didn't seem at all impatient or anxious to escape the conversation. What was it going to take to get him to see that Eileen was not the right girl for him? And she was definitely still a girl in many ways. This was horrible. She had to put a stop to it, but at the same time, she couldn't have him go complaining to Eileen, turning her daughter against her.

She laughed softly. "I'm not sure how we got off on that. I suppose because I was making the point that, to be perfectly blunt, you're a bit old to be starting a family. I know I couldn't do it at this age."

"Well, we're different people, aren't we? But it makes me happy that you see a future for Leeny and me."

That name made gooseflesh run down her back. And that was not at all what she'd meant. Was he playing games? Surely he realized she saw through him? They were the same age, and Eileen was practically a teenager. "You'll be in your mid-sixties when your child graduates from college. Even if you had one right now." She laughed. "Imagine when Eileen wants to step aside from her career to travel, and you'll be in your eighties."

"I get it that you're concerned about our age difference," Ned said. "But Leeny and I have discussed it. We agree it's not important. Age is the last thing you want to think about. When you enjoy the same lifestyle, are interested in the same hobbies, are philosophically in agreement, and have similar activity levels...I could go on, but those are the things that matter, and we have all that. To find someone who is a so-called *appropriate* age but lose half of that? We both said, no thanks."

As if God wanted to prevent her from speaking another word to this idiot, Eileen's key scraped inside the lock, and the door opened. "Thanks for the text," Eileen said. She closed the door and shrugged off her coat. She crossed the room quickly and kissed Ned, a kiss that lingered until Stephanie had to look away.

After another eternal minute, they separated from each other, and Eileen picked up her coat and purse. She started toward her bedroom. "I'll change my top and shoes, and then I'll be ready. Five minutes."

Stephanie felt ill. There had to be a way to stop this. Now.

When Eileen was out of earshot, Stephanie leaned forward on the couch. She brushed away the sudden sharp pain of recognition that Eileen hadn't given her a kiss or a hug hello and, in fact, hadn't even acknowledged her presence. She spoke softly. "Ned, I think if you really love Eileen, you'll give some serious thought to what you're doing. She very much wants to have children, and you'll be robbing her of that. You'll be robbing her of a husband in her golden years, and you'll be forcing her to choose between her faith and whatever it is you believe."

He gave her a warm smile. "Thank you for being honest. I appreciate knowing what's on your mind."

Before Stephanie could compose her thoughts to say more, Eileen came into the room and shrugged on the coat she'd dropped on the chair. "Let's go. I'm starving."

Ned stood. "It was good talking to you, Stephanie."

She said nothing. When the door closed, she let herself fall sideways onto the couch. She cried for a long time—until the sun went down and the room grew dark.

Finally, she got ahold of herself. Without even a snack to tide her over, having missed dinner as she drowned in her grief, she left the apartment. Her Bible was tucked safely inside her bag. Just as she was about to go out the door, she ran back to her bedroom and lifted her new gun out of its case. With only one shooting class so far, she wasn't confident she was that skilled with it, but after that man following her, she knew she had to bring it along. From now on, whenever she was out after dark, it would be safely tucked in her bag.

The situation facing her was so desperate, so heartbreaking, she needed the comfort of the church walls around her while she prayed. She needed God to know she was serious about this. She needed Him to know she would go out at night, deal with the drunks and rowdies on the subway, to give herself to dedicated prayer.

The church doors were left unlocked from six in the morning until midnight every day of the week. Some said it was risking vandalism, but her pastor believed it was important for people to have access when they needed to be alone, when they were struggling, when they wanted to fall on their knees before God and feel the quiet comfort of the sanctuary.

Thankfully, the building was empty. She went to the altar and slipped her shoes off her feet. She knelt with her purse strap wrapped around her ankle, just in case someone snuck up on her. She spent nearly an hour until her legs ached and her back was stiff. She pleaded for guidance regarding her precious little girl.

CHAPTER 39

*T*rystan had barely pulled his chair up to the desk and was just starting to enter his computer password. Neither of those actions were complete when he heard Diana's voice just outside his doorway. "Got a minute?"

He looked up.

Without waiting for his response, she stepped inside, closed the door, and pulled a chair up to his desk. He almost groaned. She didn't have to say a word. He knew she was there to talk about Stephanie's photographs. He'd known the photos were inadequate when he'd glanced through them. Because Alex hadn't taken near her usual quantity, there weren't enough for Diana to complete her microexpression analysis. He couldn't help wondering if Alex's minimal contribution had been deliberate, shining a spotlight on Stephanie's weakness. It was Alex's mission to prove to him that Stephanie wasn't equipped for the role she'd begged for. Still, Alex and Stephanie both insisted the photo session had ended abruptly and prematurely, so maybe it was as it appeared on the surface.

"How are things going?" he asked. "Despite the fireworks recently."

She rolled her eyes, then got straight to the point, her usual style. "I don't have enough photographs of Matt Sherpa. We need a follow-up session."

It was so refreshing to talk to someone who wasn't oozing with neuroses or going out of her way to challenge every little thing that didn't suit her. "Stephanie is still coming up to speed," he said. Defending her was instinct now. He didn't even have to think of something kind or excusing to say about her, the words spilled out as if he truly believed them. And yet, as he spoke, he knew he did not. Alex had been very perceptive about that. "Do you have any suggestions?"

"Yes, send Alex alone."

He looked at her, overcome yet again by the helpless guilt that plagued him constantly. In the beginning, he'd believed that offering the co-photographer position to Stephanie would ease his guilt, but for some reason he couldn't explain, the guilt had intensified. Maybe because he knew she wasn't capable, and he felt even worse because he was putting her in a position where she was bound to fail. He was failing himself by not showing any leadership or addressing the tough choices a business owner had to make to be successful.

No matter how much he turned the situation around in his mind or talked to Alex and Stephanie, he couldn't see a way out of it. Alex made it sound so simple, but from what he'd seen, she had a tendency to slash and burn her way through life. He didn't want to hurt Stephanie. Nor did he want to be the victim of her rage if she ever found out about Eileen. She had the potential to be vindictive.

What had he been thinking, telling Alex about that? Had he truly believed that telling her would enable her to come up with some brilliant, perfect solution? There *was* no solution. He'd wanted to scrape the problem out of his own head and place it on someone else. He felt guilty, but no one could absolve him. He'd made a colossal mess. And if Alex was to be believed, he'd managed to give Stephanie the impression he might be interested in a relationship with her. It was turning into a nightmare.

"I can't do that," he said finally. "You know we need two photographers."

"We do, but the second one doesn't have to be Stephanie. She's good at office management and scheduling and that sort of thing but doesn't have any creative vision or intuition. She doesn't think outside the box, and she's too self-conscious to interact with clients in a provocative way."

He looked at her, staring through her, feeling the defeat seep into his bones. He sighed. "I'll schedule an appointment with Matt and go with Stephanie."

Diana looked at him as if he'd disappointed her.

"Anything else?" he asked.

As he spoke, she was already standing, then making her way toward the door in that gliding, efficient way she had.

To escape his anxiety after Diana was gone, he immediately placed a call to Matt Sherpa. Matt was available later that afternoon. Before their scheduled appointment, he took Stephanie to a coffee shop and went over the basics of what they were trying to achieve. She was oddly compliant, so maybe she had taken to heart what he'd said over dinner.

When they walked into the office at Matt's church, Matt was seated at his desk, the phone to his ear. He wasn't speaking, simply nodding his head, making comforting sounds every few seconds.

"We should wait outside," Stephanie said in a low voice. "It sounds like a crisis counseling call."

Trystan couldn't see the reason for excusing themselves, they had an appointment. But before he could respond, Stephanie grabbed the edge of his suit jacket and tugged at him, forcing him to follow or create an awkward scene.

They seated themselves in the reception area. He wondered where the office assistant was. Her desk looked too neat for her to have just stepped out for a moment. Stephanie pulled her camera out of her bag, leaning toward Trystan, pressing her shoulder against his arm. He wriggled his chair slightly, trying to give her more space. She looked at him, smiling.

She returned her attention to the camera, but she didn't move away, keeping her arm close to his. He stood and went to the window. "So you're sure you feel comfortable with what we're trying to achieve here?" he asked.

"Of course."

"Lots of close-ups. I can't emphasize that enough. No talking about yourself. That's critical. You have to get *him* talking, so he'll stop thinking about the camera."

"I know all of that. There's no need to remind me so often."

He nodded once.

Twenty minutes passed before Matt came out of his office. "Sorry about that. Pregnant teenager."

"Oh, I understand," Stephanie said. "A minister never knows when he's going to be needed. You can't schedule human suffering, or God's intervention, for that matter."

"True," Matt said. "So," he clapped his hands once. "Photographs."

"Let's go back into your office," Trystan said. "We can—"

"Remember, I'm running the show." Stephanie gave Trystan a beaming smile.

He felt ill. This was not ever going to work. He could feel it in every bone of his body. How on earth had he ended up in this situation? Their work had been going so well. Maybe he just needed to look his guilt square in the face and agree to live with it. He needed to stop fearing Stephanie's rage if she found out about him and Eileen.

Stop giving into fear, or destroy his business. Those were the choices.

He sat silently in an easy chair in the corner of Matt's office while Stephanie *ran the show*. She relished her control, directing

Matt like he was a model posing for a fashion line. She talked non-stop. She asked him questions, but before the man could get going on any topic, with any depth, before he could lose himself in what he was saying, Stephanie interrupted with anecdotes that she felt related to the question she'd asked. In most cases, they did not.

All Trystan could see was Matt politely listening to her, a bland expression on his face. An expression that would give Diana absolutely nothing to work with. At his first coaching session with Matt, Trystan was going to have to make a point of digging into Matt's unexpressed thoughts, to find some way of making up for what they'd lost. Now, he worried Matt was thinking he'd paid an awful lot of money to listen to a needy, fanatical church-goer ramble through irrelevant pieces of her life story.

When Stephanie was finished taking pictures, Trystan had a headache.

CHAPTER 40

*W*hen I'd told Kent I was moving, I thought he would show some disappointment that I wouldn't be so conveniently located. I thought he would admire the fact I was looking for a nicer, larger place. Instead, he obsessed over why I was moving when I had the best apartment in our building. And then we got drunk, and he obsessed over my body, and then I didn't see him for a few weeks. Not at all.

Usually, I would run into him on the stairs or on our landing at least a few times a week, but nothing. Since we'd hooked up, I'd sometimes received text messages from him, although they were never simple *how-are-ya* messages. They always had a purpose—dinner or drinks or sex without any preliminaries. He was obviously also minimalist in his approach to communication. Now, he'd disappeared from my life, and it nagged at me that he was hunting down Victoria.

When I finally texted him about getting together, it turned out I'd been right. He'd spent a ridiculous amount of time hanging out near the coffee shop where he thought he'd seen her. He was hoping for another encounter, determined to talk to her and find out why she'd disappeared from our building and what more she'd learned about Rafe's murder, if anything.

How had we gone from my excessive curiosity to his? Why couldn't he retreat to his detached self? The more chilling question was—Had I done something to pique his curiosity? Had there been a slip of my tongue, an impulsive comment that made him recognize there was something not quite right about my relationship with them, with Rafe's murder, and with Victoria's sudden evaporation into the ether?

I'd invited Kent to my place. I ordered a lavish Indian dinner and picked up two nice bottles of wine. I needed to know exactly where his head was. I needed to find a way to shut down his curiosity for good.

Now, as I arranged the cheap serving bowls I'd grabbed from Duane Reade, hoping to make the dinner look less like takeout, he was sitting on my couch, sipping wine, watching me. Was he thinking that I looked like a gracious hostess? Was he basking in the savory aromas filling my apartment? Was he thinking about sex? Or was he wondering what I knew about a man found dead in a hotel room, presumed to have been killed by a sex worker or a furious ex-lover? The police had settled on the belief that a sex worker killed Rafe, or possibly, a pimp, because a woman enraged and heartbroken over rejection would not have been so meticulous to leave the place spotlessly, bloodlessly, free of skin cells and strands of hair.

"Are you ready to eat?" I asked.

"It smells great."

"Thank you."

He laughed. "Are you taking credit for something other people prepared?"

"I paid for it. I carried it home."

"You're too much sometimes."

"Thank you."

He laughed again but didn't say anything more.

We sat across from each other and began scooping jasmine rice and lamb and chicken and vegetables onto our plates. I topped off the wine glasses from which we'd only had a small taste while I put out the food. I pushed my chair back and went to the kitchen drawer.

"What did you forget?"

"This." I pulled out a short, fat candle. I placed it on a dish at the center of the table, lit it with a match, and turned off the kitchen light. The lamp in the living room and the candle gave the room a romantic glow. It felt less like a kitchen table in a tiny one-bedroom apartment and more like an intimate dinner.

"I have the impression you're avoiding me lately," he said.

"Why do you think that?"

"I know you know more than you're saying about Victoria. Ever since I saw her, you don't want to talk to me. Now I'm even more curious."

I smiled and took a sip of wine. "I've been busy at work. I told you about all the issues with Stephanie."

"Yeah." He started eating. A moment later, he placed his fork on the plate. "Have you heard from Victoria at *all*?"

I shook my head.

"Neither have I. What about the police? Any more questions?"

I shook my head. "I think they've accepted it might go unsolved. And Victoria has moved on, I suppose."

"He was a weird dude, but she really did love him," Kent said.

"Yes, but since he's dead, what else is she going to do? Stay in an apartment that has his touch on every single surface? Live in the middle of a shrine? Hang out in the city he loved, where all the restaurants and parks and stores remind her of him?"

He shrugged. He picked up his glass and swirled the wine. He took a sip. "This is really good."

"Thank you."

He laughed.

In that moment, I knew it was time for me to move on. Kent

needed to meet someone else so he would forget about me. The memories of my connection to our former neighbors would fade. We'd had fun together, but he wasn't as interesting as some guys I'd known, or the imagined man in my mind, so there was no reason to postpone the inevitable. He was not someone I would be with on a long-term basis. In the past, long-term connections hadn't usually crossed my mind, but lately...

My plan for Kent was risky. It had some potential for backfiring, but it was a perfect fit for the situation. "Do you want to see pictures of my new apartment?" I asked.

"Okay."

I pushed my plate to the side. I went to the couch and got my phone off the end table. I opened the photos and brought up the ones I'd taken of the apartment Eileen and I liked the best. I handed the phone to him. "It's a high-rise. It wasn't my first choice, but I love the area—right near the Hudson. It's closer to Central Park, and there's good security. There's a laundry room in the building."

He swiped his finger across the screen, not pausing long on any of the photos and not speaking a word. When he was done, he handed the phone back to me. "Looks nice. Looks pricey."

"It is more expensive."

"And two bedrooms."

I nodded. I hadn't told him about Eileen because it didn't fit my plan for making him run screaming away from me.

"What do you think about sharing it?" I asked.

"What?"

I stood and went around the table, I settled myself on his leg and wrapped my arms around his neck, leaning my head against his. "We've been—"

"Slow down. I don't think I'm...we're ready for..."

I pulled away and gave him a pouty look.

He scowled. "Did you put a deposit already, just assuming I'd agree?"

I nodded.

"That's not cool."

"I thought we were—" I grabbed my phone. "I found the most amazing store. I want to get all new furniture. The stuff I have was kind of cheap, and it's not going to look all that great in another year or two. And you hardly have anything." I laughed softly, thinking of his worshipful approach to the stark but soothing atmosphere of his apartment.

He didn't look around the room to verify my assessment of my furniture. He stared at me, holding my gaze. "Are you serious? I thought this was kind of a casual thing with us."

I blinked several times. I tapped my phone and pulled up a website. "Look at this. And see that awesome bookcase with all those glass jars. It would be nice to really decorate instead of just having the essentials."

"I hate shit like that. I thought you knew that."

He lived his minimalist beliefs to the core, and maybe I was going over the top, deliberately trying to scare him with the thought of accumulating home décor, but I needed him out of my life. I needed to silence his questions as soon as possible, or I might be forced to resort to a more drastic solution. It seemed a shame to kill someone for being too curious, especially since I'm far too curious than is normal, or wise.

He shifted his legs, trying to wriggle me off his lap. I gripped his neck more tightly and pressed my head against his even harder as if I meant to merge our skulls.

"What are you doing?" he asked.

"I thought you were really into me."

"I am. I just think it's way too soon to live together. And I'm kind of pissed that you went and rented an apartment, assuming I was going to help. Because I'm not." He pried my arms away from his neck and gently nudged me off his lap. He stood and picked up his wineglass. He swallowed what was in it and placed it near the edge of the table. "I think I should head out."

"But aren't we going to—"

"I'm tired. I didn't realize it until I had all that wine."

I avoided looking at the bottle that still had at least two pours left in it. I didn't want to undermine the excuses he was flinging at me.

"I'll touch base later, K?"

I nodded. "Sure."

I moved toward him. He backed toward the door. "Sorry I can't help you clean up."

"No problem," I said.

"And to be clear..." His hand was already on the doorknob. "I'm not in a position to move. So I hope you can get the deposit back."

A moment later, he was gone. I put away the food and washed the plates and Kent's glass. I took the wine bottle and my glass to the couch. I tugged off my boots and curled my legs up on the cushion. I poured a generous glass of wine and took a sip. It was quite good.

I felt confident that the most I would see Kent would be his messages across the screen of my phone. And I was pretty sure Victoria had slipped to the back of his mind, if she hadn't fallen out entirely, in the face of having his way of life threatened.

CHAPTER 41

 ortland, Oregon

* * *

MY MOTHER'S solution to my wicked transgression—*the most wicked and heartbreaking thing I'd ever done, piercing the soul of god*— was to stalk me.

I was no longer allowed to participate in the carpool. She drove me to school in the mornings and waited while I entered the building. She showed up after school to make sure I actually went to the after-school study club, and she came to pick me up when it was over, always coming inside to greet me, rather than letting me walk to the car like the near-adult that I was. She said I'd lost the privilege of being treated like an adult. Her face didn't reveal the slightest suggestion that she didn't realize the ridiculous nature of that statement. I was already a quasi-prisoner, without several of the privileges my brothers had enjoyed, or other kids my age, even other *girls* at our church.

As if all that wasn't enough, she sometimes showed up at the school during lunchtime. She lurked around the office and made friends with the administrative staff. She talked to my teachers. And eventually, she managed to find out that Brady was the boy who had *stolen my virtue.*

Of course, Brady and I could no longer see each other unless we cut a class or two, and it was difficult to do that when I didn't know when or where my mother would show up. The guillotine hanging over my neck was that if I did anything that was displeasing to god—and that was broad territory—she would tell my father that I'd tossed away what belonged to my future husband. So far, she was seeking guidance in prayer about whether or not my father should be informed.

"I don't know," she'd said, more times than I could count, "I don't like keeping secrets from your father. God doesn't like me keeping secrets from the man He's given to protect and care for me. But I know this would hurt your father so deeply, I'm afraid he might not recover. I don't want to destroy his relationship with you. I don't want to damage his relationship with God. It might cause him to doubt his success as a father, as your protector."

I didn't care how she wanted to explain it to herself, I just wanted to avoid him knowing. I didn't want to be locked in my room with a tutor brought in for homeschooling.

So it didn't seem smart to try to cut class to be with Brady. We hung out as much as we could, but we were dying. Our bodies ached for each other, and after a while, we began to pull apart a bit because it was just easier. Feeling him close, standing beside my locker, or walking through the hallways holding hands, was too much. It was easier to stay far away.

My mother's next step made me realize that maybe I had gotten some of my craftiness from her. She approached Brady in the parking lot, knocking on the window of his car and introducing herself. Then she invited him to dinner.

I was a little surprised he accepted my mother's invitation. It made me wonder if he had a sadistic streak and wanted to watch me squirm. Maybe he was curious about this strange religion he'd stumbled upon. On the outside, our church looked like thousands of churches across the country and around the world. But inside those doors, it was a little different. Very different, according to some of the Catholic and Baptist kids I knew at school.

Dinner was planned for a Friday night. My mother made roast beef, scalloped potatoes, green beans, a salad, rolls, and two kinds of pie.

"Dinner smells awesome," Brady said as he stepped inside. It was the first time he'd entered the house through the front door. I was sure it would be the last.

My father came into the entryway and extended his hand. "Mr. Mallory."

"Hi. I'm Brady."

"Welcome to our home." My father gave him a tight smile. We went into the living room, where my mother served potato chips with onion dip. I thought it was a little much since potatoes were coming with dinner, but it was delicious and helped ease the tension on Brady's face, and on my father's face. It gave my mother something to keep her busy, along with checking on the dinner and finishing up the salad. I was the one in trouble, and I seemed to be the only one who was relaxed and strangely excited about how the evening might unfold.

My father fired questions at Brady, wanting to know the ages of his sisters, what his father did for a living, if his mother worked outside the home, and where his grandparents lived. He wanted to know what subjects Brady preferred in school and what kind of grades he got. He wanted to know his plans for college and a career.

"Does your family go to church?" my father asked.

"No." Brady grabbed a potato chip and scraped it across the dip. The chip broke, and he fished out the gooey scrap from the bowl.

"Why not?" my father asked, ignoring the gooey collapse of the chip.

"Come on," I said. "That's like asking me why my family does go to church."

"No it's not," my mother said. "It's obvious. Because we have faith."

"Then it's obvious for him," I said. "They don't have faith."

Brady laughed.

My mother glared at me, then gave a knowing look in my father's direction. I decided I had better let things play out and not offer any commentary. Brady and I were probably history anyway, so if they pissed him off or made him uncomfortable, it didn't really matter. Again, I wondered why he'd even agreed to come over. Maybe he thought they would like him. Maybe he thought if they liked him, they would let us hang out together.

He had no idea what he was getting into. And he also didn't realize that if he wasn't a church-goer, and by that, I mean hard-core, baptized, Bible-reading church-goer, there was no way they would ever like him. For my father especially, liking someone meant god had put his stamp of approval on their forehead. Otherwise, he couldn't be bothered.

Of course, my father was polite and respectful to people we met out in the world—neighbors and store clerks and servers in restaurants. But he was polite because he was always on the lookout for an opening to insert his invitation to become acquainted with god on a first-name basis.

"I guess I believe in God," Brady said.

"You *guess*?" My father said. "Does your belief influence your life? Does it give you comfort? Do you have a personal relation-ship with your Savior?" My father had several more questions, I could tell, but he paused there for a moment.

"Uh, I don't know," Brady said. "I would never kill anyone." He took the largest chip in the bowl and scooped up a large glob of dip. He shoved the whole thing into his mouth.

I was sure he hoped the obvious movements of his jaw would shift the conversation away from him.

It didn't. My father waited patiently until Brady was finished chewing.

From there on out, scattered through dinner, my father mostly asked questions that came from the script for his evangelistic visits, designed to get Brady to see he needed salvation.

When dessert was finished, and Brady said he should get going, he didn't try to kiss me goodbye, even though my parents were in the other room.

CHAPTER 42

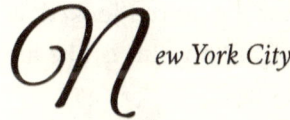 ew York City

* * *

DIANA and I left the office together. As the elevator doors opened on the ground floor, I asked her whether she wanted to grab dinner at a taqueria. It was almost six, and lunch had been a noodle bowl at my desk, which had left my stomach yearning for more by the middle of the afternoon. Now, I felt ready to faint from the gnawing in my stomach.

The place I suggested was only three blocks away, and now that we'd transitioned to daylight savings, it was a great time to walk. Rays of sunlight sliced down the sides of the high-rises, making it feel almost like mid-afternoon.

"I love daylight savings," Diana said. "It feels magical walking in the sunshine even though it's evening."

I wasn't sure about magic, but I agreed it was pretty awesome.

When we were seated at a table with a yellow oilcloth covering, plates of street tacos and rice and beans steaming in front of us, a large bowl of luscious-looking guacamole in the center, we clicked our glasses together—Diana's lemonade and my beer. I liked that about her. She didn't drink, but she never made a fuss about anyone else doing it—a beverage was just a beverage.

As we ate, we talked about work, mostly about our clients. We debated which clients in the current batch would be most helped by Trystan's coaching and who had revealed the most surprising facets in their photographs.

"It's kind of funny," Diana said. "Even though Stephanie's photos of Matt Sherpa were almost all non-starters, leaving us with about three usable images, I think it might be enough."

"Why?"

"I was really annoyed at first. I told Trystan he needed to go with her and make sure she did it right. But the more I looked at that one photograph...the shot of you hanging on him is like an entire novel when I look at the details of his face."

I laughed. "Really?"

"Matt had a huge issue with you being that close to him. He was embarrassed because he felt slightly aroused, but he was also terrified and a little angry, guilty and confused."

"It's kind of funny the way it worked out. I did that to shake things up. I had to get Stephanie to stop making it awkward and all about her. When I tried to make it sound alright to Trystan, I realized that preachers, or any man in power, get hit on a lot. If he wants a flock of five thousand people, he'd better—"

"A flock?" She took a sip of her lemonade.

"That's what they call it."

"Like they're sheep? That's kind of ironic."

I laughed and scooped a chip through the guacamole. "I never thought about that. I wonder if preachers, or their followers, realize what they're really saying about themselves."

"Anyway, it's a great photo."

I didn't know what else to say. I was so tired of Stephanie. I hated that I'd started wondering if I'd met my match. No matter what I did, she managed to twist the situation in her favor. As far as I could tell, it didn't seem like Trystan was going to take my advice.

"I told Trystan the photos didn't work," Diana said. "But the more I looked at that shot, I think I can give him the readout he needs for the next step in Matt's coaching. So thanks for making that happen." She took a bite of her fish taco. She seemed to be looking past me. Her gaze was fixed so intently on the window into the kitchen behind me, I wanted to turn to see what was so fascinating. But then she blinked and returned her attention to me. "I also told him to send you out alone, but he didn't like that."

I took a sip of beer and dug into my second taco.

"I'm worried he's going to destroy this company if he doesn't get a grip. She isn't working out in that role. She was an awesome admin, and he should just give her a raise and more responsibility, but she shouldn't be a photographer. She shouldn't be interacting with clients for anything but scheduling."

"Do you think he wants this venture to fail?" I asked.

"What makes you ask that?"

"I don't know. Just trying to figure out an explanation, I guess."

"I don't know what it is. It almost feels like she's blackmailing him." Diana laughed and drank more lemonade. "Who knows."

For a moment, I thought about telling her what I knew, but it wouldn't fix anything. It felt like the four of us were frozen in amber, like those insects from millions of years ago. We were all fully formed, but we couldn't even flicker an eyelash. And pretty soon, we might be dead, at least his company would be. "Do you think we're losing clients?"

"No. But if he keeps sending her, and if he sends her alone...I don't know. It will be a slow trickle that we won't notice at first. It's not as if people will leave just because she makes them uncomfortable, but it's sure going to make it almost impossible to do my job, and that will have a long-term effect. They might back out and not say why. And the referrals will go down."

After that, we started talking about going for another hike, but we didn't make plans. Then Diana told me about her sister, who was living in the UK for six months. She thought she might visit her since she'd never been.

"And you'll have a free place to stay," I said.

"Yes. But not just that. I miss her."

"Did she live in New York?"

"No. Chicago. But it feels different with her so far away."

I didn't see how that would matter, but she looked very serious, so I kept my mouth shut. For once.

After dinner, we parted at the subway entrance. The moment I was alone in my seat, I started thinking about my new apartment. The pictures I'd shown to Kent had been of our favorite, but someone had already rented it because Eileen hadn't said anything more about actually starting the process or suggested when she would be ready to move.

I pulled out my phone and looked at my last message from her. Three days ago. She hadn't mentioned the apartment or moving. I let the screen go dark and held the phone in my hand, staring at it as if that would bring a message from Eileen, suggesting we schedule another hunting expedition with the goal of filling out an application on the spot.

My train reached my stop, and the phone was still dark.

As I walked to my apartment, I thought about Kent. I was pretty sure he was going to keep some distance from me, but I still wanted to get my move underway. It wasn't just about escaping from his curiosity. After touring all those slick, modern apartments, everything at my place looked grungy in comparison. All the little flaws that I used to find charming now seemed like nothing but decades of neglect.

When I moved in, I'd scrubbed the place to the bone. I kept it as clean as was possible, but now the worn spots on the carpet and the way the windows stuck because of too many layers of paint, and the dark stain in the kitchen sink...there were a hundred little things like that. Before, I'd considered them the price of living in Manhattan, but now, I was beyond impatient.

Inside my apartment, I yanked off my shoes and walked to the bedroom, shedding the top I'd worn that day as I moved, tossing it onto the bed. I changed into a yoga outfit and did some stretches near the foot of my bed, thinking about how glorious it would be to have space to move between my bed and the window, thinking about a shower with thundering water pressure and a refrigerator that didn't have cracks in the produce drawer and scratches on the door.

I mixed a martini and settled on the couch. I put some music on my tablet and picked up my phone. Without considering how I should say what I wanted to say, I tapped out exactly what was in my head in a message to Eileen.

Alex: *I want to be in a new place by May 1. Are you coming or not?*

She answered right away, which was good. But what she said was not so good.

Eileen: *I have to talk to my mom.*

Alex: *What's taking so long?*

Eileen: *I need to find the right time. She's going to blame Ned and I don't want that to happen.*

Alex: *Who cares?*

Eileen: *I told you, I don't want to hurt her. And things aren't good with her right now.*

Alex: *Are you going to live with her forever?*

Eileen: *No.*

Alex: *Well I need to move. So let me know by the weekend if you're coming with me. We can check out some more places and put down a deposit.*

Eileen: *I don't know if I can.*

Alex: *No hard feelings, but I'm ready. So just let me know.*

She responded with a thumbs up, and I wondered what would

happen. I didn't want to cut her off. I would be able to find a much nicer apartment with a roommate. But I didn't want to wait for two years. I hoped she would figure out there was no good time. Stephanie was always going to be manipulative, hurt, blaming, and angry. Eileen just needed to be ready for that.

CHAPTER 43

*A*lexandra and Diana had already left for the day. It was twenty past six, and Trystan sat in his office, wondering when the hell Stephanie was going to leave. He was starting to feel like a prisoner in his office. He knew if he walked past her door, headed to the lobby, she would call out to him, and he'd be forced to talk to her for twenty minutes. Things between them had been awkward since her second poorly managed photoshoot with Matt Sherpa.

No one had given her feedback on her photographs, although she'd asked several times. He didn't even have to look at them. He'd watched Matt while she took the photographs and knew she hadn't captured anything useful. Now, they were at a standstill. He couldn't continue allowing her to work as a photographer, and he didn't have the stomach to fire her. She refused to take any guidance. She believed her work was brilliant. She'd even used that word.

He wanted her to go home. He didn't want to walk past her office, a fly thinking it could sweep past the sticky web of a spider.

The next time she asked about the pictures, she wasn't going to let him escape with a vague answer about not having gotten to it yet. It had been two days, and that excuse had worn itself to shreds. He opened a browser window and clicked to a news page. That should keep him occupied until seven. Surely by then—

Suddenly, Stephanie was standing in the doorway. Her hair was soft around her face, her eyes large and prominent with liner and shadows. She wore a white dress with a neckline that was not only slightly low for her, it was inappropriate for an office. Had she changed clothes? He tried to remember what she'd been wearing earlier. Had he actually seen her at all that day or only heard her voice in the breakroom while he tried to avoid the coming confrontation?

It disgusted him that he'd allowed her to gain such power over him. He felt like he'd become a completely different person over the past few months. The build-up of guilt, the confusing, combative relationship with her, and the sudden change in his relationship with his daughter...he sighed.

"Are you okay?" Stephanie's voice was filled with concern, but with her, you never knew when that would change. It could happen before he had time to blink, the seemingly normal personality replaced by a growling menace. He sometimes wondered if she had a split personality. It wasn't the kind of thing he was familiar with. He wondered whether he needed to enhance his education with some graduate psychology courses.

"I'm fine," he said.

"I don't think you are." She walked into the room, the white dress flowing seductively around her body. "Now that you and I are getting to know each other on a personal level, you should know you can share your feelings with me. I won't tell a soul. I'm good at keeping secrets."

He gave her a smile that probably looked more like a grimace. "Shouldn't you be heading home?"

"I was reviewing my photographs of Reverend Sherpa. I wanted to highlight the most telling ones for Diana. I have to say, it's pretty exciting working as the photographer. For one thing, I feel more like a key part of what we're doing here. But also, I never realized how fascinating it is to study people, to read their test results and essays and then examine their faces to intuit what's holding them back."

"You don't need to do it all," he said. "We each have a role. All we need from you is a broad selection of photographs in which the client is captured without consciously posing for the camera."

She nodded, her hair moving gently around her face. She stepped closer to his desk. Instead of pulling over one of the chairs, she remained standing. She placed her fingertips on the edge of the desk as if to balance herself. "You seem really tired. Kind of sad," she said.

"I'm not."

"If you're sure you're okay, then maybe I can talk to you about something I'm struggling with."

He sighed, hoping it wasn't loud enough for her to hear. What was wrong with him? He should act like a man. Stand up, get his laptop bag and coat and walk out the door. He owed her nothing. Why was he crumbling like this? Possibly his daughter's impending move so far away from the center of his life had caused him to lose his center.

Stephanie settled herself on the corner of his desk. She looked like she was striking a pose she'd adopted from a 1940s film. The flesh of her hip spilled over as if it wanted to creep toward him. He shivered.

"Are you sure you're okay?" she asked.

He nodded.

"This isn't very comfortable." She laughed and stood. She turned and glanced toward the guest chairs arranged near the small conference table. Her gaze traveled to the bookcase in the corner of the room. She walked toward it and picked up the photograph of his daughter. She studied it for several seconds. "She looks just like you."

"That's what I've been told."

She returned the photograph to the shelf. "You've had this same picture for a while. How old is she now?"

"Fifteen."

"Time flies." She walked back toward his desk, and despite her stated discomfort, seemed to think sitting on the corner was a better choice than pulling over one of the chairs. "Children are a treasure, but also enormously challenging, and sometimes heartbreaking."

"She's with her mother most of the time."

Stephanie nodded. "That makes sense. For a girl. But I'm sure it's hard on you, since you're such a devoted father."

"Am I? I'm not sure about that."

Stephanie's eyes looked glassy as if she were about to cry for his loss or his failure, he wasn't sure which it was.

"It's funny we're talking about your daughter. The thing I wanted to tell you about involves my own daughter. A parent's concern for their child never ends. Of course, you probably know that from your psychology background. From our clients."

He said nothing. Why was she doing this? He wanted her to leave. Now.

"My daughter is missing her father. I've only just realized the hole he left in her life is the reason she's choosing inappropriate men. So I hope you'll keep fighting for time in Katie's life, even if it's a lot of work."

"I'm not interested in discussing my daughter."

"I'm not trying to pry."

He felt something crack inside as if he were close to giving up...on everything. "Actually, I won't be seeing her much at all. I've lost a custody battle with my ex-wife, and she's moving to Singapore for a new job. My daughter can't wait to go. So..." He shrugged.

"Oh, that's awful. I'm so sorry."

"Maybe it's for the best."

"How could it be for the best? She needs you."

"She has her step-father."

She gave him a sharp look. "She still needs you."

"She knows I'm always a text or a phone call away."

"And she knows you can easily fly to Singapore, right? Or she can come home to visit. Maybe you'll end up seeing her more when she comes home to visit, she'll want to stay for a while, see her friends…"

He pushed his chair away from the desk and tapped his computer to lock the screen. "I don't know. I really don't want to talk about it."

"I'm here to listen," she said. "Whenever you do want to talk."

He gave her a nod and moved from behind his desk. "Are you leaving?"

"I need to finish a few things."

"Well, don't stay too late." He went to the door, and even though it wasn't necessary because there was a sensor, he pressed the switch to turn off the lights.

In the darkened room, Stephanie's white dress seemed to glow. Her hair was luminous, and her face was hidden in shadows. She moved toward him and stopped just a foot away. He could feel the heat of her body as his own turned cold. What the hell was she doing? He stepped quickly toward the doorway and out into the hall. "Good night, Stephanie."

"You seem like you're in a hurry." She followed him into the hallway.

"It's been a long day. And tomorrow night, I have a client dinner." Why was he explaining himself to her? "Okay, then. See you tomorrow." He strode toward the small lobby and across it to the outer door.

Stephanie called after him. "I thought you would want to see how well the photographs turned out."

"Not tonight." He pulled the door closed behind him to cut off any more chatter from her. As he stood waiting for the elevator, he couldn't stop glancing at the closed door, expecting her to come floating into the hallway in her white dress, riding the elevator down with him, and following him home.

In some ways, the whole thing, especially with that dress, made him feel it had all been a dream.

CHAPTER 44

Stephanie shivered during the entire subway ride home. The white dress she'd slipped into, standing in the women's restroom after Diana and Alex were gone for the day, had looked great on her. It was something she'd purchased without Eileen's input. A dress Eileen didn't even know she owned. It felt good to have some secrets from her daughter since Eileen was so very good at keeping them from her mother. It was petty and not how a parent should think about their child, but she couldn't help it. She was feeling petty. She felt helpless, and that always made her petty.

It seemed as if life had a way of flipping itself from side to side. When everything was going well between her and Eileen, her job had been demeaning and infuriating. Now that she was successful in her career, moving into a more important and interesting role, her relationship with Eileen was falling apart.

She gripped her arms, trying to keep warm. The coat was perfectly adequate over her normal workday clothes, but her bare legs and thin shoes, not to mention the exposed skin of her breastbone, made the coat feel like it was made of tissue paper.

Trystan had seemed to notice the dress, she'd felt him looking at her in a slightly different way, but he hadn't complimented her, and he'd gone out of his way to avoid touching her.

Trying to talk to him about his daughter, trying to connect as one parent to another, hadn't worked. She understood that was how men were a lot of the time. It took effort and patience to get them talking about their feelings. She should have thought more carefully about that. Especially her expectation that he would share feelings about his daughter. He was probably struggling with his ego, feeling like a failure as a father. She knew she could help him with that, but she needed to get him to open up. He probably just needed more time, another layer of trust.

Now that she knew he had a spiritual life, she could also encourage him to look for guidance in the Bible and in prayer. In the end, God was the one who needed to provide the help Trystan needed in knowing how to approach his relationship with his daughter.

The train came to her stop, and she stood, glad to be moving again, hoping for some warmth.

Her walk home was uneventful. Now that it was light in the evenings, she hadn't felt the need to carry the gun every day. Carrying it had made her nervous, irrationally afraid that she might be stopped on the train and her purse searched. She hadn't seen that creepy guy in over a week, which also made her feel more relaxed.

She slid her key into the door of her apartment. As the door swung open, she was assaulted by the odor of alcohol. She half expected to find Eileen and Ned partying it up. Instead. Eileen was sitting on the couch, a look of uninhibited rage on her face—her cheeks red, her eyes glassy and staring, and her body tense. Beside her on the end table was a glass of wine and the half-empty bottle.

Stephanie was surprised she could smell the alcohol so clearly. It was on Eileen's breath. She closed the door and glanced back at Eileen. "You look upset."

"I want to know what the hell this is."

Stephanie left her coat on, hoping Eileen wouldn't notice the dress. "What do you want to know?"

"This."

Stephanie looked at Eileen. Her head was lowered, her gaze fixed on the coffee table. Stephanie wasn't sure why she hadn't looked in that direction right away. She supposed the wine and Eileen's angry expression had caught her attention and held it.

Lying in the center of the coffee table was her gun. "What were you doing in my room?"

"You have no leg to stand on with that, Mother. After you went through my things."

"That's different. I'm the..." She'd meant to say the adult, but that didn't really fit anymore. "I'm your mother," she said. Her voice sounded limp, trying to placate.

"Why do you have a gun? And it's loaded! Or it was."

"Because we live in a dangerous city and—"

"New York is not dangerous," Eileen said.

"Don't be naive."

"Yes, there's crime, but...it doesn't matter. A gun is not the solution, even if we felt unsafe, which we don't."

Stephanie walked to the table. She picked up the gun as she passed by and continued to her bedroom.

"Where are you going?"

"I'm putting this back where it belongs. Under my bed, where it's close by, and where you should not be snooping." A moment later, she was in her bedroom. The box for the gun lay open on her bed. From the corner of her eye, she saw Eileen was standing in the doorway.

"I don't want it in the apartment," Eileen said.

"I'm the parent here. You don't get to tell me what to do."

"I thought we were both adults. Equals."

"We are."

"You're not acting like it. I don't want to live in a place that has

255

a loaded weapon. It's not safe. Don't you know that more people are killed by their own guns than the number who stop intruders?"

"This is a dangerous city, and I don't feel safe."

"We have a security lock on the main door. And locks on our apartment door. We don't need a gun."

"I do." Stephanie picked up the cartridge that Eileen had removed and tossed on the bed. She reloaded the gun and placed it gently in the box, closed the lid, and shoved the box under the bed.

"So now you can't sleep without a loaded gun under your bed?"

Stephanie slipped off her shoes and carried them to the closet.

"How is that going to help you?" Eileen's voice was shrill, possibly audible to people in the apartment next door. "You're not thinking clearly."

"Don't talk to me like that," Stephanie said.

"I don't understand what's wrong with you. You don't need a gun. It's not safe, and it scares me—trying to figure out why the idea even came to you."

Stephanie faced her daughter. "I met someone in my photography class who suggested it. She pointed out how women are always getting hassled and assaulted when they simply try to walk down the street."

"A gun won't stop rude comments. You don't need it. I want you to get rid of it."

"No."

"What if someone did break in here? You would never get to it in time."

"I'm more worried about creepy men lurking in alleys."

"Oh, come on. There aren't any creepy men lurking anywhere near our building."

"A man was bothering me, asking me to light his cigarette, and then he followed me. He was making comments."

"Where was this? When?"

"Just two blocks from home. A few weeks ago."

"What kind of comments?"

"I don't want to get into it. He scared me."

"So you're going to carry a gun every time you walk home from the subway? Why didn't you have it with you today if it's so important for protecting your life?"

"It's also for peace of mind. I don't like feeling that a stranger is in control of how I feel, of my security."

"Then why didn't you have it with you?"

"With daylight savings time…I only feel unsafe in the dark."

"You sound crazy, do you know that?"

"I'm not crazy, and it's cruel of you to say it."

"No one carries a gun around Manhattan."

"Tamara does. And she said a lot of women she knows have a gun in their purse."

Eileen laughed. "That's sick. Do they think we live in the wild west?"

Stephanie shrugged. "You should try it. You might be surprised. It really made me feel like I had the upper hand, for once."

"I'm not afraid."

Stephanie put her hands on her hips. She stared hard at Eileen's mocking face. "Well, maybe you should be. There are a lot of not very nice people in the world."

Eileen backed into the hallway. She reached for the doorknob and began pulling the door closed. "You've lost your mind. I want you to get rid of that gun. I'm serious about not living in a house with a loaded weapon. It's not safe. It destroys *my* peace of mind."

"Maybe I should invite Tamara over for dinner. She can explain how willfully ignorant you're being."

"No thanks. I'm going to spend the night at Ned's. I can't sleep, knowing it's there. When I come back tomorrow, it needs to be gone." She pulled the door closed with too much force, and the wall trembled.

It was comforting to see that brief shiver of an inanimate object. It made Stephanie feel less alone as if the angels of God were trembling beside her, feeling her fear.

CHAPTER 45

 ortland, Oregon

* * *

ALTHOUGH BRADY HAD LEFT AS FAST as he could get out the door
after being center-stage with my parents, he was still very much
into me at school. Two days later, he cornered me beside my open
locker, pressing me up against the metal doors surrounding me.
"We have to figure out something." He kissed my neck.

This kind of thing wasn't allowed at school. The only affection
allowed was holding hands in the hallways. Making out got you
detention. They were very specific about what kind of touching
was considered an infraction—sliding hands inside of clothing,
making *lewd* gestures, sticking out your tongue and wiggling it, air
kisses...really, anything you could imagine that teenagers might
do when they're around someone they're going out with or are
hoping to hook up with.

"I don't know what we can do," I said.

He kissed me, sliding his tongue into my mouth. This was very
unlike him, at school. Usually, he was worried about getting

caught, afraid it would affect his status on the football team, which was often used as a very effective punishment for kids who were into sports.

He pulled away. "Think of something. I'm dying here."

"So am I."

"You're smart. You're much better than I am at sneaking around, especially since you have to work a lot harder at it."

He was right about that, but I'd spent a lot of time trying to come up with solutions to the hovering presence of my mother, and my mind remained blank. She was always popping up. And the stick she was using was a powerful one—my father.

Even though Brady had endured dinner with my father, even though he'd heard some of my stories, he really had no clue what the man was like. And it seriously would not have surprised me if my father decided to lock me in the house until I was eighteen. I couldn't risk that.

I think my mother worried about that too because it was unusual for her not to tell him what I'd done. She'd kept secrets once or twice before, but it wasn't the norm. In this case, she'd never come back to me with her final decision. But I sensed in the way she looked at me, and her veiled threats, that she'd decided not to tell him, for the time being.

"I have to be careful," I said.

"You should report them for child abuse."

I laughed. "I don't think getting grounded or being given curfews are considered child abuse."

"What about how she won't let you even walk home from school or take the carpool?"

"It's not child abuse, and you know it." I kissed his jaw.

He put up his hand. "Don't touch me. Until you figure this out, I'll have to institute a hands-off policy."

I poked him in the stomach. "What was that kiss about?"

"Come on," he said. "There has to be something we can do."

We started walking toward our third-period classes. My mind

spun, as it had since the door closed behind him when he left our house that night, but still nothing came to me.

"We can try cutting school for the whole afternoon and get you back here before the end of the day."

"That won't work. She's turned my teachers into spies."

He sighed.

As I sat in my English Lit class, I didn't hear a single word of the discussion of *Catch-22*. I kept trying to look at my daily schedule as if it were a diamond I was holding up to the light, turning it around and around, looking for the perfect alignment of light and stone to create a red glow.

Before I could come up with a brilliant plan, my mother threw another curveball. "Why don't you invite Brady to dinner again."

I stared at her, trying to decide what to say. I had assumed she was under the impression we'd broken up. I hadn't mentioned him at all, and I was pretty sure her spies on the high school faculty hadn't seen us because we'd been very careful there as well, aside from that one incident near my locker.

"Don't stare like that," she said. "It makes you look stupid."

"I'm not sure..."

She waited. She stared at me, which made me want to advise her not to look stupid, but I was too busy deciding what I wanted to say. Finally, after a long pause filled with too much staring, I said, "I don't think we'll be together much longer."

Her eyes nearly bulged out of her head. "But you gave your body to him! You need to make it work."

"Make it work?"

"In God's eyes, the two of you are married."

It shouldn't have been a surprise to hear this. I knew our church believed this, I knew my parents believed this, but I was unsettled to hear it applied directly to me.

"You should invite him over. If you don't feel comfortable with your father talking to him yet, invite him over after school. I can get to know him in a more casual way." She smiled as if this solved everything.

"I'll see." I slipped out of the room and ran up the stairs. As I sat at my desk, staring out at the inviting branches of the oak tree, I hoped she might forget about it. I would flood her ears with information about my schoolwork, stories and gossip from youth group, anything I could think of. Maybe, there was a slim chance she might forget. But I knew I was ridiculous in my hope. My mother would never forget the boy who stole my most valuable asset.

She continued to nag me to invite him over, and I continued to put her off.

About three weeks later, I came out to the parking lot after school. My mother was in the car, as usual. I opened the passenger door, and there was Brady sitting in the back seat. He gave me an awkward grin.

"Look who I found!" My mother's voice was shrill and triumphant as if she'd captured a leprechaun.

"Hi." I slid into the car and buckled my belt.

The drive home was filled with my mother's chatter. At the kitchen table, she unfurled an endless stream of questions for Brady while we ate oatmeal cookies and drank hot chocolate.

When the cookies were gone and the mugs empty, Brady stood up. "I should head out."

"I'll drive you back to your car." She looked at me. "Are you coming?"

Of course I was going. I needed to know what else she would say to him.

During the drive back to the parking lot, she talked to Brady as if she were giving a mini-sermon, perfectly designed for the travel time from home to school. She told him about god's view of marriage and the sanctity of the human body. She told him we were married in god's eyes but that we needed to cool off and wait until we were older to make it legal with the government. It was a believer's duty to follow all laws and government regulations, she said. Then she said she liked him, and my father thought he was alright, but it might take some time to win him over. She said it would be really helpful if he started attending our church. That would gain my father's approval more quickly than anything else. Once he was established at our church and baptized, he should come to dinner once a week.

When we pulled up beside his car, Brady, who hadn't said more than two words, rocketed out of the back seat, waving at me as he hurried to his car. Two days later, he broke up with me. It was probably for the best.

My mother was devastated. She never forgot him. Even though I was frustrated with the way she'd treated him, I never forgot that she kept my secret from my father. It was the first thing I thought about when my father called to tell me she'd gone to paradise. I sure hoped so. She deserved it.

 *ew York City*

* * *

AFTER HEARING Eileen leave the apartment, Stephanie stripped off all her clothes, leaving the white dress and her underwear in a heap beside the bed. She slid between the sheets, feeling very wicked and very free with the cotton caressing her bare skin. She'd never slept naked, and she wasn't sure what had made her decide to do so now. It felt natural—wanting to be rid of the dress because it reminded her of how Trystan had ignored her, and not wanting to spend another minute on her feet, not wanting to go to the trouble of brushing her teeth and putting on a nightshirt and all the others things she'd done for more nights than she could possibly count. The days of following the identical routine stretched behind her in an endless stream of sameness and lost time. Her life was sliding through her fingers, and nothing was turning out as she'd imagined it would.

No one understood her. No one cared about her feelings. No one respected her career. And no man had ever loved her body.

She was probably months, maybe even weeks, from passing the point of no return, heading toward that place where she would be less desirable with every passing day. Realistically, she was already there and had been for years, but this was different. Lately, the decay had become more obvious.

She turned onto her side. She shouldn't be having these thoughts. It was pure lust. Ever since her shopping trip with Eileen, since she'd begun to put effort into making herself look good, she'd also begun desiring more from life. But instead of getting more, she felt that the money spent and the daily effort that went into her appearance were all for nothing. That realization sharpened her sense of loss until it was a constant, driving pain.

She turned off the bedside light and closed her eyes. The weight and coolness of the sheets felt sensuous on her skin. She hadn't experienced something like that for a very long time, probably never. It was different from the shivering cold of being on the subway in a flimsy dress. This was a coolness that relieved the desire burning in her blood and bones.

What would it be like to have a good man? Not like that awful man who used her as a study object, a science project for social behavior. But a really *good* man. A truly Godly man. A man like Trystan.

How had she never realized he believed in God? All these years she'd worked with him, and he'd never said a word. Now, here he was talking about the Bible and considering what kind of behavior God wanted from his creatures. Maybe facing the loss of his daughter made him more willing to open up. Earlier, she'd been frustrated he hadn't shared enough of his feelings, but maybe he'd shared far more than he had with anyone else. The rest would come in time.

She took a deep breath and let her body sink into the comfort of the mattress.

She pictured the inside of her church, the simple altar decorated with cascades of white flowers. She didn't care what it cost. Besides, Eileen had incredible amounts of money now, and she knew Eileen would gladly give all she could to provide a beautiful wedding for her mother. A second chance at love, and life.

Behind her eyelids, Trystan appeared in a charcoal gray tuxedo. He was gazing at her with such unfiltered adoration it made her gasp.

She placed her hands on her breasts and allowed her mind to recall the notes of the wedding march. She saw herself in a simple white gown, not unlike the dress she'd worn that day, but floor-length. In her arms was a spray of long-stemmed white roses.

As she walked toward Trystan, the faces of the attendants and the preacher faded and disappeared. Only Trystan's face was sharp and clear inside her daydream. She moved slowly, almost gliding, enjoying his smile as it grew broader. A look of desire and love filled his eyes. When she reached the altar steps, he took her arm. He moved close to her side until their hips were touching. He leaned down and kissed her, his lips soft and warm on hers. A gentle, perfect kiss. Not without passion, but subdued and appropriate for public display.

Together they walked up the steps toward the minister.

The preacher spoke to them about the true meaning of love, then read the words of the traditional marriage ceremony. When he was finished, they exchanged simple gold bands. They kissed, more deeply this time, and then glided back down the aisle, past their friends and family, hardly recognizing a single face as they walked out into their future.

Stephanie put her hands to her face. It was wet with tears. She wiped at her eyes, then gently patted the tender skin beneath them. She blinked hard and sat up. It was a wonderful daydream. Who knew what was going to happen. Life could be very surprising. It hadn't been all that surprising for her, but it *could* be. God was opening Trystan's heart to her—showing him they had the most important thing of all—a spiritual foundation. It was really the only thing that mattered in a marriage.

She could trust that God was going to put that into Trystan's heart, if He hadn't already. But at the same time, it wouldn't hurt to give a little nudge. She needed to get him out of the office again, away from Alex, that was for sure. It was almost as if Alex poisoned the air they breathed in their suite of offices, making it impossible for Trystan to think straight. Maybe that's why he'd never shared his faith with Stephanie. It was telling that the first time he'd mentioned it was when they were eating dinner together, far from the office, hidden from Alexandra.

She would invite him to dinner at her apartment. It was more intimate than a restaurant. If Eileen was out, and she was most of the time now, they could talk freely. She would make a nice dessert, so he felt welcome to linger. She might even buy some of that scotch he liked to drink. She could offer him an after-dinner drink, and then he would relax and settle into her couch, and they could really get to know each other on a serious level.

All she needed to figure out was a solid, plausible reason for the invitation, something that would overcome his concerns about mixing his personal life with the professional side. It was possible she was going to have to look for another job very soon. Although sometimes husbands and wives worked together. They ran small businesses together, working side-by-side, deepening their connection...so it might work. She'd have to take that part one step at a time.

CHAPTER 47

The apartment felt hollow. Eileen had left her bedroom door open when she left, which was not her usual habit. This made Stephanie feel as if Eileen was welcoming her mother to snoop to her heart's content, having taken anything she didn't want discovered to that man's apartment. Instead, Stephanie pulled the door closed and went to the kitchen to make a pot of coffee.

She was going to be late for work. She'd overslept, much of the night filled with pleasant dreams of married life. Then, a single nightmare intruded, wiping out the beautiful dreams and waking her at two in the morning, shaking and cold. Ashamed that she'd slept naked, she'd slithered out of bed and pulled on a nightshirt. After that, it was difficult to fall back to sleep. She'd twisted her sheets into a coil, moving around for another hour or so, trying to find a position that would allow her to settle back into unconsciousness.

Where was Eileen? Didn't she need to come home to get ready for work?

The fight with her daughter had created the dream-piercing nightmare that she couldn't recall in detail, only the feeling of it.

Trying to think of words that might patch things up between them was what had kept her awake. Finally, she'd worked out what she wanted to say, and she'd assumed they would have a few minutes before they both left for work. It had never occurred to her that Eileen might not only sleep in that man's bed, but that she would take all of her things and dress for work in his...in that moment, she realized she didn't even know where he lived.

She'd drunk two cups of coffee, eaten a scrambled egg with chopped tomato, and taken her shower, and still, Eileen wasn't home. She picked up her phone and opened the text window. Her finger was poised above the glass as she tried to think about what she would write.

What if Eileen was still asleep? What if they were...

She dropped the phone into her purse and grabbed her coat. Maybe having a day to let things settle out would be good. She could distract herself with work. During the ride home, she could refine what she wanted to say.

But that evening, when she unlocked the door, the apartment was gloomy with late afternoon light. She knew, without calling her name, that Eileen wasn't there. She went to Eileen's bedroom. The door stood open, the room untouched since the night before.

She heated frozen chicken enchiladas and allowed herself a small glass of wine. Too keyed up to read or pray, which probably would have been the best thing to do, she went into her bedroom and got her gun out from under the bed. She took it out of the box and held it, feeling the weight in her hand.

Why was Eileen so angry with her for buying it? Didn't she want her mother to feel safe? She'd made such a big deal out of it. She'd acted as if Stephanie was stupid, unable to care for it responsibly. She wondered if she should have hidden it better. She raised the gun, holding it in her right hand as the instructor had shown her. She aimed it at the window and wondered what it would feel like to have the weapon explode in her hand, to see a bullet rocket out, to watch it pierce the chest or skull of a human being. It was too horrible to think about, but it still made her feel like her life was in her own hands. No one could hurt her. Ever.

She put the gun back into the box and went into the living room. She turned on the TV and poured a bit more wine into her glass. Even though it was Friday night, she was certain Eileen would be home any minute. Surely Eileen wanted to smooth things out between them as badly as Stephanie did. Surely the disagreement had nagged at her, disrupting her sleep and interfering with her focus at work, making her heart tight with sorrow.

It was almost eight-thirty when she finally heard a key in the lock. She turned off the TV and swallowed the rest of her wine.

Eileen was wearing jeans, a hoodie, and running shoes. So... she'd taken more than her work clothes to Ned's place. In fact, there was something about her clothing and her movements that suggested she was just dropping by, not planning to stay.

Stephanie smiled at her. She loved her daughter with an intensity that sometimes felt like pain. It was impossible for Eileen to understand that kind of love. With any luck, she might someday, but not now.

"Hey," Eileen said.

"It's good to see you." Stephanie waited for Eileen to apologize. There were definitely more things on Eileen's side that needed apologies. And really, Stephanie hadn't done anything wrong at all. It was legal to own a gun, and it was a sensible thing to have in the apartment of two women.

Eileen moved toward the couch. "Is it gone?"

"No."

"I was serious. I can't stay here with it in the apartment. So I guess I'll pack a few more things and hang out at Ned's until you have a chance to get rid of it."

Stephanie patted the couch beside her. "Let's have a good mother-daughter talk. We can work this out."

"There's nothing to talk about or work out. I already told you my views and aren't going to change."

Stephanie picked up her wineglass. She remembered it was empty and placed it back on the table. "What do you think is going to happen? It has a safety lock. There are no small children around..."

"I think if someone broke into the apartment, which is so remote, I can't even guess at the odds, he would overpower you and take the gun. If you did manage to get a shot off and injured him or even just scared him, he might kill you. Just for spite."

"That man who wanted me to light his cigarette scared me. He followed me."

"There are people all over the streets and—"

"There wasn't another soul. I was alone, except for cars going by, and no one was looking at me. It was terrifying. It's cruel to pretend my feelings don't matter."

"I didn't pretend your feelings don't matter. But I don't want you to get into an argument with me and end up shooting me."

A shriek escaped from Stephanie, something instinctive that she hadn't seen coming. She felt as if Eileen had smacked her face. "That would never, ever happen. Ever."

"We lose our tempers. Things happen."

"It makes me physically ill that you would think that."

"I want you to get rid of the gun."

Stephanie sighed. Eileen was stubborn. It was a good trait in many ways. She was strong. If she would attend church more frequently, at all, really, it would be a good quality to have for telling people the truth about God's plans for the world. "What am I supposed to do? To protect myself?"

"I thought God was watching over you."

"That's not a very nice thing to say."

"But that's what you believe, isn't it?"

Eileen was right. Stephanie hated to admit it, but what did God think of her gun? Had she even asked? She'd been seduced by the things Tamara had said, captivated by the idea of feeling powerful. Still, there were weapons in the Bible—swords, spears. It wasn't as if there wasn't a place in the world for weapons. Until heaven triumphed over hell, there would be wars and battles. There were evil people all around.

"What good does it do you if some guy wants a cigarette lit and hassles you a bit? The gun is in a box under your bed."

"I told you, I carried it with me when it was dark. But now..." She turned her head slightly, not wanting to meet Eileen's gaze. Eileen was right about that too. What good was it doing her under the bed? She'd bought the smallest one they had so it would be easy to carry in her purse.

"Well, I don't want it here. Period." Eileen walked out of the room.

Stephanie went to the kitchen and poured a splash of wine into her glass. She took a sip. Was it wrong to lie to your daughter? Sometimes, not being entirely truthful was necessary. Only God had a right to know all the secrets of her heart. She didn't owe her daughter an explanation. She could keep the gun in her purse. If there were an intruder, that would be better anyway.

She poured the wine down the drain. She went to Eileen's door and knocked.

When Eileen opened the door, Stephanie gave her a warm, motherly smile. "I'm sorry. I didn't mean to frighten you and—"

"It's not about being frightened. It's—"

"As I said, I'm sorry. And I'll get the gun out of here. Tomorrow after work."

Eileen smiled. She gave her mother a hug. "Thank you. And thank you for respecting me, for treating me like an adult with an equal voice here."

Stephanie nodded. "Of course. I raised an amazing woman."

Eileen laughed, but then she closed her door, and Stephanie didn't speak to her or hear a sound from the bedroom for the rest of the evening.

CHAPTER 48

*A*fter I gave Eileen her ultimatum for finding an apartment, things moved fast. A few days later, she texted me that she'd told her mother she was moving out but gave no details. Even when we met for coffee to strategize our hunting expedition, she didn't say much except that Stephanie understood reality, and she'd promised she wasn't going to let the move destroy their relationship.

"To be honest, I think she was so relieved I'm not moving in with Ned, it helped her accept that I need my own place."

"Does she know you're living with me?"

"Please don't turn that into an issue."

"I'm not. I'm just asking. I do work with her, remember. It might come up."

"She doesn't know yet. One thing at a time."

I took a sip of my coffee. I wasn't going to do anything to undermine Eileen, so I would keep my mouth shut at work. I was sure Stephanie would make me aware the moment she found out.

We identified three apartments, including one of the previous ones we'd visited, and figured that was enough. "Every place has its good points," Eileen said. "Looking at more than a few just makes the decision more complicated."

I agreed.

By lunchtime, we were finished checking out all three. We'd decided on the Riverside Boulevard place with a view of the Hudson.

As we ate angel hair pasta, with three kinds of mushrooms in a light, creamy sauce and sipped wine, I finally hinted to Eileen that there were things she didn't know about me.

I didn't tell her I'd tried to fly under the radar as much as was possible on our tiny, wired planet, to use cash, to keep my life from being discoverable on the internet as much as possible. What I did tell her was that I had an angry ex-boyfriend who couldn't know where I lived. So far, I'd *done a good job keeping ahead of him.* Then I asked her to consider my need to stay hidden, and to be responsible for the paperwork and the background check, to put her name on the lease. I would pay her rent every month, in cash, more than half, to compensate for asking her to be the one with her name all over everything.

She stared at me as if I'd told her I'd found a horn growing just above my hairline, and soon, I would be a unicorn. "Why didn't you mention it before?"

"It's kind of embarrassing," I said.

She frowned. "You never get embarrassed. And besides, why should *you* be embarrassed because he's an abusive creep?"

I shrugged. "I just don't like talking about the negative parts of my life."

She nodded. "I get that. I'm the same way, more or less."

I smiled. "So it's okay, then?"

"You sound different."

I realized I was trying too hard to be coy, to sound meek and in need of help. That happened every so often. I forgot to align the person people knew with the story I was using to get myself into the best possible position. "Maybe he makes me feel like a child, so that part of me comes out."

"Oh, Alex. That's awful. I'm so sorry."

"No worries," I said.

"And you absolutely are not paying more than half. It's not a problem to have my name on the lease."

It took a few weeks for everything to get worked out. During that time, I started boxing up the few possessions I had—mostly clothes and makeup and my pitiful supply of dishes. I told the building manager I would be leaving. He gave me a triumphant grin. I could see him fantasizing about a tenant he could more easily control. I saw him thinking about the increase in rent and how that would make him look like a good manager in the eyes of the owner.

During that time, I went to work and came home, went running and out to eat, met with Eileen and shopped, walking slowly up or down the stairs every time, but I never saw Kent.

Moving day arrived like a holiday gift. Two very good-looking students from NYU were loading my boxes and few pieces of furniture into a small truck, muscles rippling in their forearms and beneath tight T-shirts. After my stuff was loaded, they would be stopping by Eileen's to add her clothes to the mix. She was leaving her furniture behind. It reminded her of being a child, so she didn't want any of it.

All new. That was her plan. I couldn't wait to go shopping together. She'd told me to get rid of my grubby kitchen table and chairs. She would buy something nicer. Something that *did justice* to the food we'd be cooking. She poked me with her elbow when she said this, making me focus even more on the positive aspects of this new venture.

Stephanie was off at a weekend church retreat, and I wondered if Eileen had arranged our move-in date based on that.

By midnight on Saturday, we were sitting on my old couch in the new living room, something else Eileen had now decreed had to go. We were sipping martinis and gazing out through the large picture window at the lights of the city.

Boxes were stacked around us. It amazed me that there were so many boxes. How had I started to accumulate so much stuff? I'd started my thirties wanting to live lightly, to not have credit cards or a cell phone, to not have a bunch of stuff I needed to drag behind me like a dead limb if I needed to move quickly.

It made me a little anxious, thinking about my avocation and wondering how that was going to work out with Eileen knowing my comings and goings, and with the feeling of being somewhat trapped by all this stuff. Of course, truthfully, I was only trapped if I thought I was trapped. There was no reason I couldn't walk away from it all. It represented a decent amount of money, but there was always more money for anyone willing to be creative and take chances.

In the end, my freedom was what mattered. Above everything. So if I got myself into a situation that demanded I leave New York, or even the United States, I would be okay starting over. It can be fun—buying new things, viewing possessions and money as things that simply flow in and out of your life, that don't need to be hoarded. It was freeing to not view it as *wasting* money.

We toasted our new apartment.

"And a new roommate," Eileen added. We clicked our glasses together again, watching the clear liquid wobble slightly.

We both took a sip, smiling at the other over the rim of the glass.

She put down her glass. "I feel like an adult for the first time in my life."

I smiled.

"That sounds insane, I know. And a little embarrassing." She turned her head, looking away from me. "I mean, what does it say about me that I'm halfway through my twenties, and I feel like a college kid?"

"Everyone has their own path."

She laughed. "Aren't you philosophical?"

I sipped my drink.

"It feels really good to be here. I love my mom, but she's…" She sighed. She poked at her olives with her finger, then licked it. "She's oppressive. And exhausting. And so controlling." She laughed. "I feel like I can relax for the first time in…maybe in forever. I have you to thank for that."

"No worries."

"Thanks for pushing me out. You did what she should have done—pushed me out of the nest."

I hoped she didn't think of me in any maternal capacity. I shivered.

I thought about Kent, the one who had given *me* a very firm shove to get moving. I also wondered if Victoria was still living in New York or if he'd been seeing ghosts.

Like Eileen, I felt as if I could relax. The tension slid out of my shoulders. I was eager to stretch out in my large bedroom, to eat good food at a nice table, and to look out at that terrific view. I also thought it was good that I no longer had the roof garden, luring me up there to enjoy a cigarette on a warm summer evening.

Everything about this change looked promising.

CHAPTER 49

*S*tephanie stood at the living room window and stared at the street below. She had a feeling that man might come creeping by, having followed her home after all, waiting all these weeks until she let down her guard. She wouldn't put it past him. His whole purpose was to terrify her, and then when she was weak and trembling, he would move in for the attack. Why had she believed he wouldn't bother her again? She was naïve. How, at her age, could she still be so naïve?

Her gun lay on the table beside her. She wanted to touch the beautifully crafted weapon, but gazing at it was almost as satisfying, for now. In some ways, it was all she had left. God had certainly abandoned her.

She forced herself to turn away from the gun. She had to keep her attention focused on what lay beyond the window. Turning to look at the empty rooms behind her was unbearable. Her empty, silent apartment. Eileen was gone, her bedroom stripped of all but the bed, dresser, and bookcase. No more framed photographs cluttering the walls, no scarves draped over the mirror. The bathroom was equally empty. There was plenty of room now for Stephanie's abundant supply of cosmetics.

The devastation of it all, the removal of Eileen's spirit and possessions, was so vast she couldn't even cry. All she could do was stare out that window.

At work these past few days, she'd walked and talked like a being who no longer possessed a soul. She wasn't even aware of what she said, even though she heard her voice speaking. She found it even more difficult to comprehend what others were saying to her. Oddly enough, no one seemed to notice. They acted as if she were her normal self, as if her words made sense.

Everyone would say it was natural, even a good thing, for a girl in her mid-twenties to move out into her own apartment. But they didn't know Eileen. She wasn't finished. That had been proven when she decided to hook up with that old man, unaware she was looking for a father and then sharing a bed with him. It was disgusting and sad and terrifying. Eileen needed to be home with her mother so that Stephanie could complete the job of raising a Godly and admirable young woman. If Eileen went out into the world half-finished, what did that say about the most important purpose of Stephanie's life? She'd failed. There was no other word for it.

She pressed her forehead against the glass. A couple passed by, their arms wrapped around each other's waists. A moment or two later, a mother pushing a stroller with a shrieking toddler came into view. Stephanie could see the child's contorted face but couldn't hear its screams with the window closed. She felt as if she were that child, being pushed around without any ability to take control of her own life. Screaming into the void that God had abandoned her.

The women in her Bible study group would accuse her of catastrophic thinking. They would tell her to shift her thoughts to something more pleasant. They would tell her she'd done her best with Eileen, and now she had to let go. They would tell her so many things, all smug experts on every part of life. They were so sure in their opinions, they seemed to believe that when they opened their mouths, the words of God were flowing from their slick, painted lips.

She picked up her gun and held it to her chest. The cold weight of it was comforting. Maybe she should turn it on herself. But then, they would win. And what if God punished her for taking her life? Her life belonged to Him, and she had no right to decide when it was over. Of course, the same could be said for shooting another human being. But if someone threatened her, that would be completely different. That was why she owned the gun. It was only for protection.

Placing it on the table again, she closed her eyes and tried to picture Eileen as a little girl. It was so difficult. The memories were blurry and fading fast. She had bits and pieces as if scraps of Eileen's life were drifting in the air around her, and her own life was scattered across the ground, pieces she couldn't put back together.

She'd taken Eileen to church every week of her life. She'd registered her for Vacation Bible School and sent her to summer camps. She'd done everything she could think of to make sure the love of God was nurtured in her daughter's heart. But she'd been blind. She hadn't realized that Eileen needed her father. Stephanie had assumed since Eileen said next to nothing about him that the hole inside her didn't exist. It never occurred to her it was there all the time, growing wider and deeper every day.

And now, Eileen was out looking to fill that space, but she hadn't turned to God in her need. Stephanie had failed on both fronts. She hadn't carried her daughter across the finish line into a life of faith, and she hadn't provided her with a father.

Still, the tears didn't come. That was probably a good thing. If they came, they might not ever stop.

It was time to make dinner, but she had no desire for food. She'd barely finished her apple at lunch. She'd had a cup of coffee in the afternoon, thinking it would make her hungry, but it hadn't. Now, the clock ticked toward seven.

Eating wasn't really the issue. It was the thought of walking into the kitchen, of thinking about food for one person. For the rest of her life, there would be a single plate on the table, one fork, one knife, one glass. It would be days before she could run the dishwasher with her pitiful contributions.

The other thing Eileen hadn't considered in her selfish desire to flee with her four million dollars was that Stephanie was not a rich woman. She wasn't even a comfortably situated one. And now, she would be paying the rent on her own. It horrified her to think she might need to find a roommate. How utterly embarrassing and shameful to go looking for a roommate at her age. How had she gotten so far off the track of her life to be standing in this apartment alone?

Wasn't God supposed to guide and take care of her? She used to feel so confident that He was speaking to her, that the things she said and did came from the awareness of His hand upon her shoulder. Now, she had no idea what she was supposed to do. When she prayed, she had trouble forming the words because her mind was so filled with all the things that were wrong—in her home, her job, and every single thought and action on her way to this moment in time.

It was dark when she turned away from the window. She'd thought her legs would get tired, and she would be content to settle on the couch with a sandwich. She'd thought she would feel the need to lose herself in mindless TV, allowing it to flood her brain with enough voices and storylines and news that the other thoughts would be shoved to the side.

She closed the blinds. She picked up her gun and carried it into the kitchen. She opened the refrigerator door and looked inside, hardly seeing what was there. After several minutes, she closed it again. She didn't even feel like a glass of wine. Something drastic was required, or she would dissolve into nothing.

The first thought that came to mind was that she should

rescue Eileen from her new apartment. But of course, that would be impossible. Eileen didn't want to be rescued.

What she really needed was a life of her own. Stephanie didn't have a place where she fit in the world. At her Bible study group, most of the others were married, and she'd never grown as close to the other women as she'd hoped. Many of them had small children. At work, she was second place to a wicked, conniving demon. She had no one. She'd thought she had Eileen, but she hadn't.

If there was a man who loved her, if she had someone she could talk to every night before she fell asleep, then all of these other problems might not cause so much pain. Even better, they might grow smaller. She would have someone cheering her on, someone to bounce ideas and feelings off of. At night, she would fall asleep in the comfort of another's arms, and she would wake in the morning excited for their shared life. She would be loved.

She couldn't form the thought that God wasn't enough, but that's what was lurking beneath this desire. Hadn't He designed each human being to need and desire a mate? He'd created women for that very purpose to begin with, and that's why Stephanie felt lost in the world. She'd been created to be a helpmate.

She opened the fridge door again, pulled out the bottle of wine, and filled a glass. She sipped her wine while she boiled water and poured it over a cup full of dried noodles and vegetables. She carried her dinner into the bedroom and went to the desk in the corner. She sat in front of her computer, placed her meal to the side, and opened a web browser. She posed a question to all the minds connected through that vast web—*How do you get a man to fall in love with you?*

CHAPTER 50

*I*t had been nearly a month since Stephanie made that weird appearance in Trystan's office, wearing a white dress that looked like it belonged at a summer cocktail party. During the intervening time, he'd dithered and dragged his feet and agonized and worried. And he'd done nothing. During that time, Stephanie had managed to provide a flood of photographs that didn't meet the requirements. He was quite sure that Devon Major, a musician, had changed his mind about working with them because of how the photography session with Stephanie had gone.

The choice was Stephanie or his company. He'd known that for quite some time, but he'd remained frozen.

He owed her nothing. Now that he was seeing things more clearly, his mind unclouded by the arguments and discussions about what was best for his daughter, he realized that it didn't matter that he'd had that night with Eileen. His frustrations with his ex-wife, his grief over the realization that his daughter was moving to the other side of the world, and worse, that she wanted to go, had become less violent. He hadn't realized how much all of that had affected him.

Now that his mind was starting to clear, he knew—what could it possibly matter if Stephanie found out? It wasn't as if she had some hold over him. All the assumed obligation had been in his own mind. He'd been kind and considerate of her feelings, but running a business couldn't always be done with kindness. Kindness would not make him a success, a provocateur admired and sought after by the most successful and powerful people in New York.

He was a fool if he kept Stephanie on as a photographer for one moment longer.

He wasn't going to wait for the perfect timing or worry about her reaction. He had to be bold and quick about this. The moment he saw her, he would ask her to come into his office.

As it turned out, they saw each other first in the break room. Diana was making coffee, and Stephanie was washing the mugs that no one had bothered to wash the Friday before. Immediately, he was thrown off balance. He couldn't quickly ask her to come to his office when she was elbows-deep in hot, sudsy water.

He chatted with Diana, filled the clean mug Stephanie handed to him, and finally managed to focus his attention on his mission. "Stephanie, are you free to meet in my office for a few minutes?"

She smiled. Her cheeks turned pink. She dried her hands and ran her fingers through her hair. "I'd love to."

He wanted to smack her. The thought shocked him. Never in his life had he thought of hitting a woman. He hadn't thought of hitting another human being at all since he was fourteen years old. What was wrong with him? He felt like he'd turned into a different person, and he didn't recognize this guy.

He walked out of the break room without acknowledging her strange, off-key response. *Don't react*, he told himself. *Don't react. Provide the information—You aren't working out as a photographer. You can continue managing the scheduling and other office tasks, but photography is out.*

Don't react to her comments, don't respond to her expressions or her outbursts; and be clear. Don't hedge and try to soften the blow. There was no softening it.

When Stephanie followed him into his office, he reached around her and closed the door. It seemed as if she leaned into him, but they hadn't touched. It must have been his imagination, his out-of-control, disturbed imagination. He went to his desk and sat down. "Please have a seat."

She gave him a coy smile. "I thought you'd pull out the chair for me."

He stared at her.

Still smiling, she walked sideways to the table, grabbed the back of a chair, and dragged it over to face his desk. She was a little rough with it, and he cringed, thinking of the microscopic tears in the carpet fibers.

"I need to—"

"Wait," she said. "Let me go first. Please. Ladies first, right?" She gave him that sickly sweet smile again.

"What I have to say will be brief. I—"

"Me first." She stood and placed her hands on the desk. She leaned toward him. "I want to invite you over for dinner. You look like you're in need of a home-cooked meal. I don't think you realize what an amazing cook I am." She grinned. "It's true. I didn't get to show my skills during that crazy Thanksgiving feast. And I hadn't cooked for my daughter lately because…well, that doesn't really matter." Her grin became larger, if that were possible. "But now, I've been cooking a lot, and I want to make you a healthy, elegant meal to thank you for—"

"No."

Her eyes filled with tears. "Please let me finish." Her voice was shrill.

He heard a shriek of laughter from the break room. When was the last time anyone had laughed in their offices? Had he ever heard Stephanie laugh? Alex must have come in, and she and Diana were talking and laughing. Maybe, it would be a good idea to go to Stephanie's for dinner. If he told her at her home, she could scream without Diana and Alex overhearing. She could carry on or make threats, or spout Bible verses, or tear into Alex, whatever it might be that would strike her in that moment. If she wanted to resign, feeling her ego had been damaged beyond repair, she would be able to do it on the spot. She wouldn't have to see the others again. Maybe he owed her that.

Just because he needed to make a clean break on the photography position didn't mean he didn't value what she'd contributed over the years. He did owe her respect. And he knew she would be embarrassed about the stripping away of what she'd begged for.

"It would mean so much to me," Stephanie said. "We could have an in-depth conversation. And you could relax and enjoy real food, not something from a restaurant."

He fixed his gaze on the wall behind her, looking at the photograph of the Sydney Harbor Bridge on a sunny afternoon. He'd taken that photo during the trip when he'd first met Alex. Over the past six months, he had eaten in a lot of restaurants and taken food home from even more. Maybe an in-depth conversation would be good. He could take the time to be sure she understood. There was a good chance she would resign, and he could talk to her about other opportunities, offer a bit of counseling.

"Sure. That would work."

She laughed, so he guessed he'd been wrong about her not laughing. The reason he'd thought that was because her laughter was mechanical. The truth was, she laughed quite a lot, but listening to her was an unsettling experience. Hearing that sound was sometimes downright chilling.

"It would *work*?" she said. "I hope you don't see this as a *chore*. Or a business obligation you'd rather avoid."

"I'll look forward to it," he said, sounding rather mechanical himself. "What day works for you?"

She smiled triumphantly. "Wednesday."

He nodded. He supposed waiting two more days before breaking the devastating news wouldn't be the end of the world.

"What did you want to talk to me about?" She was still leaning over the desk, giving him a ridiculous grin.

"We can talk Wednesday."

"Perfect." She clapped her hands, spun around, and walked out of his office.

CHAPTER 51

*A*fter Trystan had agreed to come over, Stephanie felt she was floating for the rest of the day. She'd expected him to turn her down. He hadn't! She hadn't misread the signals like she so often seemed to with nearly everyone she knew.

When she left work Monday evening, she'd been filled with a sensation of supernatural energy. She'd stayed up all night, scrubbing the apartment more thoroughly than she had the entire time she'd lived there. She'd always taken pride in her apartment, but this deep cleanse was fueled by energy that seemed to come from out of nowhere. She wanted the walls to glisten, the lightbulbs and lampshades free of even a speck of dust, and the grout in the bathroom pristine white, the chrome polished until it sparkled.

She wasn't at all tired as she watched the city grow light around her. She went into work early and looked through the list of clients who were scheduled for upcoming photography sessions. For the next two days, Alexandra's name was on every single one. That was strange. She wanted to ask Trystan about it, but she didn't want to spoil the lead-up to their evening. She would wait. There would be an opportunity over dinner. Or, it could wait until their connection was strengthened.

Since there wasn't much to do, she spent the afternoon at her computer, planning the menu for her dinner. After work, she went to the store, and at home, she began prepping. She started with the dessert—a peach pie. She spent the evening in the kitchen, finally sliding into bed at ten past midnight. She took off all her clothes, and now, she felt inclined to spend the entire night naked.

On Wednesday, Trystan arrived about ten minutes late, which didn't worry her. He was a busy man. When she opened the door, his breath smelled of alcohol, so she supposed he'd met someone for a drink. A client, probably. She wouldn't comment on it. She smiled and welcomed him inside.

She already had a bottle of cabernet breathing. She'd read about how important it was to open red wines well before you served them. She was learning a lot about wine. She was eager to make up for lost time, all those years of believing God didn't want her to enjoy something He'd created for that very purpose. She handed a glass of wine to Trystan, directing him to settle on the couch. She arranged a plate of vegetable spears and dip and another with cheese and crackers on the table in front of them.

"This is a lot of food," he said. "And whatever you're roasting smells excellent."

She smiled. "We don't have to eat it all, but appetizers are nice with the wine, don't you think?"

He nodded. He didn't reach for any of the food.

"Do you want a cracker and some goat cheese?" she asked.

"Sure."

She prepared a cracker and a slice of cheese and handed it to him. They talked about their clients for a while, and then Trystan's daughter. Stephanie had thought about it the night before while she made the pie, planning a list of questions to get him talking. He wasn't as chatty as she'd thought he might be, but he answered her questions and sipped his wine. His glass was almost empty. She'd assumed they wouldn't have a second glass until they sat at the table, but she couldn't leave his without. Besides, he kept looking at the glass as if he longed for more.

She poured a bit more for him. She was not going to get drunk. She'd bought two bottles of wine because she knew he liked it, and she didn't want to embarrass herself by running out. But that was quite a lot of wine, and she was determined not to have more than a few glasses herself.

He seemed more relaxed once they were seated at the table, although he was talking even less. The wine should have made him loosen up. It should make him want to tell her everything that was in his heart. She tried asking about his childhood and got nowhere. She told him about her relationship with God, hoping he would talk about his own, but he was absolutely silent on the role God had in his life.

He was relishing the food, so that was good. The first bottle of wine was empty, and she'd only had a glass and a half. "Do you want more wine?"

"Absolutely," he said. "It's perfect with this delicious meal."

"Save room for dessert."

He nodded. "I'll try."

She told him about Eileen moving out, amazed by the calm in her voice. It was possible she felt calmer about it because talking about her feelings to another human being was comforting. It was something they shared—losing a child's physical closeness. She wondered if he realized they had that in common. She didn't feel she should point it out. He might think it wasn't quite the same since Eileen was technically an adult.

"Should we eat our pie in the living room?" she asked.

"Sure."

"I can make coffee, if it won't keep you awake all night." She laughed.

"I'll just have another glass of wine. There is something I wanted to talk to you about."

"I hope it's not work. This should be a fun evening, no more work talk allowed." She giggled softly.

"It will be brief." He took a swallow of wine.

"Are you okay?" Risking everything, but feeling as if it was the right thing to do, as if God were moving her limbs for her, she placed her hand on his leg. He didn't seem to react. At least, he didn't shake her off.

He was gazing into his nearly empty wineglass.

"Trystan?"

He placed his glass on the end table. "I've probably had more to drink than I should have."

"So have I." It wasn't nearly as much as he'd consumed, but for her, it was a lot. Luckily, her body was more acclimated to alcohol now, so she wouldn't have a repeat of that drunken display on Thanksgiving. Of course, that hadn't just been the alcohol. That had been provoked by Alex, and she was the furthest thing from Stephanie's mind right now. Or she should be. She took another sip of her wine.

Her hand was still on his leg.

"I really need to discuss—" he said.

"Don't worry about it now. I'm sure it can wait." She leaned toward him.

He closed his eyes.

Taking a breath and holding it, she rested her head on his shoulder. This was too good to be real. She felt amazing. Her body was warm and liquid, and the wine enhanced the feeling of melting into him. What would it be like to hold him? To kiss him? To do even more? She couldn't believe this was happening. God cared for her after all, and He'd placed this wonderful man in her life! She just needed patience.

She turned her head, looking up at his jaw. His eyes were still closed, but she didn't think he was sleeping. He was enjoying their closeness as much as she was. She brushed her cheek along his jaw. It was so smooth. He must have shaved for her! Moving away from him slightly, she turned to face him. His eyes remained closed.

"Trystan?"

"Mmhm."

"Are you falling asleep? I guess you had a couple drinks before you came here."

He moved his head in a slight nod.

"It's okay." She inched closer, gazing at his eyelids, his dark lashes, all the tiny flaws and imperfections of his face that weren't obvious until you were up close. She brushed her lips across his.

The touch made his eyelids flutter. "What?" he said.

She pressed her lips against his, and a moment later, she felt his mouth soften and join with hers. Then, his tongue slid between her slightly parted teeth. The sensations pulsing through her body were almost too much to bear. She felt slightly ashamed of how her mind raced toward thoughts of taking off her clothes, unbuttoning his shirt, releasing his belt buckle…

Suddenly, he moved away. "Oh my God. Stephanie."

She spoke in a whisper, not sure she could generate enough energy for a normal tone. "Yes?"

"What are you…what's…" He stood. "I think I passed out for a minute. I need to get going."

"But our dessert." Why had she thought first of dessert? What had just happened outweighed dessert by every measure imaginable. She wasn't even hungry, didn't want anything in her mouth but the taste of Trystan.

"I'm very tired. I'm so sorry that happened. I think I was…and I…please, please forgive me." He crossed the room and opened the door.

"*Forgive* you?" She laughed. "This is the most wonderful night I've had in…" Her breath caught in her throat.

He looked at her as if her face had transformed into something unfamiliar. She touched her cheek, wondering what he saw.

"No. I'm sorry, so very sorry." He stepped out of her apartment and closed the door.

She shoved herself off the couch and raced across the room, yanking open the door. She stepped into the hallway. He was gone. She stood there for a long time, numb and filled with indescribable joy.

CHAPTER 52

*S*tephanie didn't want to go to church with wine on her breath, but at a few minutes before eight-thirty, the doors would still be open. The thought of making it through the night without a clear message from God about what had just happened was intolerable. She left the food sitting on the table, drying and hardening in the pots and pans. She blew out the candles, changed into jeans and a sweater, and went out.

Walking to the subway was pleasant, knowing the gun was in her purse, ready to protect her. She felt her stride was easier, and there was less tension in her body. This was how it should be. Women should be able to walk at night, in any neighborhood they pleased, and feel secure. That had been denied her most of her life, and the feeling now was one of enormous power. She smiled, breathing in the warm night air.

The subway was nearly full, which surprised her on a Wednesday night, but she supposed the warm weather had brought everyone outdoors, escaping their small, dark apartments into the light of spring. She smiled at the beauty of her thought. She should write it down, maybe compose a poem. This thought broadened her smile. Already Trystan was bringing out another side of her—an entirely new person to replace the one who had been calcifying within a thick shell for so many years.

The lights inside the church were on, which made her feel safe as she pulled open the door. Although she had her gun, she felt a prickle of anxiety at the thought of kneeling with her face toward the altar, the doors to the street unlocked behind her.

Standing in the center of the room, she turned in a circle, looking up to the rafters and around the entire space, trying to decide where she should go that wouldn't leave her so exposed. If she positioned herself close to the altar and off to one side, the doors would be to her right. She would keep her purse open beside her.

As she settled onto her knees, making sure she was comfortable before she started, the doors opened with a clank. She jerked her head to look, then almost cried with relief as two older women stepped inside. She sighed and closed her eyes. It was fine. No one would enter a church to attack people in the middle of New York City on a spring evening.

She remained on her knees until they ached. She told God all her thoughts about Trystan, outlining what a wonderful man he was and how she felt like Ruth, lying at the feet of Boaz until he saw her and knew they were meant to be married.

Finally, her knees ached so badly, she had to stand. She hated doing it because she hadn't received any insight, any sense of a message coming into her heart. She glanced toward the seats where the women had been. They were gone.

As she stood there, still longing for a clear sense of direction, the lights seemed to brighten. She felt her hands start to shake.

When she turned, a woman was standing a few feet away on the opposite side of the altar. She wore a light blue dress that hung below her knees. Her hair was long and tangled, and she had tired-looking sandals on her feet, but her cheeks and nose were red, her skin shiny. She smiled at Stephanie. "The answer is yes."

"What?"

"You want an answer. We all want answers. Yours is yes."

"Who are you?"

"I'm another living soul. Like you."

"How do you know I want an answer?" Stephanie asked.

"Everyone does."

Stephanie wasn't sure whether she should be elated that God had sent an angel to reassure her or worried this woman was deranged and might attack her. Or maybe she wasn't real. Maybe a mere five hours of sleep in the last three days and all that wine, along with the feelings Trystan had aroused, were causing hallucinations.

"Do you go to church here?" Stephanie asked.

The woman smiled.

"Do you?"

"Does that matter?"

She supposed it didn't. But this was making her nervous. She pressed her hand against the side of her purse, feeling the outline of the gun. Did she have time to pull it out? Could she remember how to quickly release the safety latch? She should have practiced that more. The minute she got home, she would. Or tomorrow. She was so tired. "I don't know what you want," Stephanie said.

"I don't want anything. I just thought I'd let you know." The woman turned and walked down the center aisle and out the doors in utter silence. The doors didn't clank as they had when the others had come in earlier.

Stephanie pulled the gun out of her purse and tucked it into her waistband. It felt awful, pressing into her abdomen, but she had no idea what might be waiting for her outside the sanctuary. She opened the door carefully and stepped out. The street was deserted. She half-ran to the subway and remained standing for the entire ride home. Now that exhaustion overwhelmed her, she was afraid of falling asleep, of becoming vulnerable prey.

Inside her apartment, she looked at the congealing food, but it was too much work to clean up. She still didn't have her answer about her next move with Trystan. Or did she? Maybe that woman really had been an angel. Even if she wasn't, God often spoke through human beings, and so many times he'd chosen plain, unimportant people.

The woman must have been an angel. There was no other explanation.

Suddenly, she felt warm and filled with excitement. She fell onto her bed, tucking the gun under the pillow. If angels were going to start showing themselves to her, maybe she would no longer need the gun. Besides, once she was sleeping in Trystan's bed, a gold band and a glittering diamond on her finger, she would feel safe and protected every night. He would never let her ride the subway alone after dark. In fact, he might insist she take cabs everywhere, no matter what time of day.

She fell asleep in her clothes and didn't wake until the sun was well up in the sky, startled by the sound of the lock in her front door turning.

CHAPTER 53

Stephanie shot up in bed. "Who is it?" She shoved her hand under the pillow and touched her gun, curling her fingers around the handle. Why hadn't she practiced with the safety latch as she'd vowed she would? Looking away from the bedroom doorway for even half a second could lead to something awful, beyond imagination. Her voice shook, despite her iron grip on the gun. "Who's there?"

"Mom?"

She slid her hand away from the gun. She pulled the blankets up to the edge of the pillow, so there was no chance of Eileen seeing it. She leaned her head back, trying to catch her breath and slow the rapid thump of her heart.

"God, it stinks in here."

Stephanie heard the sound of a living room window sliding open. She inched toward the edge of the bed. She was still wearing her clothes from the evening before. She wasn't even sure what time she'd arrived home after that angelic visit. Maybe she'd been in the creature's presence for hours. Perhaps days had passed. She hadn't slept this well in a very long time. It was the sleep of certainty, the peace of being touched by God. She smiled and got out of bed. "I'm in here, sweetie."

A moment later, Eileen was standing in the doorway. She wore comfortable shoes, faded jeans, and a tight-fitting white T-shirt with a pleated jacket over it.

"No photoshoots today?" Stephanie asked.

"Why are you home? Alex texted me and said they were worried about you."

Stephanie laughed, ignoring Eileen's glaring eyes.

"She said they called and sent texts. Why didn't you respond?"

"I overslept. What day is it?"

Eileen stared at her, the glare softening slightly as her brow wrinkled with concern. "You don't know—"

"I slept so well. It was heavenly." Stephanie let out a deep sigh.

"It's Thursday. Why is there food all over the table? I think something spoiled. The roaches will be here any minute if they're not already poking around in the kitchen."

Stephanie moved closer to her daughter. "It's so good to see you. Let me give you a hug."

Eileen wrinkled her nose.

Stephanie laughed. She wasn't going to let Eileen spoil her mood. She had been visited by God, and she was loved by a man whom God had dropped into her life. He'd simply been waiting for the scales to fall from her eyes.

"So what's with all the spoiled food? Are you okay?"

"I have a new man in my life." She giggled at the expression on Eileen's face. She felt a peacefulness inside, knowing that she and Eileen were peers again—two women who could share their experiences of being in love. For now, it didn't matter that Ned was too old. Eileen would figure it out soon enough and find someone better.

"That's a little sudden."

"Not really. I've known him for ages."

"Who?"

"Trystan."

"Trystan, your boss?"

Stephanie laughed. "Who else? Not many men have that name."

"You're dating your boss? I don't think that's a good idea."

"He's not really my boss. We all treat each other like peers."

"Until it's time for a raise, or there's a disagreement or…" Eileen took a step away from her.

"Actually, I could use your advice. I don't want to put him in a difficult position."

"*Him*? I'm worried about *you*."

Stephanie smiled. "I'm fine. He really cares about me. And it turns out he's a believer. I never knew that."

"And now you do? How?"

"Things he's said to me. Recently."

"Is all that spoiled food because he was here? For dinner?"

"We kissed." Stephanie felt her face burning, amazed by how fast the heat had spread through her veins. She wondered if Eileen noticed. She didn't seem to.

"Mom, please be careful."

"Of what?"

"He's in a position of power over you. Please don't tell me you're that naïve."

"I'm not naïve."

"It's not a good idea to be in a relationship with your boss. You should know that."

"Okay. Fine. I'm sure for some people, that's true. Now can I get some advice?"

"About what?"

"I need to know if I should invite him over again or let him make the next move."

Eileen stared at her.

"What do you think?"

Eileen crossed her arms. She glanced to the side, then spoke without looking Stephanie in the eyes. "I think you should look for another job if you're dead set on seeing him. And I don't think you should make any moves at all, especially since you already invited him over here."

"I can't just wait for him. I think I'm too old for that." She giggled. "And he's very cautious."

"It's a mistake to be in a relationship with him. He has total power over you."

Stephanie laughed. "No he doesn't."

"You need to find another job. Or tell him to forget it."

"Why would I do that? We're in love."

"In love? Are you serious? You just...how long has this been going on?"

"Forever, in God's eyes."

"How many times have you gone out?"

"Counting the times we talked about my career, we've had—"

"No. How many dates? When you both knew it was a date?"

"That's a funny way to put it."

"How many?"

"I don't think that matters."

"And I think refusing to say how many matters quite a lot."

Stephanie sighed. "Let's not argue. It's been so long since I've seen you."

"Five days." Eileen shrugged off her jacket. "Let me help you get this cleaned up. Text Alex or Diana, and let them know you're okay."

Stephanie let out a short, sharp laugh. "They don't care."

"Yes, they do."

"I'll let Trystan know."

"Big mistake. Text Diana or Alex." Eileen turned and walked toward the kitchen, tossing her jacket on the couch as she passed through the living room.

Stephanie turned and dug her phone out of her purse. The battery was almost dead. She sent a message to Trystan then another to Diana. Both responded almost immediately with a thumbs up. It was good to know Trystan was so worried about her. She smiled as she plugged her phone in. She pulled the bedroom door closed to add another layer of protection between the gun and Eileen. Although, it didn't really matter anymore. Eileen had said she couldn't live with the gun in the apartment, and then she'd moved out anyway. Stephanie was glad she hadn't caved to Eileen's irrational fear and gotten rid of it.

The clank of dishes and rush of water drew her toward the kitchen. In that brief time, Eileen had already cleared the table and scraped the food into the garbage. Now, she was digging dried-out pasta from the pot, dropping it in clumps with congealed cream sauce into the can.

She worked quickly while Stephanie watched. Stephanie knew she should help, but Eileen was moving so fast, seeming to open the fridge and slide plates into the dishwasher and wipe the counter in a graceful, fluid dance. Stephanie closed her eyes. She didn't think she could keep up.

"Are you okay?"

The water shut off, and Stephanie opened her eyes. "I'm fine."

Eileen wiped her hands on the towel. "I left the pans to soak. I need to get back." Eileen glanced at her watch. "I promised Al—"

Stephanie pulled back sharply, trying to read Eileen's expression, trying to figure out the reason for the sudden halt in her words. "Aren't you seeing Ned anymore?"

"Of course I am."

"You promised someone something, and you weren't about to say Ned. Is it one of your agents?"

Eileen shook her head. "No. I—"

"Alex? Were you going to say Alex? And *back*... where? Are you...is she your *roommate*?" Stephanie sucked air into her lungs and let it burst out.

"Yes."

Eileen stared at her with such defiance, Stephanie thought she might as well stick her tongue out, just as she had when she was seven years old. That habit hadn't lasted long. Stephanie had seen to that. But apparently, the defiance had festered inside Eileen for all these years. No one ever told you that. Focusing on stopping behavior didn't allow you access to the inside of a child's mind, where the real trouble was.

"I can't believe you would betray me like this," Stephanie said. "I don't know what to say. I—"

"Don't start. I don't want to hear it. Now you know, and I don't have anything else to say about it." Eileen walked into the living room and picked up her jacket and purse. "I'm worried about you. I doubt you're going to like me saying this, and you'll probably ignore me, but I really think it would be helpful if you would see a therapist."

"I don't need therapy."

"You need to talk to someone objective. You need to get some insight into what you're doing. All of it. Your hatred of Alex, this relationship with Trystan…"

"I already have it figured out. When you listen to God, you don't need a therapist telling you what to do."

"They don't tell you what to do, they provide a sounding board and ask questions so you can see where you need to make changes in your life."

Stephanie smiled. "Thank you for washing the dishes. Let's get together for lunch soon. I miss you."

"Are you kicking me out?"

"I need to get ready for work." Stephanie went to the door and opened it. She stood there until Eileen walked out. Neither of them spoke another word. It was probably better that way. Both knew everything the other was thinking. They had for a long time.

CHAPTER 54

*W*hen I arrived home from work, Eileen was sitting on the couch—my old one, because we hadn't even started looking at furniture. Simply emptying boxes had taken a ridiculous amount of time. I'd thought it would be faster than packing, but I was wrong.

Two icy fresh martinis stood on the table in front of Eileen.

"Nice," I said, then turned and started toward my room.

"I need your help," Eileen said.

"I'll be back in a second." In my room, with enough unoccupied space to spread my arms out and spin around, I stripped off my work clothes, tossed them onto the bed, and pulled on a sundress. It was still coolish outside, but I felt like dressing for the soft blue sky, fading to evening outside my window, especially after wearing slacks and a jacket all day. Now that I had this large window in my bedroom that allowed me to wake to the sky every morning and fall asleep looking at the stars, I felt more in touch with the natural world. Maybe the pleasure I felt in that meant I wouldn't remain in New York City forever, planning my burial like Diana was.

I returned to the living room and settled beside Eileen. I picked up my glass. "What are we drinking to?"

"Nothing. We're just drinking. There's a problem...with my Mom. I hope you can be objective and help me, that you can put your feelings about her to the side. I trust your insight, and I desperately need it, so I hope you can do that."

"Absolutely." I smiled and sipped my drink. I had no feelings for Stephanie that needed to be put aside. I had self-preservation. And I had opinions, which would remain solidly in place. You can't really change an opinion when it's based on something you've witnessed almost every day for months.

"My mom is in love with Trystan."

I laughed. "I don't think so."

"She told me. And it's worse...she thinks he's in love with her."

I took a long, soothing swallow of my drink. The news wasn't at all surprising. It was a shock to hear it said, but immediately, I could see the whole train of events as if I'd been watching a wide-screen movie pass by my eyes. I could see Stephanie reading into everything and misinterpreting everything else.

"How in God's name did she get that idea?" Eileen's voice was a pitiful wail. "I told her she needed to find another job. Now. But she laughed it off."

I nodded. That would work well for me. I wondered if there was any way Stephanie might listen to her daughter. Probably not, but the moment of satisfaction when I briefly thought she could slide easily out of my life was pleasant.

"I think she might be...unbalanced, maybe?" Eileen picked up her glass and ate two of the olives but didn't take a drink.

I'd been told to put my opinions aside, so I figured I could do that after all. Eileen hadn't told me to change them but to put them on the shelf. She and I had just started to get the sense of being roommates, and I didn't want to chase her away even before I got a chance to decorate my new apartment and before I had time to meet a new guy and invite him into this fabulous place where we could eat in style, and have sex in style. It occurred to me that I needed a new bed.

"Do you think there's any chance Trystan has fallen for her?" she asked.

I thought about his relationship with Eileen. I wondered how much of this was Eileen being creeped out or worried her mother would find out about her hook-up with Trystan, and how much was genuine concern for Stephanie. I was guessing most of it was the first part. I was also sure she was worried about the damage control that would fall to her if Stephanie's fantasy love life and her career all blew up at once. I supposed I should be thinking seriously about that as well. What if Eileen invited Stephanie to stay with us for a while? I coughed several times.

"Are you okay?"

I nodded. "Just a spasm in my throat."

"Do you think the feeling is mutual?"

"I haven't seen anything from him that would make me think he's into her. I'm pretty sure it's the opposite—he wants to get rid of her. She's not doing a great job as a photographer."

Eileen nodded as if this was something she'd already known. "Then she's imagined the idea of him being interested, right?"

"Probably." I could definitely speak to Stephanie's over-active imagination, the imagination that allowed her to think she had a great rapport with our clients. The imagination that enabled her to believe the things she did about the invisible world. "She has an active imagination."

"I know. And she reads people wrong. All the time. She thinks he's in love with her!"

I nodded. I sipped my drink and put down my glass. I wished we could stop talking about Stephanie, unless she was going to look for another job. In that case, I could talk all night. Right then, I wanted to walk to the window and look out, savoring my martini. I wanted to put on music. And I was getting quite hungry.

I didn't smell anything from the kitchen, so I imagined we would be getting takeout.

"What do you want me to do?" I asked.

"I don't know."

I turned away from the window. Her eyes were filled with tears.

"I don't mean to be dramatic," she said, "but I'm afraid for her. I worry that she's…I went over there, and she was sound asleep at ten-thirty on a weekday morning. There was food on the table from last night, and the kitchen was a mess. The place stank like sour milk. I cleaned it all up, and she just stood there, watching me, closing her eyes every few minutes. It felt as if she wasn't sure where she was. And when I first went into her room, she asked me what day it was."

"I don't know what to say."

"Maybe you could talk to Trystan."

"I don't think that would work. He knows she and I don't get along. He'd just think I was trying to create trouble for her."

"What should I do?"

"There's nothing you can do. She's going to do what she wants."

Eileen sighed. Finally, she took a sip of her drink. "She always has."

"You could talk to the preacher at her church, maybe. To see if he could get her to see a doctor." I knew none of this would work, but it seemed like Eileen was expecting me to give her a solid way to keep her mother from blowing up her life, and I supposed that's what a good roommate should do—provide solutions. That, or just listen.

"I feel so helpless," she said.

"What does Ned think?"

"I haven't talked to him about it yet. You know my mom a lot better than he does."

"You could just let it play out. Like you said, she does what she wants. We all do, really."

She laughed. "Maybe. I don't want her to get hurt."

"You can't stop that from happening. If she thinks he's in love with her and he's not, there's nothing you can do to make her feel better."

"You're right. I know you're right. Why do you see things so clearly?"

I shrugged. It seemed obvious—when you're not drowning in emotions, the water looks clear.

"I hate seeing her life going off the rails. Maybe I just don't want to deal with the fallout. This isn't how it's supposed to be. The child isn't supposed to be worrying about her mother's love life. My mother is supposed to worry about mine." She sipped her drink. "Although she does that too, and I wish she'd stop." There was a bitter tone in the laughter that followed.

I nodded. "She won't listen to you. So just let it play out. And maybe if she wakes up, then you can get her some help." It was a lie. I knew it was a lie, but there was nothing else to say, and I sure didn't want to talk about it for an hour and end up in the exact same spot.

CHAPTER 55

$\mathcal{T}$he next morning, I woke with a headache. This was the result of two martinis, followed by two glasses of wine. Eileen and I had then gorged ourselves on Chinese food, lots of noodles and rice, because we needed something to soak up the alcohol and to settle our nerves after a circular conversation. There had been two martinis because we ended up talking about Stephanie for another hour after I'd thought we finished.

Despite the headache, I arrived at work a few minutes before eight. Diana was in her office. I smelled the coffee, and she waved as I passed by. I filled a mug, popped two Ibuprofen into my mouth, and went to my office. I was ravenously hungry from all those carbs and nothing but an orange for breakfast. I thought about going out, but I could feel my adrenaline pumping in anticipation of the day.

No matter how much I liked Eileen and didn't want to see her so upset, I was quite curious to see how the Stephanie-in-love scenario would unfold.

Trystan came in around eight-thirty, and finally, at nine-fifteen, Stephanie showed up. She swished down the hall like she owned the building.

I had a horrifying picture of the future flash across my mind—maybe Trystan did like her, maybe they would hook up, maybe my job, that was getting a bit hellish at times, would descend to the third circle, or even further. I shivered. I took a sip of my fourth cup of coffee and vowed it would be my last for the day.

I tried to busy myself reading profiles of the clients I was scheduled with the following week, but my mind wouldn't focus. I read the same sentences three or four times and still didn't know what they said. I went into the break room and poured my coffee down the drain. I washed the mug and opened the fridge to grab a lemon sparkling water. I checked the drawer for meats and cheese. There was a small block of cheddar cheese wrapped in plastic. I cut five slices, arranged them on a small plate, and returned to my office to wait for the show to begin.

By lunchtime, I was exhausted from keeping my attention at full alert. The offices had remained nearly silent all morning, with nothing but the click and tap of computer keys. Trystan hadn't even made any phone calls. I felt like we were all waiting for the sky to let loose with pounding thunder and torrential rain.

Diana closed her door while she ate leftover soup at her desk. Trystan went out. Stephanie also closed her door but appeared not to notice it was lunchtime. I walked two blocks to a deli and ordered a roast beef sandwich with a side of potato salad. I bought an energy drink that claimed it would detox my system. It was unlikely, but it was better than spending the afternoon sucking down more coffee. I realized that this dance, or whatever it was, between Stephanie and Trystan could go on for days, weeks. I wondered if Trystan even knew he was in a dance.

At four o'clock, I heard Stephanie get up and walk into the hallway. I didn't hear her in the break room, and she hadn't walked past my office, so I figured she'd gone to see Trystan.

I slipped out of my chair and went to my doorway. Diana's door was still closed. I peeked out into the hall. Trystan's door was open, and Stephanie was in his office, but I couldn't hear what she

THE WOMAN IN THE CHURCH

was saying. I walked toward his office, staying close to the wall, desperate to hear. Of course, the conversation might erupt any minute, and then I'd have no trouble hearing. If one of them saw me, they would probably not be pleased, but things around there had deteriorated so badly, I wasn't sure I cared. There wasn't a lot I could do to make it worse. I moved closer to Trystan's doorway.

"All I'm saying is that I was so sorry you had to rush out," Stephanie said.

"I don't want to discuss it." Trystan sounded tired, not even energized enough to get angry. "I only came over because I need to tell you something."

Stephanie didn't respond. I pictured a smile spreading across her face as she imagined him expressing his love. From behind his desk—that sounded passionate.

"You're not working out as a photographer," Trystan said. "I know that's hard to hear, and I know you put all you had into it, but your photographs aren't useful."

I heard a tiny shriek from Stephanie.

"If you'd like to resume your former role, you were fantastic at it, and I'd love to have you supporting us again."

I rolled my eyes.

"But if you want to give me your resignation, I'll understand that as well."

Stephanie laughed.

This was followed by several moments of silence. I could feel my breath moving in and out, worried that the utter silence would make the sound of my lungs audible to them. I was being slightly ridiculous, standing in the hallway like a child listening to divorcing parents speak their final words to each other, but I couldn't stop. I had to know where this was going.

In some ways, Stephanie had managed to get the upper hand with Trystan. There was no way he was going to come out of this feeling pleased with himself, no matter what happened. I'd watched the man slowly decay over the past few months as he allowed Stephanie to dictate how he ran his business, how he treated his other employees, and what her job should entail.

My mind spun back to the day she'd appeared in the office with her new hairstyle and makeup. I knew then she was up to something, and I'd watched it softly detonate every week—a slow-motion explosion. The funny part was that I didn't think she'd ever had a plan. She seemed to react spontaneously to nearly every situation she encountered. And yet, looking back, it appeared to be a very definite plan.

Had she been in love with him all along? If she was starved for affection, if no man had paid attention to her for twenty years, she might easily create a fantasy prince charming out of Trystan.

"I don't need your decision right now," Trystan said, finally. His voice was weak, and I pictured them—gazes locked onto each other, daring the other to speak first. Of course, he had lost that standoff because he was a peacemaker.

"This doesn't make any sense." She laughed softly. "What about last night?"

"I told you that was a mistake. A terrible, terrible mistake that I deeply regret."

"That's a lie. I could tell what you were feeling."

"You can't trust the human body to always be truthful. I'd had too much to drink. I was extremely stressed because I've been worried about having this conversation with you."

"Why would you worry about talking to me? We understand each other, you know that."

"Because I'm telling you that you can't be a photographer. And I wasn't sure you would take that well."

"You have a very low opinion of my talent," Stephanie said.

There was another long pause. I shifted my position, flattening my back against the wall, so I felt more comfortable. I might be there for a while.

"Can you tell me you understand what I'm saying? You can have your old job or resign," Trystan said.

"I'm not resigning."

"Good. I'm glad to hear that."

"I mean, maybe I won't work at all after a while. Once you and I...well, I don't want to jump the gun." She giggled hysterically.

Now I understood Eileen's concern. I'd always thought Stephanie was quirky and disturbed. I'd known she was neurotic and had a fantastical view of the world that she shaped to her own liking. But now, I wondered if she was actually medically unbalanced. Her laughter had a strange, manic quality to it.

"Stop," Trystan said. "What are you doing?"

"I need to be close to you. It was so good to hold you last night. I feel almost wicked saying these things." She giggled. "But I know that what God put between a man and a woman isn't truly wicked. The world has just twisted it around to make it that way with adultery and fornication. But now that I know you're a child of God, and now that we've kissed, I know that God brought us together. I feel so blessed that he's given me to you. And if you need to take things slowly, I can be patient. Because I know what's—"

"Get off of me," Trystan said.

This was followed by more silence.

"Stephanie." There was a crash and a little shriek.

I glanced toward Diana's door. It was still closed. If she came out and saw what I was doing, she wouldn't think well of me, but I also wondered whether, deep inside, she would want to do the same thing. She just wouldn't, ever.

Stephanie was crying now. "Hold me. Please hold me. I *need* you to hold me."

"Can I call someone for you?" Trystan asked.

"What are you talking about?"

"I think you need to go home, you need someone to talk to."

"I need you!" Her voice rose.

Diana's door remained shut. Maybe she had her headphones on.

"There's nothing between us," Trystan said. "Yes, okay, I kissed you, but I didn't even realize it was you. I would never do that. I'm not attracted to you, and there is no relationship between us. And to be sure we're absolutely clear, I don't have the same religious beliefs as you. Not even close."

"You can't be saying this. What's wrong with you? God told me you love me. I dreamed of our wedding. You...maybe He just hasn't revealed it to you yet. But I know you're attracted to me. The way you kissed me was..." Stephanie was whimpering. Each time she paused for a breath, a moaning sound came out of her.

"I'm not attracted to you. I never have been, and I never will be. I think you should leave. Go home and rest. Take next week off to sort out what you want to do."

"This isn't right."

"This is how it is."

"No!"

A moment later, Stephanie flung herself into the hallway, racing toward her office, her pink silk blouse fluttering around her like a kite because she was moving so quickly. She didn't even notice I was standing there.

Then, she burst out of her office, and I blinked hard. She was holding a small gun in her right hand, clutching it close to her stomach. Again she barreled past me. I lunged toward her, grabbing at her blouse. It tore, leaving a ribbon of pink in my hand.

As I reached for her again, I nearly fell into Trystan's office. I crashed against Stephanie, and she kicked me, landing the heel of her shoe with incredible accuracy right on my kneecap. I cried out and grabbed my leg, trying to regain my balance. She hadn't budged, as if my body falling against hers felt like nothing more than a stiff breeze.

"Give me the gun." I held out my hand.

She looked at me, staring into my eyes, moving her arm until the gun was pointed at me. She smiled. "You think you can tell anyone whatever you want, and they'll do it. Not me."

"Trystan isn't in love with you Stephanie. He's into someone else, and you can't change..." My words trailed off as Stephanie whirled to face Trystan.

"You betrayed me." Her voice had dropped to a low, eerily soft tone.

"There's nothing to betray." Slowly, Trystan pushed his chair away from his desk. He stood, raising his hands in front of him. "Let's sit down and talk."

"Who is it? Her?!" She waved the gun toward me. "Of course it's her. You've always had a thing for her. The very first time you brought her here, I saw you drooling all over her. Telling everyone what a talented photographer she was. Ha. Everything she wants, she gets, and you believe her instead of me. You were meant for me! You only like her because she's young and hot and—"

"Why don't you put the gun on the desk?" Trystan asked. "Then we can talk this out."

Stephanie whimpered. "You didn't deny it. So it's true." She let out a bellowing cry of pain. Then, suddenly calm again, she spoke softly. "She's not going to get you."

I felt the explosion of her gun with every cell. Once. Twice. Three times. I watched as Trystan folded in upon himself, blood pouring out across his white shirt. He collapsed onto the floor.

I bolted for the door before she could turn her attention back to me. I threw myself out into the hallway, racing to my office. I slammed the door and locked it, then scurried to the opposite corner in case she decided to shoot through the wood.

I tapped my phone.

Alex: *Stephanie has a gun. Don't come out. Lock your door.*

Diana replied with a horrified emoji.

Alex: *I'm calling 9-1-1.*

As I told the dispatcher what had happened, I heard another shot.

CHAPTER 56

*I*t was Saturday afternoon. I was sitting in my new living room, enjoying the silence and spaciousness of my apartment. Not that I was already tired of my roommate, but after the previous day, the freedom from human voices spewing overwrought emotions was a great relief.

I'd slept only two hours the night before.

First, there'd been the mess at the office. By the time paramedics and police arrived, Trystan was dead. I was pretty sure he'd died moments after the bullets sank into his body. Even those brief moments were so unpleasant I thought I might be sick. I loathe blood, it's why I always avoid any kind of weapon that might cause blood to flow out into the world where it doesn't belong. I tried not to think about it soaking into the carpet, splattered on the walls. And that was just Trystan's.

The last shot I'd heard while I was talking to the police dispatcher about Trystan, was Stephanie shooting herself.

That night, I'd been the one to tell Eileen about it.

I didn't text her. I didn't call her. I waited until the police said we could leave. I picked up pasta from an Italian bistro, along with freshly baked sourdough bread. I wasn't sure she would want to eat, but I thought I would be prepared. I also bought two bottles of wine.

At the apartment, I put the food in the kitchen and asked Eileen to sit beside me on the couch. "I need to tell you what happened with your mother."

Her eyes widened. I'm sure in her wildest imagination, what had happened didn't enter her thoughts. She probably saw images flickering through her mind of Stephanie crying, screaming, the police called, perhaps. Maybe an unwilling visit to the psych ward at Bellevue. But not what I was about to tell her.

"She was talking to Trystan how she felt, but he cut her off and said she had it all wrong. He wasn't attracted to her."

"Oh no." Eileen picked up the glass of wine I'd poured for her and took a long swallow. "She's going to be—"

"There's more. Let me just tell you everything."

"She was getting kind of upset. She sat on his lap, I think, and he pushed her onto the floor. She started crying, and then she ran back to her office and came out with a gun."

"She told me she got rid of it!"

"You knew?"

Eileen started crying. She leaned against the back of the couch and gave into her despair. "She met some woman who...never mind. It doesn't matter. I found it in her room, and she promised she'd get rid of it."

"She shot Trystan."

Eileen gasped. "Oh, no! Is he...?"

I nodded. "She shot him three times. In the chest. It was pretty bad."

Eileen was sobbing now. I placed my hand on her arm. "After that, she shot herself."

A scream came out of Eileen that was like nothing I'd ever heard.

I kept my hand on her arm and squeezed gently. This was way

outside of my territory. I had no idea how I was supposed to comfort someone when I needed so little of it myself.

She cried in waves, her tears and gasping breaths slowing and then escalating again. She sat up slightly and fell against me, resting her head on my shoulder. I felt bone meeting bone and the hot wetness of her tears. I put my arm around her shoulders and let her carry on.

After a while, she whimpered. "I'm an orphan."

Those were the first words out of her mouth. It reminded me that even though I'm not like others, I'm not a complete anomaly of nature, in that most people think first of themselves. For a moment, I felt less like an outsider.

"She was so unhappy. Her whole life, as far back as I can remember, she's been angry and upset, and..." She gasped for air, her shoulders heaving against me. "It's so unfair. Some God she believed in, right?"

I said nothing.

"Now, she'll never have a chance to be happy." A convulsive sob shook her body.

I tried to think about whether there was anything else to say. I didn't think I should tell her that the reason Stephanie shot Trystan was because she didn't want me to have him. Would that make her feel better or worse? I wasn't sure.

After a long while, she sat up. She took a few sips of wine and wiped at her face.

I went into the bathroom and returned with a box of tissues. She was sipping her wine—very tiny sips, but without letting up. The glass was almost empty.

"Do you feel like eating something?" I asked.

She shrugged.

I was starving. "It might help you think."

She laughed, tears spilling out of her eyes. "How will eating help me think?"

"It will distract you."

She gave me an understanding smile. "You're hungry."

"A little."

We went into the kitchen. I heated the food and placed some butter and a container of grated parmesan cheese on the table. While we ate, she talked about her mother and how Eileen felt a huge relief that it was all over. And at the same time, how she felt like she wanted to die herself...because it was all over.

She told me about growing up with Stephanie. Even though Stephanie had been so unhappy, she'd done a lot of fun things with Eileen. She explained that church wasn't so ominous back then. Eileen had loved going to Sunday School. She loved the stories and crafts and the other kids. She remembered lots of good things about her mother and how Stephanie had focused all her energy on being there for her child. She told me that whenever she asked about her father, she was told that God was her Father. As a child, that made her feel good, special, because she'd gotten the idea that her father was better than any human father. It wasn't until she made the connection that God called Himself the father of all human beings that she felt betrayed.

By the time she was done talking, she'd managed to make Stephanie into an interesting, complicated person. She almost seemed like someone worth knowing. And I suppose when you know the details of another person's life, every human being is worth knowing. It was a strange picture she'd painted—of a woman who was embarrassing to her daughter, loving, rigid, thoughtful, giving, confused, slightly unbalanced, and then completely unbalanced.

Eileen had loved her.

Now, she felt like the center of her life had been carved out of her.

CHAPTER 57

*I*t was almost summer by the time things got sorted out with Trystan's consulting business. Because the company was still a functioning business legally, the payroll service continued to issue checks to Diana and me. We were assured by the accountant there was plenty of cash on hand for the foreseeable future while things got sorted out.

We met Trystan's ex-wife and his daughter at the funeral. They weren't all that interested in us, and I suppose that makes sense, given the circumstances, and that we'd never met. Who knows if they had even heard our names.

Then, everything turned in a surprising direction.

It was a Wednesday morning. Diana and I were meeting for our weekly breakfast to catch up on things and marvel over the limbo state of getting paid, and telling clients someone would be in touch soon, but doing nothing to earn our paychecks.

"I made an offer to buy the client list and the methodology." Diana didn't smile or change her expression at all to mirror my widened eyes. She bit primly into a slice of bacon and chewed it carefully. Trystan's ex-wife did not want the business. She wanted whatever cash she could extract.

"You want to keep this going?" I asked.

"There's huge potential. And there were some things I think Trystan could have done better, so…" She smiled.

"What did you offer?"

"Unless you want to do this as a partnership, and you'd like to make a joint offer, I don't think I should say."

I smiled. "It would be great to keep working with you. I like taking photographs. I like looking at people's goals and figuring out how to help them, but I'm not a good candidate for a partner."

"How do you know?"

"I know."

"What does that mean?"

"Let's leave it at that. But I hope you'll consider hiring me back." As I said those words, I knew I had to figure out a plan at some point. If I didn't, other people were going to shape my life, and I would just be going along for the ride.

"Absolutely," Diana said. "I should know if she accepted my offer by the end of the week."

I studied her face. She was smart, and she knew pretty much every aspect of the coaching work Trystan did, so it made sense, but she suddenly looked very young.

It was impressive to think about a black woman, barely thirty, who would be shaping the careers of some of New York City's most powerful people. It gave me a bit of a thrill to think about how it would be to work for a woman again. It made me think of the only other woman I'd worked for—Tess. And it made me think about how I'd been treating life like a bit of a game—fun and good times. That would never change, of course. I would always want fun and good times and toying with people to be part of what I did. But if I wanted to win, I needed to think about my game strategy.

Diana's offer was accepted. Two weeks later, I unlocked the office door on a Monday morning, walked inside, and saw the coffee table in our lobby strewn with fat books of carpet samples, furniture catalogs, and paint chips. This was going to be different, and I was pretty sure it was going to be a lot more fun.

Another thing had struck me while I was running through Central Park a few mornings after Diana told me she was working on becoming my boss. I was growing this small circle of women around me, and I wasn't sure whether that was a good thing. They really had no idea who I was.

A NOTE TO READERS

Thanks for reading. I hope you liked reading about Alexandra as much as I enjoy writing her stories. I'm passionate about fiction that explores the shadows of suburban life and the dark corners of the human mind. To me, the human psyche is, as they say in Star Trek — the final frontier — a place we'll never fully understand. I'm fascinated by characters who are damaged, neurotic, and obsessed.

I love to stay in touch with readers. Visit me at my website: CathrynGrant.com

To find out when the next Alexandra Mallory novel is available, you can sign up for my new book mailing list here: Cathryn-Grant.com/contact.

As a thank you for signing up, you'll receive a free Alexandra short story — Death Valley.